The Little Green Men Murders

A Jim Guthrie Mystery

Rick Neumayer

Literary Wanderlust | Denver, Colorado

Published in the United States by Literary Wanderlust LLC, Denver, Colorado.

www.LiteraryWanderlust.com

ISBN Paperback: 978-1-956615-33-3
ISBN Digital: 978-1-956615-34-0

Printed in the United States of America

Dedication

To Cora Rouse Neumayer,
my beloved wife and best friend

Chapter 1

When my phone rang, the *Ariel* was pitching and bobbing in the chop of a passing coal barge. A faint tap-tapping on my line made me slide my feet off the ice chest and tug with the tip of my rod to set the hook. Then I grabbed my cell.

"James Guthrie Investigations," I said. Multi-tasking.

It was a sweltering Thursday afternoon in August. I was glistening with sweat, standing now in the foredeck well of a borrowed twenty-two-foot pontoon.

"Jim, this is Jessamine Tilford. Jessamine *Barrett* Tilford."

"Of course, the senator's daughter. Thought I recognized your voice."

"You remembered. How sweet."

Thought, hell. I'd have known that sexy, throaty growl anywhere. Even as a teenager, she sounded like Lauren Bacall. But I remembered her vividly as a wild, good-looking, eighteen-year-old redhead.

"How are you, Jessamine?"

I started reeling in my catch, wondering what the grownup version of her would be like. Fifteen years ago, she was a radical animal rights activist who had been jailed for breaking into a laboratory and letting all the test animals out of their cages. She claimed at the time that researchers were cutting off their limbs and sewing their eyes shut.

"I'm fine. But my husband isn't."

"Your husband?"

"Travis Tilford. We've been married for three years now. We met in film school at UCLA and decided to start working together. One thing led to another ..."

Film school? "I'm sorry to hear there is a problem. What seems to be the trouble?"

The monofilament abruptly went slack. I put my rod and reel aside, knowing I'd lost my fish. I wouldn't have eaten it—or anything out of the Ohio River—anyway. Unlike my day job, fishing was strictly catch and release.

"Travis has been kidnapped."

"What?" This was serious and startling news. Many hostages are never released even after a ransom has been paid. Should I tell her this?

"Sorry to just drop it on you like this, but there's no time to mince words. If I don't pay the ransom by tomorrow morning, they're going to kill him."

"Tell me what happened."

"He disappeared while we were shooting interviews for a documentary."

A documentary about what, I wondered. "Where was this?" "Hopkinsville. At the Little Green Men Days Festival."

"Hopkinsville?" A small city in far southwestern Kentucky. "Where your mother grew up. This doesn't have anything to do with John Drake, I hope?"

"No, I don't see how it could, since you put him in prison for the rest of his life."

The boat was rocking. I grabbed the port handrail. Drake was Cybil's first husband. Jessamine had never met him until he began tormenting her mother, first by stealing her dog, and then by abducting her. I kept him from murdering Cybil, and I recovered her dog.

"At the Little Green Men Festival, you say? I think I read something about that. What is it?"

"Back in the 1950s, aliens in flying saucers supposedly visited a local farm. They've been celebrating it ever since."

"Weird. Okay, lots of people around, but nobody saw or heard anything? Travis just vanished?"

"It was early, not much of a crowd yet. We needed a boom mic, so Travis went back to the truck to get one. The parking lot was off by itself, where nothing was going on. I was less than a hundred yards away when it happened, but I was so focused on what I was doing that I didn't see anything. It shouldn't have taken Travis more than a couple of minutes. When he didn't come back, I tried to call him. Then I went looking for him. But the truck was gone and so was he. I asked around, but nobody had seen him. My phone rang. I picked up when I saw it was Travis. 'Where are you?' I asked. But a man's voice I didn't recognize said he had taken him."

"Can you remember the exact words? Whether there anything noticeable about his voice? Did he sound like he was educated? Have an accent?"

"Listen for yourself. I keep my phone on auto record while we're in the field."

I heard clicking and static, then a high-pitched, nasal voice with a Kentucky twang. "We have your husband. Here's a video."

Jessamine said, "It's Travis, Jim. I'm sure of it."

"Can you forward the video to me?" When I got it, I saw a man lying on a dirt floor in what looked like a cellar. He was tied up and gagged but seemed alive.

More intermittent noise. Then Jessamine asked, "Is he all right? Put him on the phone so I can talk to him."

"No," said the kidnapper's voice, "he's not doing any talking right now. We make the rules, not you. We want a million dollars in small, unmarked bills. Or he's dead."

"But we don't have that kind of money."

"You raised enough money to make a movie, didn't you? Get

the million bucks or else."

"The movie is only a documentary, and we've already spent all our money on the script, cast, and crew."

"I don't care. If you ever want to see your man again, you'll get me my money. Stay by your phone for more instructions." The line went dead.

"When did you get this?" I asked.

"Ninety minutes ago. I'm driving back to my parents' horse farm in Oldham County."

I checked my watch. A few minutes after two. "Have you called the police?"

"No."

"Why not?"

"They threatened to kill Travis if I did."

"That's scary. I understand. But kidnappers always say that. I assume you're asking for my advice. If I were you, I'd call the police right now."

"I can't. I don't trust them. I'm afraid they'll be more interested in catching the kidnappers than saving Travis."

I blinked as a sudden gust out of the southwest blew in my face.

"Maybe, but they're still your best bet. The police have the experience, resources, and can make objective decisions. Whereas loved ones are easily manipulated."

"I got the kidnapper to cut his demand in half," she said.

"You did?" This was a little hard for me to believe. Maybe Jessamine was tougher to manipulate than I thought. "How did you manage that?"

"Ten minutes after the first call, he phoned again. Seemed that I had convinced him we didn't have the money."

"But you do, or your family does." Horse-breeders generally had deep pockets.

"I go by my married name, you see, and Travis is not wealthy. The kidnapper doesn't know that I'm a Barrett."

"Good thing or he'd have wanted more."

"Exactly what I thought."

"Did you record the second call?"

"Yeah. Here it is."

"If you can't raise a million, how about half?" said the same voice as before.

"I'll try to get the money," Jessamine said.

"You'd better pay up, or that will be the end of him. Be in downtown Hopkinsville by eight tomorrow morning, alone, and with the money."

Then the caller hung up.

"I was terrified," Jessamine said.

"He sounded jumpier, more erratic on this second call," I said. "You took a heavy risk by haggling, but it paid off. If you had agreed to the kidnapper's original demand, he might've raised the amount, assuming you could afford to pay more. Even so, half a million is still a lot of money. I wonder if he'd be open to further negotiations."

"Never mind that. My father has agreed to pay. That's why I'm going home—to get the money. I talked to Dad right before I called you. He insisted I come and meet with him in person."

Ah, her rich, powerful father still wanted to call the shots, even when it meant life or death for his son-in-law.

"I assume even he doesn't keep five hundred grand in cash lying around the house."

"No, but he told me he had a cooperative banker. They were that way if you kept enough of your money on deposit, he said."

"Whether or not he pays it, though, once someone goes missing, the chances of getting them back safe go down by the hour. There's something else you need to know. Even when paid off, kidnappers don't always release their victims."

"What are the chances they'll live up to the agreement?"

"No way of knowing. You've been lucky so far. But trying to handle this by yourself probably won't turn out well. That's why you need to call in the cops."

"I don't intend to handle it by myself. I'm not calling for

your advice. I'm calling to hire you to help me get Travis back."

"I'm a detective, not a miracle worker. How do you think I'm going to do that?"

"I don't know how, but you did it before, and I believe you can again. Last time, it was Mom you saved without calling the police. This time it's Travis."

Jessamine sounded a little breathless now, maybe on the verge of hysteria. "The kidnappers hold all the cards. At best, they'll take your money and release Travis. At worst, they'll just take your money."

"I believe you are our best hope of keeping that from happening. I'm desperate, and I'll pay you well to take the case."

Hearing this put on a professional basis reminded me how much I needed the work, as I was between investigations. Since the pandemic, little money had come in. But expenses still went out. I had given up my office, working from home now. From what I'd heard, I feared for Travis Tilford's life. Still, if I didn't take the job, Jessamine would find someone else to handle it, probably someone less skilled.

"Okay, I'll do it. I'll need you to sign a contract. We can work out the details later. Now the kidnapper was very specific about the amount of the ransom and when you were to be in the downtown area in the morning. Any ideas about where exactly it might take place?"

"Not a clue. Downtown Hopkinsville's not that big, though."

The wind had gone, leaving me miserably hot, and I mopped my brow as I stared across the river toward Indiana. "Lucky for us. You say you're headed for Louisville?"

"Yeah, I'll be at the farm in about an hour or so. Can you meet me there?"

I said I would and hung up.

I headed back to shore, tied off the *Ariel* at my next-door neighbor's dock and by the time she was shipshape, I had sweated out the two beers I drank. I climbed the small bluff to the old fishing camp where I lived, a rustic concrete box surrounded by upscale resort homes, a few miles upriver from Louisville. I inherited it from my great uncle, who built it back when the area was woods and wetlands. I loved living on the river. And I didn't care what my neighbors thought.

It was ninety-four degrees and one-hundred percent humidity—shorts and T-shirt weather. Nevertheless, after stripping and showering, I opted for a short-sleeved dress shirt and khakis. I could always shed the office casual look later. I got a standard contract, grabbed my go bag out of the bedroom closet, and unlocked the gun safe. A double barrel twelve-gauge pump shotgun was useful for almost any shooting situation. I put mine into a black polyester tote bag, along with a back-up .38, extra ammo, and some GPS mini trackers.

After locking up the house, I stowed both bags in the trunk of my Mustang and stashed my .45 semi-automatic in the glove compartment. The Mustang was dented, dinged, and scratched with high mileage and significant wear. But I knew a guy who kept it running smoothly, and it started right up, as always, with that signature rumble.

I put it in gear and headed for the horse farm.

Chapter 2

It was a twenty-minute drive from my house to the Barrett place off U.S. 42, the winding old two-lane highway that used to be the main road between Louisville and Cincinnati. Now it was quieter and had a more moneyed look with rolling fields and black rail fences. Barrett Farm was shielded by a heavy iron gate attached to massive fieldstone pillars. I pressed the security button, said I was Guthrie, and the gates swung open.

I went up a shady lane, passing pastures of romping, grazing Thoroughbreds. Halfway to the house was a blind curve. On my first visit here long ago, a speeding Porsche whipped around it and ran me off the road. I was sitting stunned in a ditch with a bump on my head as the Porsche stopped and backed up. The driver leaned her head out the window to say sorry, then went on her merry way. My introduction to Jessamine Barrett.

I hoped now I was dealing with a more responsible adult.

A faint smell of fresh manure lingered in the air as I passed a peaked-roof horse barn and came to a stacked stone fence, where I parked. I followed an azalea-lined path to an ancient log cabin with a sprawling steel and glass addition. The front door was hewn from oak with hand forged hinges, an iron handle instead of a doorknob. Bluegrass aristocracy. Hooking my shades over my top shirt button, I knocked. The maid answered, a large, dark-skinned woman in her sixties wearing a lavender blouse with matching tennis shoes.

"Hello, Mr. Guthrie. Nice to see you again," she said, her tone somber.

"Nice to see you, too, Mrs. Jackson."

"Mrs. Barrett's expecting you."

"What about Jessamine?" I asked.

"She's not here. I believe she's meeting Senator Barrett at his bank."

Mrs. Jackson ushered me through the two-room pioneer structure, with its chinked log walls and hand-sawed hardwood floors, to a hallway decorated with fine watercolors of Thoroughbreds and jockeys in racing silks, all painted quickly with big brushes and good technique. Watercolors are unforgiving. Make one mistake and there's no correcting it. I preferred acrylics—cheaper and easier to use. I painted in the spare bedroom, which since the pandemic also served as my office. Some are surprised to learn that a grubby private eye would have a passion for art. But I do, painting landscapes mostly for myself but sometimes showing my work in a gallery.

The hallway led to a contemporary sunroom with a cathedral ceiling and a wide glass southern exposure. More art on the other walls—realistic oil paintings, sketches, photographs. All professional quality, and all dogs. The rug had a doggy design, and end tables were overflowing with doggy bric-a-brac. Next to a huge, life-sized stature of an Irish wolfhound stood the keeper of this canine shrine, looking out the big window. After announcing me, the maid withdrew.

Cybil Barrett, Jessamine's mother, turned and faced me.

"Jim, I'm so glad you're here. We're all terrified." She sounded hoarse, her voice cracking with tension, and seemed nervous, harried. Having a family member kidnapped will do that to you. It's such a cold-hearted, unpredictable crime.

"I came as quick as I could, Cybil."

She glided over and clamped her cold hands around my arm. "Thank you for coming. This is just unbearable, horrifying. Jessamine just can't lose Travis—"

"I'll do everything I can to keep that from happening," I said.

She flashed a smile. "I know you will. Just having you here makes me feel better."

"Jessamine's not back from the bank yet, I take it?"

"That's right. She and Shelby will be along any time now. Come sit down with me."

With the clock ticking and the kidnapper's deadline growing ever closer, I was itching to get started. But there was no way to rush this.

"You know, you haven't changed at all," she said, and drew me toward a Louis XIV settee.

Not liking its flimsy look, I swerved to an armchair instead.

"Neither have you," I said.

We were both lying, of course.

When I first met this small, slender, auburn-haired woman, she was in her mid-forties but working hard at staying thirty. Now at sixty, she still had her figure, but had traded the plunging neckline for an embroidered peasant top. She had some wrinkles and sagging skin but I detected no signs of cosmetic surgery. I was still a rangy six-three and two-twenty-five, but with crow's feet now and an alarming number of shaggy gray hairs.

After an uncomfortably long moment of silence, she said, "So, still detecting after all these years."

"Unfortunately, crime never goes out of style," I said, feeling more antsy by the minute. "How's your dog?" In this setting, an inevitable question.

"I'm afraid Magoffin has gone to that great kennel in the sky," she said, hiding her grief behind hard-boiled irony.

"I'm sorry. That was a tactless question."

"As I recall, you were always a little skittish around him."

Small wonder. Next to Cybil's dog, the hound of the Baskervilles would pale. Her Irish wolfhound stood over seven feet tall on his hind legs, with a wiry gray coat, foot-long snout, and tennis ball-sized eyes.

"I have another wolfhound now, Maeve."

She smiled as I looked around apprehensively, listening for the click of ten-penny toenails on hardwood. But no dog appeared. I was going to ask about her husband when he and his daughter came in, each toting a briefcase that looked heavy, presumably full of money. While Jessamine smiled at the sight of me, Barrett regarded me with consternation.

"What's he doing here?" he asked.

Testy as ever.

"I called him," Jessamine said.

Barrett looked at her with frustration. "Why didn't you tell me?"

"I knew how you'd react."

"I told you we didn't need anyone else's help. Certainly not his."

Shelby had big white teeth, shaggy brows, and eyes so dark they seemed burned into his deeply tanned face. In his boots, jeans, and short-sleeve denim work shirt, he looked as if he might have been out chopping brush. He was much the same as I remembered him, but older and grayer.

"We've been all through this, Dad."

"Yes, we have. And I told you what needs to happen," he said, in a voice used to ordering people around.

I sat there quietly, letting it play out. Shelby Barrett was providing the ransom money. If he really didn't want me around, this could be a short visit. Whether I stayed or went was up to Jessamine. I'd been reluctant to get involved. But now that I'd sunk my teeth into this, I didn't want to let go. And time was slipping away.

Jessamine planted her huaraches wide apart like a boxer about to put up his dukes. "I love you, Dad, but you don't get to tell me that."

Barrett seemed ready to take up the challenge.

Other than their combativeness, I saw little physical resemblance between them. Barrett was wide-bodied and thick-necked like a wrestler. Jessamine was svelte in shorts and a blue T-shirt. She had her mother's hair, one long strand curling at her throat.

"Damn it, Jess. I told you—*explained* to you—that I'd deliver the money myself," Barrett said.

"No, you won't. You'd probably wind up kidnapped yourself. I'm afraid of what might happen to Travis if we don't get some professional help."

"I see. You want my money, but not my counsel or involvement." Barrett slammed down his briefcase, which looked sturdy. Half a million in twenty-dollar bills weighed over a hundred pounds—I'd done the math. I hoped the cases were made of extra thick cowhide and heavy gauge steel, with padded leather handles.

Jessamine set hers down, and in that rich deep voice of hers said, "I'm already doing what you want by not calling the police. You've made me come home and wait. Let's just get on with it and save Travis, all right?"

Not calling the cops because Barrett didn't want them was news to me. Jessamine had said she didn't want them because they might get her husband killed. I understood why Barrett didn't want me involved. He'd been furious when I exposed some of his family's dirty laundry to rescue Cybil and he had never gotten over it. But that didn't explain why he wouldn't want police assistance. Unless there was some political angle. Or maybe he just wanted to be macho and in-charge.

"What we need to focus on," Jessamine continued, "is saving Travis's life. That's what matters, isn't it? Even if it is your money?"

"I thought that's what we were doing," Barrett snapped.

"Stop it, both of you," Cybil said. "That's enough. Now let's all sit down and discuss this rationally."

I was surprised when they sat down. Jessamine gave me a

pleading look.

Time to speak up.

"Senator, I know I'm not your favorite person, but Jessamine's right about this. Doing it yourself is a bad idea. You don't have the experience and you're too important to put yourself at risk. You're a public figure. If you were recognized, the kidnapper's demands might go way up. They might even try to abduct you. Even if you don't want to work with the police, you still need someone who's done this before."

"I suppose that means you?" Barrett asked, still fuming.

"Jessamine thinks so. You don't have time to get anyone else."

"At your usual rates?" Barrett asked.

I told them what I'd need. Jessamine reached for her purse.

"I'll take care of it," her father said.

"No, you've already done enough."

She wrote out a check and handed it to me.

I passed her a contract. "I'll need you to read this and sign it."

I placed her check in my wallet. When I had her signature, I pocketed the contract. "All right, now I need a recent photograph of your husband."

Jessamine lifted her phone out of her purse. "I'll text you one. Then can we go?"

"Sure." She seemed barely able to contain her impatience, and that was understandable. I was anxious to get on with it, too. But we couldn't afford to go off half-cocked. Part of my job would be calming her down. I was pondering how to do it when Travis Tilford's picture appeared on the screen of my phone. I was looking at a waist high shot of a man taken in front of a thick grove of evergreens. He looked deeply tanned, with curly dark brown hair and beard stubble that had not touched a razor in days. His khaki vest had about twenty pockets. Dark sunglasses and an orange baseball cap—apparently the one in his captor's video—completed his scrappy, outdoorsy appearance. Travis

Tilford struck me as more the bush pilot type than a movie director.

"Will that do?" Jessamine asked.

"It's fine. He looks like a survivor. Tell me more about him."

Travis was thirty-two years old. He kept himself in good shape and was in perfect health. He was also level-headed, not prone to panic in a crisis.

"Good to know," I said. His life might depend upon it.

"Can we go now?" she said.

"Take it easy, Jess," I said, hoping to soothe.

But her annoyance and frustration were growing.

"Why is this taking so long?" she mumbled under her breath.

"I need to know more facts. Try to be patient."

"Patient, hell!" she said, looking exasperated.

"I know. It's tough. But you need to answer my questions."

The stolen vehicle was an old white GMC van big enough to haul their film equipment. She'd written down the license number. I copied it into my well-worn pocket-sized notebook. Upon my request, she showed me the video she had recorded, working her phone until a man appeared on screen.

"Are you sure that's Travis?" I asked.

"I'm positive. That's the stupid orange baseball cap he loves so much lying beside him."

"Thought I recognized it." We replayed the thirty-second video. I studied it. No blood was a plus. I listened for background noises. Heard traffic, air conditioning, muffled talk. Possibly, the kidnapper was indoors and near a roadway when he called and might not have been alone. Not much to go on, though the latter could prove significant.

"What's your sense about the kidnapper? Was he trying to disguise his voice at all?"

"Hard to say."

I asked who else knew about all this.

"Only the people in this room. Possibly Mrs. Jackson, but she has our trust," Jessamine said.

"What about Travis's folks? Does his family know he's been kidnapped?"

"His parents are both dead. He's an only child and has no one else. Can we wrap this up, please, and go?"

I looked at Barrett. "Do you know of anyone who might be harboring a grudge against you or your family, senator? Political or business enemies? Anyone who might try to get back at you?"

"By kidnapping my son-in-law? No."

"Okay. Last but not but least, Jessamine, tell me about your documentary film. Hopkinsville's not exactly a movie mecca—or a tourist magnet. Why make it there?"

"Because of the festival."

"The Little Green Men Festival? What haven't you told me?" Shelby looked about ready to pop.

I hoped she wasn't going to say Travis had been kidnapped by aliens.

A flush crept across her cheeks. Clearing her throat, Jessamine said, "There's another video. Two, in fact. It's a long story."

I couldn't wait to hear about this.

Chapter 3

"Why am I only hearing about this now?" I asked, miffed and wary.

"I was in a hurry. I'm showing them to you now." Jessamine collected her laptop and played a short YouTube video titled: "Mysterious monolith discovered in the forest in Hopkinsville, Kentucky." It began with a tall silvery column standing in a clearing in the woods. In front of the column was a masked figure dressed in black.

"This is the video we made last night," Jessamine said. "That's me in front of the camera. Travis is behind it. We shot the video around two a.m. at Kelly Station Park."

"Why? What's the purpose of this?"

"It was a publicity stunt to promote our movie about the great monolith craze of 2020." She looked at my blank expression. "You don't remember?"

I shook my head.

"That November," Jessamine said, her pitch sinking even lower as if she were narrating the video, "some bighorn sheep counters in a helicopter saw a metallic flash in a remote Utah desert canyon. When they went down to investigate, they found a monolith deeply embedded in the red rock floor. Like everyone else who saw it online, Travis and I were fascinated and wanted to know what was going on."

"So, what was going on?" I asked.

"That's what our documentary is about."

"Seems a little thin for a movie."

"That's what I thought, too," Barrett said.

"But it isn't! Who puts something like that out in the middle of the desert like a ship in a bottle and waits five years for it to be found? Then the other monoliths began popping up all over the world. They found one at an archeological site in Romania, another on a mountaintop hiking path in California. Even one made of gingerbread in San Francisco. Over a hundred on five continents. And then it just stopped. Where did they come from? Who did it and why? That's what the movie's about."

"So, where did they come from?" I asked, getting interested in spite of myself.

"It's still a bit of a mystery," Jessamine replied. "Lots of speculation. At first, some assumed it was aliens. Others thought they were some bizarre form of devil worship, so they started tearing them down. Another school of thought was they were a Banksy-style art installation."

"Banksy?"

"The infamous vandal," Barrett said.

"Shelby, please," Cybil said.

"Come on, Guthrie," Jessamine said. "Try to keep up. Banksy. The famous yet anonymous graffiti artist whose tags always stir up a media frenzy. Like the silhouette of Mona Lisa aiming a bazooka that Banksy spray painted on a brick wall."

"Somebody else's brick wall," Barrett pointed out.

"It's social commentary," Cybil said.

"Oh, that Banksy," I said. "You're saying nobody knows for sure who started the craze?"

"That's right, although various claims have been made. I'm rooting for aliens myself," Jessamine said.

"Aliens," I said.

"Benevolent ones," she said. "Although maybe not."

"How does that explain what you did?"

"What's to explain?" Jessamine seemed excited now, her dread momentarily forgotten.

"Travis and I felt it was a sign from the film gods. Since we were already in California, we started there, documenting one monolith site after another, from Atascadero to Santa Clarita to San Luis Obispo. Unfortunately, by then all the monoliths were long gone and so were the people who had first-hand knowledge about them. We'd have to track them down, and it would be costly. Making a film, any film, is ruinously expensive. Even low budget indie films cost $750,000 on average."

"What funding did you have?" I asked.

Jessamine looked at her parents. "Dad staked us, but we were almost out of money when Travis had a vision."

"A vision?" I echoed.

"Epiphany, stroke of genius, whatever you want to call it. We had our set designer fabricate a monolith prop, one that looked like the original but was ultralight. He made it using foam and a steel rod to hold it together and provide ballast."

"Where is the monolith now?"

"It was in the truck when Travis disappeared."

"What were you hoping to achieve?"

"If enough people saw the video, it would attract new investment. We decided the best place for others to find our monolith would be at the annual Little Green Men Festival in Hopkinsville. It attracts all kinds, from weirdos and visionaries to UFO believers and conspiracy theorists. We wanted to hear what they would say about the monolith."

After watching her video again, I said, "You mentioned two videos. Let's see the other one."

Shot with a shaky hand-held cam, this video offered a behind-the-scenes version of making video one. It recorded one masked figure recording another using stage lights on tripods. After about thirty seconds, the monolith was disassembled and, with the lights, put into a white panel truck that drove off slowly into the night.

"Wait. The kidnapper used Travis's phone to call you with the ransom demand. But this video was made earlier than that—before the kidnapper got his hands on Travis's phone. How?"

"He called on our motel room phone late last night."

"How did he know where you were staying?"

"He must've followed us there from the park."

"That means he could be watching your room. We'll have to be extremely careful."

"The extortionist said he was sending us a video and demanded fifty grand *not* to release it."

"Because you were perpetrating a hoax," I said.

"No more so than any of the other monolith makers. We preferred to think of it as an August Fool's joke. But I guess now the joke is on us." Jessamine's thin smile faded. "Anyway, after we watched it, Travis laughed at the guy. 'Go ahead, expose us. All publicity is good publicity,' he said."

"This could be very bad news," I said.

"Why do you say that?"

"Travis may have made the guy mad by mocking him. If so, the kidnapping may be as much about getting even with Travis as about money. If it isn't just a for-profit scheme, paying the ransom won't work. If it's about having power over Travis, or hurting him, we'll have to take a different approach."

"Like what?" Jessamine asked.

"Using force."

"But they'll kill Travis if we try anything," Jessamine said.

"Maybe they'll kill him if we don't."

"That's a brutal thing to say," Cybil said.

"Yes, but it had to be said. Kidnapping is a capital offense, punishable by death. That means the kidnapper has nothing to lose by harming his victim after he's collected the ransom."

"What can we do?" Jessamine said.

"We can trace the kidnapper's phone number. Try to find

out who, and where, he is."

"Can you do that?"

"Yeah. I know a guy."

Jessamine gave the phone number to me. I wrote it down.

"Now, what do we know about the kidnapper?" I asked.

"Not much," Jessamine said. "Except he's a ruthless criminal. And he was at the fair."

"We know more than that," I said. "This doesn't feel like a well thought out crime. If nobody else knew about the monolith ahead of time, the kidnapper must have stumbled across it. Who would be out in a hayfield in the middle of the night?"

"Somebody high on space juice who had passed out?" Jessamine said.

"My thought exactly. Maybe he wakes up, sees a strange light in the woods, and staggers over to investigate. Seeing the monolith, he whips out his phone and sets in motion this half-baked extortion scheme."

"We know he's greedy," she said. "But willing to accept less than his first demand."

"He also took a huge risk in snatching Travis in broad daylight in front of possible witnesses. So, he's impulsive. Probably angry. And making mistakes. Not a pro. Considering all this, I'd advise you to pay the ransom."

"But I thought you said we might have to use force."

"We might. But we must find Travis first. Let's insert a GPS tracking device with the money. If the kidnapper doesn't release Travis as promised, at least then we'll have some way to hunt him down and rescue Travis."

"That's your big plan?" Barrett sneered. "Anyone who watches television knows about GPS trackers. The kidnapper will probably just take the cash out and dump the briefcases."

"Probably, but this can still work. Open one of the cases," I said.

Frowning, Barrett unsnapped the catches. Inside the case were thick bundles of cash.

"Okay, suppose he takes the money out and dumps the cases like you said. Criminals are lazy by nature, always looking to turn a fast buck the easy way. It's unlikely the kidnapper would do any work he didn't have to. And he has already revealed himself as no criminal mastermind. I very much doubt he'll go through every cash brick carefully enough to find a hidden tracker this big."

I pulled a quarter out of my pocket and held it up.

"It sticks to surfaces and has a built-in SIM that communicates to an app on a cell phone. What you see on the phone is a GPS map with the money's location lit up."

"You could be wrong about how the kidnapper will behave," Barrett said.

"Possibly. But I'm not. This is our best shot."

"Do we have enough time to get them?" Jessamine asked.

"I brought some with me."

Next, I explained my plan. We'd follow the kidnapper's instructions to the letter—except for the trackers—pay the ransom, and hope he let Travis go. He might. But if he didn't, I'd follow and take Travis away from him.

"All right," Jessamine said.

"Are you sure that's what you want to do?" her father asked.

"I'm sure. Let's go." She stood up.

I got to my feet. "Any questions?"

"Oh, Jessamine, I wish you hadn't ever gone down there. You know Hopkinsville's always been unlucky for me," Cybil said.

"It'll be all right, Mom," Jessamine said. "I'm going to bring Travis home safe."

"Keep us informed," Barrett said.

"We will," Jessamine said.

Neither of our cars was exactly invisible. But we might need them both. We decided to drive separately. Barrett insisted on personally stowing the briefcases in Jessamine's trunk.

And then we got moving.

Chapter 4

We flew along southbound I-65 at high speed in the rush hour traffic, passing clusters of warehouses and manufacturing facilities. As we left the city behind, I used the hands-free cell device that was my Mustang's only new feature to call my hacker and give him the phone number to trace for the usual fee.

Then I focused on driving, which was necessary just to keep up with Jessamine's cannonballing. Why was she driving so fast? I wondered if she was taking out her fears and anxiety on the road. Unfazed by the congestion, she phoned me. We weighed our options for tonight. When I mentioned getting another room, she said Hopkinsville was booked solid for the festival. So, we had no choice but to share the one she already had.

"I'm not sure that's a good idea. The kidnapper could be watching your motel. We don't want to scare him off or lose the element of surprise. Besides, that would be certain to raise eyebrows."

"If you're worried about what my husband might think, don't be. He'll understand."

"I'm not so sure about that."

"What do you suggest instead?" she said, picking up the pace even more when the interstate shrank from ten lanes to six.

"You know, we don't have to be there until tomorrow morning," I said.

"What's the matter? Won't that Mustang of yours keep up?"

It would, and I roared along behind her. I really didn't know what to do about lodging, so I said, "Play it by ear." As she swerved between two semis, I asked how she was doing.

"Oh, swell."

I envisioned a pained stare, a white-knuckled grip on the steering wheel, and muscles jumping under her skin. Or maybe that was just me trying to keep up. We raced through farmland and forest, and reached the knobs still in one piece, where the semis slowed down for the climb. Then we played the dangerous game of flooring it to get around them, adding more tension to our already nerve-wracking journey.

"What did your mother mean about Hopkinsville being bad luck for her?" I asked.

"You know she's from there," Jessamine said. "That's where all her troubles began."

"I must have forgotten," I said. "It's been a long time."

"Yes, it has."

"Tell me how you met Travis," I said, hoping to distract her from her fears and reduce her speed. I'd have better luck slowing down a cruise missile.

"We met at a party. I overheard this cute guy saying that fifty-thousand indie features get made every year, but only one in a thousand ever reaches an audience. I told him that was depressing. 'Better to know what you're up against from the start rather than find out too late,' he said."

"Makes sense," I said, weaving across two lanes of traffic as the pavement rushed by.

"He also pointed out that if you let that stop you from making your film, then it was certain nobody would ever see it."

"What sort of films was Travis interested in making?"

"He was still searching for what he called his 'one true subject.' But once he found it, nothing would stop him from making the film. 'No budget? No problem.' He'd fight for it no matter how long it took. I really admired him for that."

"Idealistic," I said. "You took similar stands in preventing cruelty to animals, as I recall."

"Being a wild-eyed radical, you mean?"

"You could put it that way," I said.

"We were both eager to make meaningful films."

Jessamine soon discovered that they had a lot in common, even though their backgrounds were vastly different. "Travis was a west coast boy, raised by his widowed mother. At an early age, he started making stop motion clay animation movies with his father's old Super8 cam. By the time we met, he already had a couple of music videos under his belt, plus a web series."

"Impressive," I said, though she had to explain that a web series meant video episodes broadcast online rather than on TV—and do so while bending perilously around a sharply banked curve.

She and Travis started going out, moved in together, and tied the knot.

"My parents had a fit because we didn't have the classic black and white, beautifully photographed church wedding. No exotic destination. No huge reception. Just a simple civil ceremony in front of a justice of the peace."

"Whose idea was that?" I asked, skeptical that she hadn't wanted the big wedding expected of Bluegrass Blue Bloods.

"Mine. Travis wouldn't have been comfortable dealing with an onslaught of entitled well-wishers. He has enough trouble dealing with me. Besides, when it comes to ceremonial displays of wealth, I'm a bit of a Marxist."

"Who owns a Mercedes-Benz," I said.

"An old one," she said.

I appreciated the irony, but less so at ninety miles an hour. "You know, Jess, if you don't want cops, you should slow down."

Although so far, I hadn't seen cop one.

"Where's the fun in that?" she said.

She had not married Tilford for *his* money. He didn't have any. But a struggling moviemaker might find it useful to have a rich and powerful father-in-law. One, in fact, who already was bankrolling his project. Had Tilford faked his own kidnapping for fun and profit? Better to keep this dark thought to myself. For now. I needed to keep my mind on the road anyway if I wanted to make it to Hopkinsville alive.

"By graduation, we had applied for several grants to fund our first film on climate change. But funding dried up because of the pandemic, and we were also in quarantine," Jessamine said.

We exited at Elizabethtown on two wheels and picked up the Western Kentucky Parkway, now 125 miles from Hopkinsville. This stretch of road was lightly traveled, thinly populated, and deeply forested. It felt almost like driving through a national forest during the off season—on a racetrack. Jessamine and I had switched off our phones for a while. But I couldn't help wondering what the former animal rights activist thought about the alarming number of mangled deer carcasses alongside the road.

Maybe that's why she eased back the throttle a bit.

That allowed me to catch my breath and go over everything I knew about the kidnapping case so far without running off the road. I started with the monolith in Hopkinsville. But was it any more of a sham than the other monoliths? Only if you claimed it was of extraterrestrial origin, I suppose, and Jessamine hadn't done that. Aside from the monolith as the triggering event, I had nothing but a video showing a kidnapped documentary filmmaker, and a variable ransom demand ranging from fifty grand to a million dollars and back to half a million. It was possible that the victim was hiding out in luxury somewhere while his father-in-law coughed up the cash to finance his film. Could Jessamine be in on such a scheme? She'd almost have to be for it to work. But would she do that to her own father?

They had a thorny relationship—and she had gone to extremes before. But always with some moral justification.

Even if innocent, that didn't make her any less dangerous. And I wasn't just thinking about her driving. Hadn't she almost gotten me killed the last time I worked for her family? She had been arrested for slapping a downtown restaurant owner who was serving exotic game. "Zebras are the quintessential zoo animal," I remembered her saying. "They're noble, beautiful, and they're a horse. Kentucky's whole heritage comes from horses—and here we are, carving them up." Before the incident was over, I'd been arrested for defending her, grabbed off the street by killers, and barely survived a fifty-foot fall into the Ohio River off the "bridge to nowhere"—an abandoned railroad span whose steel approaches were torn down—when I stepped into a hole in the crossties while running for my life.

Ah, nostalgia.

Outside Hopkinsville, I phoned Jessamine and arranged for us to take the first exit. Pulling well off the road into a rocky parking area, I got my .38 out of the trunk and slid in beside her.

"Do you think I'll really need that?" she asked when I showed her the gun.

"Not when you're behind the wheel."

She thought about that before grinning.

"Better to have the gun than not, just in case," I said. "Ever shot one of these?"

"Once, a long time ago."

I showed her how to use the revolver safely. "You have six chambers, but leave one empty to keep from shooting by accident." I removed the bullets. Told her to always point it in a safe direction. And to keep her finger off the trigger until ready to shoot. "Never point it at anyone unless you mean to shoot them—and if so, aim for center mass." I tapped my chest. I showed her how to line up the shot as if pointing her finger, then to gently squeeze the trigger. She dry-fired the gun a few times, and I reloaded it.

"Do you want to wait back at the motel or come to the crime scene? Either way, it won't do for us to be seen together. And it could be dangerous. That's why I'm giving you the .38."

"I'm coming with you," she said.

Hopkinsville. Population of thirty-one thousand. The shady streets, windowed storefronts, and small clapboard houses made it seem like a typical small southern city. Traffic was heavy through downtown. We slogged by newly restored government buildings, seeing out-of-county plates and bumper stickers evoking flying saucers and spacemen.

JUST VISITING THIS PLANET.
WE ARE NOT ALONE.
READY FOR ABDUCTION.

I hoped Jessamine had missed the latter.

Congestion eased somewhat as we left town and headed north on a two-lane highway paralleling the CSX railroad tracks. The countryside was mostly farmland with some houses and an occasional church. Driving at legal speed—never a certainty with Jessamine—we covered the distance from downtown to Kelly Station Park in under ten minutes. As we reached the turnoff and went across the railroad tracks onto Old Madisonville Road, I saw SUVs and pickup trucks lining the narrow country lane. Up ahead were flashing blue lights and a uniformed deputy directing traffic.

Jessamine phoned to say the parking lots were probably full and our best bet would be to pull off here. I agreed, and we parked there on the grass. She'd kept her engine running for air conditioning purposes. I moved up to the Benz and got in.

"Stay in the car while I walk around, get a feel for this place," I said.

"No way," Jessamine snapped. "I didn't come along just to be cooped up in my car."

"I understand. But we shouldn't be seen together."

"So, keep your distance."

"This car will really stand out here among the pickup trucks. What if someone breaks in and steals the ransom money while you're out hobnobbing?"

"That's unlikely. And I don't know how to hobnob."

"It's probably a lost art."

"Besides, you're the one who's going to stand out like a sore thumb dressed like that. I thought private eyes were supposed to keep a low profile."

I looked at my clothes. "I'll change. Where's the gun I gave you?"

"It's in the glove compartment."

"Take it with you. And remember, we don't know each other."

"I'll keep one eye on the car while I'm shopping for out of this world fashions," she said.

With all that settled, I got some shorts and a T-shirt from my go bag and put them on while mostly shielded by the Mustang.

Country rock music was playing loudly as I started toward the park, which was across the road from a jumble of house trailers and a swath of clutter. It reminded me that we'd come to the opposite end of the spectrum from wealthy horse farm country. Noting something unusual about the entrance to a nearby parking lot, I decided to cut across the road. It was a green golf cart occupied by posterboard cutouts of waving little green men. Not your traditional small metallic humanoid aliens, but large, pointy-eared, green-skinned, goblin-like ones with big claws, oversized eyes, and bulbous heads sprouting antenna. Beside them was a sign:

DESIGNATED FLYING SAUCER PARKING ONLY
VIOLATORS WILL BE BEAMED OUT
AT OWNER'S EXPENSE

Thinking I'd hate to pay those towing charges, I cut through the cars, rusty pickup trucks, and SUVs and moved toward the midway. It was busy for a blistering Thursday afternoon. The promoters must have been pleased by the turnout. Hundreds of festival goers seemed to be having a good time. This included all ages, from unflatteringly dressed older folks to young women with bare midriffs, jangling bracelets, and tattoos. Long lines formed at the refreshment stands and striped tents. The booths were filled with Little Green Men Festival themed merchandise, ranging from commemorative quilts and T-shirts to buttons and DVDs. Kiddie swings and an inflated wading pool had been set up, along with picnic tables and acres of folding metal chairs.

In many ways, this festival was the same as an ambitious but plain old country fair. People waited, sweating, for a turn at the portable red, yellow, and orange carnival rides. Or for a seat on a long flatbed trailer pulled around by a tractor. Children rode in a three-car, black, and red cartoon choo-choo train.

But the kids were all wearing alien masks or face paintings, as were some adults.

With all this going on, it was hard to believe someone could be kidnapped without anyone else noticing. Of course, not that many were around earlier this morning when Travis was abducted. Still, it was a brazen attempt. That said something about who I was dealing with.

I came across an information booth inhabited by a volunteer clad in a Kelly-Green LGMF T-shirt and cap. Her nametag read "CHRISTY." Wisps of gray hair showed above her ears.

"Where can I see this monolith that I've been hearing so much about?" I asked.

"Oh, I'm sorry. I'm afraid you're too late. It's gone," she said.

"Well, shoot, Christy. I came all the way down here from Louisville to see it."

She frowned sympathetically. "I don't know if anybody really saw it, other than online. It disappeared right away. It's been a huge draw, though."

"Think it was aliens?"

"Who knows? Fun to imagine, though, isn't it?"

She seemed fairly level-headed, so I risked asking, "This festival sure is unusual. How the heck did it ever get started?"

Christy lowered her vinegary western Kentucky twang to a confidential level. "Well, the city needed something. Back during the Clinton administration, government restrictions on raising tobacco had killed Christian County's cash crop. Unemployment tripled. Stores and factories closed. Young people fled in droves. We had to act. So, we came up with this festival."

"Why aliens? Why not Fort Campbell helicopters? Or soybeans?"

"We had two possibilities. One was the historic railroad depot, which once was the only place between Louisville and Nashville where you could drink alcohol legally. Passengers hopped off the train, got a drink, and hopped back on again. Hence the nickname *Hoptown*."

"Interesting. And possibility number two?"

Christy mopped at the small beads of perspiration clinging to her forehead. "The alien invasion of 1955 when they came to the Sutton farm just down the road in their flying saucers. Liked to have scared people to death, popping their little green faces in and out of doorways and windows. The farmers fired shotguns at them, but it didn't do any good. Eventually, the aliens left."

"So, it was either the train station or aliens?"

"That's right," Christy smiled. "We went with aliens."

"Have they ever come back?"

"Ah, that's the question, isn't it? We get a wide range of people here for this festival. Some of them take all this *very seriously*."

"For instance?" I smiled.

Looking around furtively, Christy said, "There's a panel discussion about to start on the bandstand. You listen to that for a while, and you'll see what I mean."

I waited for her to say more. Instead, she nodded at a poster I hadn't noticed.

"Please join us," it read. "Ours is a movement born of

outrage. Yet our shared hope is for a better universe that inspires people globally to show up and take action. As we mark this anniversary of the 1955 invasion, we invite you to join us in celebrating the change that occurs when people have the courage to demand a future where human rights are enjoyed by races from all planets."

What a bunch of gobbledygook.

Outrage. Take action. Demand.

But then I wondered if Travis Tilford's captor could have been motivated by this gibberish when he saw them monkeying around with the monolith. It seemed loony, but not as loony here as it would have back in Louisville.

I thanked Christy, picked up a brochure, and moved on.

Now I was wondering if the kidnapper was a local or a visitor. If he would stay away from here or return to the scene of the crime. My eyes swept the crowd for anything that looked unusual. But hell, everything looked *unusual.* Kentuckians loved outdoor fairs of any kind. But I hadn't expected all this hustle and bustle here just to celebrate an alleged alien invasion of a hayfield. Maybe it would help Jessamine and Travis garner more attention for their project. Wouldn't matter much if he didn't survive, though.

The park, I soon discovered, had only a trio of permanent attractions. One was the roofed bandstand Christy had mentioned. It was bedecked with sponsor banners and an American flag. Onstage, a three-piece band played loud electric guitars. The talk about little green men must have been next. But I didn't wait for it. The second permanent feature was a beautiful stone sundial shaped like a flying saucer. Unaccountably, it had the Ten Commandments written on it.

The third and signature attraction was a massive silver pavilion, also shaped like a flying saucer. According to my brochure, it measured 38-feet wide and weighed 2.5 tons. Nevertheless, it was said to be capable of "hovering" while lighting up and emitting smoke.

This, I would have to see. But apparently it only happened at night.

On top of the pavilion was a cockpit-like clear bubble where little green men sometimes waved. There was a tongue-like metal ramp that could serve as a sliding board.

This was such an Alice in Wonderland kind of place that I began to wonder if I was dreaming or awake, and whether something as serious as a kidnapping could have taken place here. But I knew it had. My next stop would be in the woods, where the monolith appeared.

I came to a small gravel parking lot near the back edge of the park. This was where Travis Tilford was grabbed, along with his truck. The tree line was about twenty-five yards away. I walked toward it on a single rock lane past parked vehicles and a playground with monkey bars, swings, and slides painted in bright primary colors. When I got to the woods, I found a dirt path and followed it a few more yards to a clearing. The place looked familiar, though somewhat different in daylight than when the monolith was here. Behind it, the land fell away sharply into a ravine maybe thirty feet deep.

I knew right away that I'd find nothing useful here, even if accompanied by bloodhounds, a decoder ring, and a deerstalker hat. The monolith was gone and there was no sign that it had ever been here. Any other forensic evidence had been trampled by curiosity seekers and would have been inadmissible in court, anyway. Not that it mattered, since my job was only to rescue Travis.

I puzzled again over what sort of criminal I was dealing with. How seriously did he take this whole alien business? He had been here for the festival. But he also was sufficiently rational and down to earth to pluck Travis Tilford out of movieland and demand a big ransom. But did he also believe in aliens? How might that impact my efforts to get Travis back? I pondered where I would hide Travis if I were the kidnapper.

My phone rang. Jessamine wanted to know how it was going.

"As you might expect. No silver bullets or magic solutions. Where are you?" I asked.

"In a tent looking at alien T-shirts. Want one?"

"No, thanks."

I told her where I was.

"Any idea where Travis is being held?" Jessamine asked.

"I was asking myself the same question. This is a rural area, and he could be almost anywhere. Maybe in an abandoned house? Or an old factory?"

"I know. It's just ..."

I waited while she searched for the right words.

"Just not what I hoped to hear."

"Look, I want to poke around here a bit longer. You never know what might turn up."

I returned to the middle of the park. On the way, I overheard a seemingly normal woman with a long braid down her back saying, "If God created this world, why not people from another planet?" Her own aunt had seen a spaceship back in the 1950s, she added.

Another woman said, "For a long time, I've thought that the government was covering it up. I think people have seen different shaped spaceships. The pictures don't lie."

Unless they're Photoshopped.

I kept moving until I came to a line for a Little Green Men Festival homemade costume contest. Some of the costumes were more imaginative than others. My favorite was the one consisting of aluminum foil pants and a green mop wig. That kid was having his picture taken with an adult clad in a standard LGMF outfit.

I went over and shook his long green hand.

"Is that costume uncomfortable?" I asked.

"Man, I'm sweating like a hog," he said.

So was I—without wearing a costume.

"What did you think of the monolith that showed up here last night?" I asked.

"Cool. Very cool." He repeated the word as if that might help lower his temperature.

"Think it was sent here by aliens?"

"It's not impossible. If we went to their planet, we'd be the aliens."

He definitely had a point there.

A few minutes later, I chanced upon a conversation and heard the word "monolith" used.

"Why do you think it disappeared?" a bearded guy in overalls asked, sipping something—space juice, maybe—from a paper cup.

"Did I mention the government?" said another.

I wondered how they'd react to the news that the Kelly monolith was a fake. I couldn't explain how I knew, so I didn't tell them.

Back at the bandstand, the musicians had been replaced by a foursome without musical instruments. The thinner, livelier of the two women was speaking into a mic. Her black hair was pulled back with a red ribbon. Clearing her throat, she said, "I'm so proud to be part of this panel of experts. When it comes to UFOs, it can be hard to know what to believe. There have always been fakes, and today anyone so inclined and with modest skills can fake a UFO video and put it on YouTube for worldwide distribution, which means that identifying the truth takes time and effort."

If she only knew.

When she noted that belief in intelligent life outside of Earth—aliens—was still more often ridiculed than not, the crowd booed loudly.

"But today it's more absurd *not* to believe in alien life," she continued. "Did you see where the Pentagon is forming a new task force to investigate UFOs that have been observed by U.S. military aircraft?" She pulled out a sheet of paper and read from it. The gist was a growing concern that unidentified flying aircraft posed a serious risk to U.S. military bases. "There is no consensus on their origin. That's a quote. If that's not proof that UFOs are being taken more seriously, I don't know what is."

I thought about military drones, stealth aircraft, and Chinese spy balloons. But nobody wanted to hear that.

Next came a fleshy-faced man with a droopy mustache.

"As our understanding of other planets, the solar system and the universe grows, we are collectively realizing that intelligent life simply must exist outside of Earth. You may be finding it difficult to uncover the truth on this subject because of government coverups and fakes. Aliens are real, and they love Kentucky. They come here all the time. Thousands of UFO-related incidents have been reported in Kentucky. The National UFO Reporting Center says about thirty out of every one-hundred thousand Kentuckians have seen some sort of an aerial phenomenon that defied earthly explanation. And those are just the ones that took the time to file an official report. Who knows how many actual encounters have occurred here without public awareness?"

As the speaker recited a litany of reported close encounters with extraterrestrials, I was doing the math in my head. It came out to about thirteen hundred, not *thousands*. Well, he was a UFO expert, not a mathematician. Meanwhile, I idly scoured the crowd for any faces that didn't seem to belong. It might have been futile, but was a step I could not ignore. And eventually I noticed two men toward the back who stood out because, unlike everyone else, they were not reacting to the speaker, only quietly talking to each other.

"How many of you have ever seen a real UFO?" the expert asked.

A surprising number of audience members raised their hands.

"Well, that just proves it, doesn't it?" he said.

Despite the heat, the shorter and plumper of the two men I'd noticed was dressed in a long beige cotton shirt and matching trousers. His uncombed, thin brown hair was shot with strands of gray. There was something perhaps not quite of this world about him and his meek-eyed expression. The blissfulness of an ascetic monk begging alms came to mind. His taller, wiry companion wore a short-sleeved shirt with bright multi-colored stripes. He had a bristly black beard, a shaved head, and tinted glasses with dark heavy frames.

"Now I want to talk to you about little green men. Have you seen any around here?"

At these words, costumed aliens started popping up. I counted ten of them. A roar erupted as the crowd leaped to its feet, clapping, hooting, and whistling. In the tumult, I lost track of the pair I was interested in. Now they were gone. I was thinking about how those tinted glasses and dark, heavy frames drew the eye away from the bearded man's face—and there was something familiar about him. I couldn't put my finger on it, though. As the symposium continued, I slipped away—sadly, without seeing the flying saucer-shaped pavilion light up, bounce, or blow smoke.

Chapter 5

Jessamine was waiting in her Mercedes with the motor running when I got back. Everything was all right, she said. Nobody had bothered her or the cash. "Learn anything?" she asked.

"Let's not talk here. It's been a long day. We both need a break, a chance to kick back and recharge. Are you hungry? Why don't we grab some takeout and eat it in your room?"

"What if it's being watched?"

"The kidnapper's probably not staking it out twenty-four seven. I won't come in unless the coast is clear."

"All right. I know where we can get a pizza. I'll order one on the way. What do you like on yours?"

I followed her to the pizza joint, keeping an eye out for a tail, then on to her twenty-room, one-floor downtown motel. By the time we got there, the sky was black. A red neon sign in front read, "Red Nebula Inn" and "No Vacancies." Below that, a disclaimer: "Nobody around here was ever caught up in a tractor beam."

Probably not an agricultural equipment reference.

No vacancies in the red brick, white-shuttered, fifties-style motor court. But plenty of empty spaces in the lot, so the other guests must have been out on the town. I watched from my car at the curb as Jessamine parked in front of room seven. She slid a key card into the lock, opened the solid white door, and turned on the lights. Then she carried two pizza boxes and a six-pack in a plastic bag into the room and shut the door. A couple minutes later, she emerged again from a yellow oblong of illumination with an ice bucket. Showing no awareness of possibly being under observation, she went to where the two legs of the L-shaped motel met and filled the bucket at a boxy self-service machine, then returned to her room.

I waited five minutes more and, seeing nothing suspicious, parked in an empty slot providing a clear view of Jessamine's room. Armed with only a Colt .45 semi-automatic and a pure heart, I ambled across the moon-mottled asphalt and knocked on her door. Jessamine parted the window's white curtains before letting me in. By then, my clothes were clinging, and the humid air oozed like freshly poured concrete.

"Welcome to The Red Nebula," she said, sounding exhausted.

The motel room was neither stylishly retro nor charmingly nostalgic, just old. It had two beds, a double and a single, with matching bedspreads of little green men. A large wall poster depicted a burst of bright crimson light in the night sky.

"Don't tell me," I said, "it's a red nebula—a cloud of gas and dust in outer space. I looked it up while I was waiting. Wonder if there's one in every room?"

"Maybe it was on sale," Jessamine said.

I strolled back to the window and peered out. Seeing no one in the lot or on the street, I asked Jessamine for her key fob and stepped outside. Sweat dripped from my pores and a mosquito buzzed in my ear as I went around to pop the trunk. Lifting out each briefcase was like hoisting a bucket of rocks.

I carried them inside and set them down on the thin gray carpet. After hanging a "DO NOT DISTURB" sign on the handle, Jessamine closed the door behind me.

"What are you paying for this room?" I asked, as I stashed the cases in the closet.

"A hundred and eighty a night."

"Seems like a lot."

"Twice the going rate. I have that on good authority."

"Whose authority?"

"The proprietor, Byron Hutchinson, Junior."

The pizzas were waiting unopened on the coffee table along with the beer. I flopped into a padded armchair and pulled two IPAs out of their plastic rings and offered one to Jessamine.

"What's he like?" I said, opening one for myself.

"Unusually candid. And well, *unusual*. Wait till you see his ears."

"His ears?"

"You'll see. Cheers." We clinked cans. "Byron Junior told us the Little Green Men Festival is Hopkinsville's answer to the Kentucky Derby. The price of everything is inflated."

"Speaking of inflated, what is this motel rated?"

"Fair, two point eight stars. I checked. It's a mom-and-pop operation. Except Pop's dead and there's no sign of Mom. Now Byron Junior runs it."

Jessamine took the other chair and sat on one knee facing a wall-mounted TV. The news was coming on, with the volume turned low. She used the remote to bring up the sound. The lead story on the local news turned out to be from Nashville, Hopkinsville having no station of its own. The TV flickered to life.

"Kentucky finally got its own monolith last night," the pert blond anchor reported.

"That's our footage." Jessamine pointed as a video of a monolith appeared on screen.

"The mysterious silver obelisk popped up in the woods behind Kelly Station Park near Hopkinsville last night, but it soon vanished," the newscaster reported. "This has prompted some locals to ask if it was the work of aliens, perhaps planting a surveillance device."

"First time I heard that one," Jessamine said. "I need to get a copy of this show."

"As word of the monolith spreads," the story continued, "fans are showing up in record numbers for the annual Little Green Men Festival, hoping to see another monolith."

Jessamine set her beer aside and turned down the sound.

"Just watching this," she said, "I feel so ... guilty for behaving normally while Travis is in danger. What the hell am I doing? I think I may be going out of my mind."

She looked like someone who'd been given a frightening diagnosis or a deadline she couldn't meet. I leaned toward her, looking into her eyes.

"Take it easy. Nobody should ever have to go through what you have in the last twenty-four hours, especially since this morning. You're probably experiencing a delayed reaction to the shock. In a situation like this, nobody knows how to feel. There's no right or wrong way. You have to cope as best you can."

"That's how you see it? Not me. I feel like a puddled mess who's about to fall apart completely."

"Take a deep breath and pull yourself together. Travis's fate depends on it."

She took a breath.

"Let's eat some pizza and drink a beer before we try to unravel this together. Okay?"

"Okay."

We opened both boxes, and each grabbed a slice. Veggie for her, pepperoni for me.

"This pizza's pretty good," I said, savoring my first bite. It had been a long time since breakfast.

"Travis loves pizza," Jessamine said, "especially with pineapple on it."

Envisioning this, I nearly gagged.

"He took me out for pizza on our first date. It was fancier than this one and a lot more expensive." She paused. "I didn't think I'd be able to eat this at all. But you're right. It tastes pretty good."

I tried to keep the conversation going to take off the edge. But making small talk proved difficult for us. We were of different generations, from different worlds, and seemingly had little in common outside trying to rescue her kidnapped husband. Instead of chatting, we wound up watching more news, weather, sports, and even traffic reports, all with the sound off, while continuing to eat.

"Feeling better?" I asked when it seemed we were both finished with the food.

"A little," she said. "I think the beer helps."

"I'd have to agree with that. Getting back to the case, I wanted to visit that festival to get a sense of the place, and now I have. What I saw there seemed like half family fun, half loony tunes. And the kidnapping itself seems like just plain bad luck."

"Doesn't matter. We can't let them hurt Travis," she said.

"We won't. There'll be no payoff without proof of life. The kidnapper has every reason to make sure Travis remains alive and well."

"Yes, but if the kidnapper doesn't hold up his end of the bargain—"

"Travis is the kidnapper's only bargaining chip. No matter how mad he is at Travis, he still wants the money, and will do what it takes to get it. We'll make sure the kidnapper knows he won't get paid if anything happens to Travis. We'll demand proof of life every step of the way. And we've got the trackers."

"It's just so scary," Jessamine said.

"I know." I had another thought. "Who else knew about your monolith?"

"Nobody but Curtis Farmer, our set designer. He built it."

"How well do you know Farmer? Are you sure you can trust him?"

"A long time. And yes, I'm sure. Curtis is our friend. And he will benefit from the movie. Besides, we didn't tell him where, or when, we were going to do this. We didn't tell anybody."

"That reinforces the idea of this being a random event."

"Random or not, I just hope they haven't hurt Travis."

"Me, too." Jessamine's anguish felt real enough. But she seemed a bit steadier now, more relaxed. Another idea occurred to me. And what good's a private eye who's not nagged by doubt? "How much has your father invested in your movie?"

"Several hundred thousand. Why?"

"Is there any way he might want to put a stop to it?"

"No. None whatsoever. Why would he? What are you getting at?"

"Just considering all the possibilities."

"My father being behind Travis's kidnapping is not a possibility, Guthrie."

"No, of course not." I set down the can as I finished my second beer. "How about this one? You've been married to Travis for how long?"

"Three years."

"Practically still newlyweds, then. But think about it. How well do you really know him? Is it possible that Travis staged his own kidnapping the way he staged the monolith's appearance?"

"That's crazy." Jessamine said, her mouth falling open.

"What if he needed to disappear?"

"For what possible reason?" she said, much louder.

"Takes a lot of money to make a film, you said. What if Travis had debts he couldn't pay?"

"No, I'd know if he did."

"Are you sure about that? Who keeps the books?"

"He does. But he wouldn't—"

"What if he needed to escape from dangerous people he owed money to and wanted to start a new life?"

"Start a new life without me? That's ridiculous."

"Is it?"

"Damn you, Guthrie." Jessamine stood up. "Get out."

"Calm down. I have to consider every possibility."

She stalked over to the door and held it open. "Consider

them elsewhere. Out."

I was experienced at detecting lies, but I was not spotting any. Maybe she'd invite me back in after she cooled off.

But she didn't.

Chapter 6

I should have known better. I'd pushed her too hard. Now I was in my car, snoozing away until jarred awake by a rhythmic rapping on my driver's window, closed against the mosquitos. Bleary-eyed, I saw a pasty-faced young man with lank black hair staring at me.

"You can't sleep here," he yelled.

Not with him pounding on my window like that, I couldn't.

I yawned, stiff as a crowbar, and rolled it down. "Who are you?" I growled, though I could have guessed from his T-shirt, which had a starburst design exactly like the one on Jessamine's wall, plus "RED NEBULA INN" lettered across the chest.

"I'm the manager. This is private property, and I'm warning you to leave before I call the police."

He sounded a bit stilted as if English was not his native tongue. There was also the matter of his ears. They were in the right place—between the eye and nose lines—but oversized and pointy-tipped, exactly like Mr. Spock's half-human, half-Vulcan ears in *Star Trek*. I wondered if they were real. They looked real. Surely, they hadn't been altered surgically. Still, people were doing weird things to their bodies these days—rings on their noses and eyebrows, tattoos on their faces.

"Look, I had a fight with my girlfriend, and she kicked me out," I improvised.

He looked dubious. "Is she registered here?"

"Room seven."

"Oh, I remember her. Good looking woman. Here with her husband. You are not him."

"No, I'm her boyfriend. Her husband was called away."

The innkeeper's disapproval was obvious. But he softened his expression when he asked, "Do you love her?"

I smiled. "Of course I do."

"And does she love you?"

In for a penny, in for a pound. "She does."

"Then why is she still with her husband?"

I shrugged. "It's complicated."

"I like complications," he said.

I was spared further dissembling by Jessamine stepping out of her room, fully dressed in gray pants and a white tube top that left her tanned shoulders bare.

"Jim, come quick," she called. "I need you right now."

"See what I mean? Gotta go."

"I don't want to stand in the way of love," Spock ears said, "but you still cannot sleep in this parking lot. Also, you'll have to register and pay an overcharge."

"Can't sign the register. You're a man of the world. You know how it is." I wasn't sure which world, but I thought a double sawbuck might pay the tariff. I pulled one out of my wallet and handed it over. "This cover it?"

"Live long and prosper," he said, and raised his palm, thumb extended, middle and ring fingers parted in a Vulcan salute.

Jessamine returned to the room. I dashed in after her.

"The kidnapper called. I'm supposed to be in front of the Alhambra Theater, a restored movie house at Fifth and Main, in twenty minutes."

By my watch, it was seven-forty.

"I'm relieved this exchange is not happening like in the

movies in some creepy, empty parking garage. But we have to go right now, and I need you to get the money to my car."

Apparently, all was forgiven. Or at least retribution postponed. I schlepped the heavy briefcases from closet to trunk, then followed her in the Mustang through light traffic on Hopkinsville's narrow one-way streets. They were hard to tell apart and made the downtown confusing. Many buildings were unoccupied, deteriorating, with "Available" signs painted on exposed walls.

At 7:55, Jessamine drew up to the curb in front of the Alhambra. I drove by the place and then circled the block. After passing by again, I found a parking space at the curb further up in front of a gray Hyundai. It gave me concealment and cover, plus a clear view in my rearview of her car and the venerable two-story brick theater. I was puzzled by the kidnapper's choice of a meeting place since it was between the sheriff's department and the county courthouse. Further confirmation of my hypothesis that he was not a professional.

To avoid attracting any attention, I waited in the morning heat without running the air conditioning. I scanned the street and sidewalks, which were new and made of brick, for anyone suspicious. Decorative iron benches, railings, and posts bearing historical plaques were obviously part of a downtown re-design as an arts and cultural center.

At 8:00, a hairy-legged runner paused at a nearby bench to stretch his hamstrings and scratch his head. I saw a green and white city sanitation truck lumbering up a rise on the next block, where three-story, dark red Victorian buildings formed a canyon. The structures had arched windows, gargoyles, and other fancy work. Originally, they might have been department stores. But now it was hard to tell what they were. The garbage truck stopped in front of each building to collect curbside trash from large public gray bins.

Two more minutes went by. Then an elderly woman and an energetic child, probably her granddaughter, both clutching shopping bags, turned into a narrow alley across the street. According to a sign, the alley had been redeveloped into *Arthur Plaza*, a cheerful-looking shopping enclave, featuring a bar and restaurant, artist's studio, antique shop, nutrition store, and a couple of boutiques. Signs for various coming events and attractions were posted.

At 8:03, a teenager in tight jeans strolled by while staring at her phone. A man with both hands jammed into his tan suit pants pockets was a few lengths behind her. Both disappeared down the street. So far, nothing much had happened, and no one had looked like a kidnapper—assuming it was possible to tell.

But when Jessamine clambered out of her car at 8:05, I knew something was up. Except for the fact that she was carrying one briefcase only—why not both—she looked like any other shopper, or perhaps a courthouse worker. I stared at her in my rearview mirror as she headed briskly along the sidewalk, stopping at the Alhambra's trash bin. Lifting the lid, she dropped the briefcase inside, then went back to her car and drove away.

I waited for further developments. They arrived along with the garbage truck I'd seen earlier. The driver of number 204 forked the theater's trash bin up and dumped the contents into his hopper. They were then compacted by a hydraulic cylinder. By my watch, the bin was placed back down on the curb within sixty seconds. Was the driver in on it? Did he know what he'd done?

As the bulky vehicle rumbled off slowly down the street, stopping at each bin along the way, my phone rang.

"What's happening?" Jessamine asked in a breathy voice.

"When you left, a garbage truck came by and emptied the bin with the briefcase in it."

"What? I assumed somebody would just reach in and take it. How does this make any sense?"

"I'm not sure. If the briefcase was crushed when the load was compacted, those cash bricks may be scattered throughout the rest of the garbage."

"That would really complicate retrieving them, wouldn't it?"

"Yeah, it would," I said, never taking my eyes off the sanitation truck. "Where are you?"

"Parked in front of a tattoo parlor on Fourth Street."

"When the kidnapper phoned, what else did he tell you?"

"That if I kept doing as he said, he'd call me back in six hours."

"Six hours?"

"And tell me where to leave the other half of the money. When he has it, Travis will be released."

"What are you supposed to do until then?" I asked.

"Nothing except wait. I assume you're following the garbage truck. But you can't pull him over and search it—or do anything. Because if you do, the deal's off."

"I see."

"Why is he doing it this way? Why not just take all the money at one time and be done with it?"

"That's what I'd do. Two pickups instead of one make everything twice as tricky and double the risk. But it could work—if we do what he says."

"How?"

"The kidnapper's probably watching the garbage truck. If nobody follows it, he may assume that it'll be safe to collect the second ransom payment, then go back for the first."

"Are we going to do what he says?"

"No, only seem to."

"But if we don't—"

"Look, I doubt that the driver is the kidnapper. But picking up a briefcase in the garbage isn't a crime, anyway. And driving the truck doesn't prove you were in on it. The driver can simply deny everything. You'd get the money back, but the cops would have to let the driver go. The kidnapper would know you hadn't done what you were told. And he'd still have Travis."

"Keep talking," she said.

"I'm not following the truck close enough to be seen. In fact, I'm not following the truck at all. I'm following the tracker. The driver's going to keep picking up the garbage along his route until he gets to the landfill. That's the only way this works."

"What if he gets the briefcase out before it reaches the dump?"

"Impossible without me noticing."

"Why impossible?" Jessamine asked.

"It takes about sixty seconds to empty one of those bins. I timed it. Even emptying several at one stop wouldn't require more than a minute or two, whereas removing the briefcase would have to take much longer. If he tries that, we'll reach another fork in the road. Having the briefcase now definitely would be a crime, so we'd have him at least. Or we could let him get the briefcase out and keep following him, hopefully, to Travis."

Jessamine was quiet for a moment. I kept watching the truck unload bins.

"When the driver gets to the landfill, he'll have to empty his load. The kidnapper doesn't have a tracker. How will he find the briefcase among all those mountains of trash?" she said.

"Good point. I'm assuming the driver is an accomplice, who will lead the kidnapper to the money later when no one else is around."

"And if he does?"

"We'll be there to follow him to Travis."

"What if he doesn't go there, just leaves Travis to die?" She choked back a sob.

"Then we'll take him down and make him talk. We can be more persuasive than the police. Hopefully, he'll release Travis, and none of that will be necessary."

After another long pause, she said, "Okay. But in the meantime, what am I supposed to do with myself? Should I go back to the motel?"

"No, they might be waiting there to make an early withdrawal.

I know six hours is going to feel like forever. But remember, we can't afford to be seen together. Try to keep busy and maybe you won't fret as much. Go shopping or sightseeing. Just stay in public places where you'll feel safe."

"What about the rest of the ransom money?"

"Leave it in the trunk. Park it on a busy street where there are people around. Try to keep an eye on it. Anything suspicious, call me, but don't confront them."

"Where will you be?"

"Somewhere air conditioned," I said.

The sanitation truck's movements remained steady and predictable. I had slept in my clothes and the humidity made me feel twice as grubby. I needed a shower and a clean shirt, but also caffeine and carbs. You always eat on a case whenever possible because you don't know how long you'll go between meals. While continuing to monitor the tracker, I went looking for fast food and found a drive-through window. Coffee and carbs, check. After eating, I took my phone and my gear with me into the restroom. After cleaning up, I felt better and went looking for air conditioning where I could camp for a few hours.

All the downtown public buildings seemed either brand new or newly restored. The huge courthouse sat on a rise with a sweeping view. The sheriff's department resembled a bank with a drive-through window. The jail had a decorative stone sign and a flower bed. The no-hassle air conditioning and peace and quiet I needed was at the public library, a well-designed, two-story red brick. I found an empty table on the second floor. With a large reference book propped up in front of me as camouflage, I prepared to settle down and watch the tracker on my phone for as long as it took.

Chapter 7

At ten o'clock, Jessamine phoned to check in for the second time.

"How are you holding up?" I asked softly.

"Fairly well."

"Where are you?"

"At the farmer's market at Ninth and Main. Where are you?"

"At the library."

"Oh, that's why you're whispering."

"Heard any more from the kidnapper?" I asked.

"No. What's the tracker showing?"

"Nothing unexpected. The garbage truck's still tooling around, picking up trash and slowly heading in the general direction of the landfill. Do you feel safe where you are, Jessamine?"

"Yeah, there are lots of customers around and nobody's taken an undue interest in me. It's nice, a covered pavilion with everything from cut flowers to jowl bacon."

"Bacon sounds good."

"Not to me," she said.

"No, of course not."

"Look, I've been up to my eyeballs in fresh fruits, vegetables, and hanging baskets for a long time. I'm going to have to move on."

"Where to?" I asked.

"I don't know yet. I may ask people for suggestions."

"Careful who you ask. Keep in touch," I said.

At 1:30, she called again. "Any new developments?"

"Nothing's changed," I said. "I'm still monitoring the tracker. Have you heard from the kidnapper?"

"No."

"Where are you now?"

"At Hopkinsville Station. I'm the only one here."

"That's not good."

"I know, but I'm running out of options."

"What's that one like?"

"Historic. It's the old L&N depot where passengers hopped off for a drink."

It was built in 1892, she said. A little one-story frame building with a tower, cupola, and bay-window.

"When a CSX freight train blew through here a few minutes ago, it felt like the whole town was shaking and I could hear the engine chuffing and the steel wheels screeching on steel rails."

I waited.

"Sorry. Guess I was waxing poetic there," she said.

"Don't worry about it. I'll let it slide this time."

"Funny, aren't you," she said.

"I have my moments."

I was noticing more about her. Like the smart, spunky way she'd stood up not only to her father but to the kidnapper. Her bravery in trying to save her husband's life. And now this creative side that I hadn't seen before, probably because I was distracted by some of her opinions. It's never smart to get emotionally involved with a client. They're always affected by the impact an investigation has on their lives. They almost always have ulterior motives. And they often lie, though I didn't think Jessamine was. But I've been wrong before. A detective who wears his heart on his sleeve needs a new tailor. And yet, despite knowing better, if she weren't my client, and married to the man I was trying to rescue, and too young for me ...

"This waiting is pure torture," she said. "I wish he would call."

At two o'clock, he did.

I jumped into the Mustang as soon as Jessamine phoned. She was to take the money to a church out on Highway 41 and leave it in a clothing donation bin behind the building.

"He promised to tell me where Travis is soon as he collected the money," she said.

I didn't put much store in that, but I told her again to follow the instructions. As I raced out of Hopkinsville, clouds were moving in, signaling a possible storm. Bugs splattered on my windshield. The wipers only succeeded in streaking the glass. I saw the small, red brick church where the drop-off was to take place but went on by, stopping half a block away in the empty parking lot of an abandoned storefront. Interestingly, the site chosen was not far from Kelly Station Park. Did the kidnapper live in this area? Would he be foolish enough to arrange this near his home? I trained binoculars on the church, which had a peaked roof, white steeple, and budget-built new addition. Ten minutes went by as I scanned the surrounding area for suspicious cars, trucks, or pedestrians.

A familiar black Mercedes turned off the two-lane highway, crossing over a drainage ditch into the church lot, and vanished behind the church. A minute or so later, the car emerged and left the lot, headed back the way it came. I drummed on the steering wheel for a few minutes until a tan Chevy Suburban with a rust spot for every one of its thirty years in existence angled into the church lot. Showtime.

I watched it disappear behind the church, then whip back out, heading southeast. I checked the two trackers. Both were blinking. As the Chevy grew smaller than the bottom line on an eye chart, I began following the second green blip on my phone.

A few miles deeper into lightly populated farmland, it changed direction. I was doing the same when suddenly a deer bolted from a cornfield into the road in front of me.

Adrenaline pumping, I wrenched the wheel and hit the brakes to avoid a collision. But it was too late. I smashed into the deer with a sickening thud and skidded off the road. The impact threw me around like a sweater in a dryer and I hit my head on the window and blanked out briefly. When I came to my car was stalled. Clouds of steam rose from under the hood. The spent force of the collision still seemed to hang in the air.

I sat there dazed, sucking in deep breaths, wondering how badly I might be injured. I didn't see any blood. My parts all seemed to work okay. But blacking out was not a good sign. And when I touched my noggin, I found a goose egg-sized lump. That worried me. A concussion can do strange things to you, like make you feel lost in a fog, which I sort of did.

Flipping on the hazard lights, I dragged myself out of the Mustang and slowly stood in an oval of sunlight. The deer I'd struck was not in front of my car or under it. I wondered if he could have run off after such an impact, but I didn't think so. Probably a white-tailed deer, the most common kind. I'd seen plenty of them crumpled up alongside the parkway today. The sight had made me cautious, but not cautious enough.

I hobbled over to the ditch and found him lying on his side, obviously in great pain, his long narrow legs and pointed hooves thrashing. Knowing that all I could do for the deer now was to put him out of his misery, I stumbled back to the car and got my .45. Then I took careful aim.

As the gunshot echoed across the fields, I lowered the gun, feeling sick about killing this beautiful creature. His hide was mostly light brown. There were white patches around the eyes, throat, stomach, rump, and tail. He was an eight-point buck, probably three-hundred-pounds. I would've had a hell of a time dragging him out of the way if he weren't in the ditch. He could've run up to thirty miles an hour, but not outrun a speeding car.

He'd probably lived in the woods surrounding the corn fields, feeding on green plants in the early morning and late afternoon. He must've crossed this road countless times before, looking for food and water. He would have had no reason to expect this time to be any different. But as John Lennon observed shortly before being murdered, life is what happens to you while you're busy making other plans.

Feeling a bit bewildered, I looked down and saw I was still holding the gun. I shoved it into my waistband and covered it with my shirt. The flashing blip on the screen was stationary when I pulled out my phone, meaning the kidnapper had stopped. If my car was in drive-able condition, I might still catch up with him before he could do any more harm.

But it wasn't drive-able, as I knew right away, even in my muddled state. When I inspected for damage, I found the front end smashed in, one headlight destroyed, and a front tire flattened. Changing the flat tire wouldn't do any good because when I keyed the ignition. The engine wouldn't start.

Shaky, with my head beginning to throb, I phoned Jessamine for help.

"Do you have Travis?" she asked before I could say a word.

I could smell ozone just before the storm clouds hovering overhead burst open, and smoky layers of rain penetrated the canopy of spreading oak tops over the road.

"No," I said, shouting to be heard over the sudden rush of noise. "But it hasn't been that long. It's still possible he will be freed."

"What's going on there?"

Rain was dripping down my forehead and into my eyes. I wiped it away.

"I ran into a deer. Now I'm stuck in the rain."

"That's terrible. Are you okay? You don't sound so good."

"I'll live," I said.

Actually, I felt miserable. My head was pounding. My shirt was sticking to my back. And the wind was beginning to howl.

"Where are you?"

I gave her directions.

"Come and get me pronto."

"I'm on my way."

As the rain swept through the gray emptiness around me, I took slow steps to the trunk, grabbed my go bag and the one containing the shotgun, and groped my way back into the car, which now reeked of oil, smoke, and wet clothes. Inside the go bag was some ibuprofen. I tapped out three tabs and swallowed them dry. Then I leaned forward with my forearms on my knees and watched as the rain lashed the glimmering road, turning it weirdly beautiful.

A few minutes later, the cloudburst ceased as abruptly as it had begun. So did the pounding in my head. I got out of the Mustang and walked over to the ditch where the deer's carcass was wedged, forming a haphazard dam against the storm water. I was still looking at it when Jessamine screeched to a stop about ten minutes later.

I yanked open her door and said, "Move over. I'm driving."

"Are you sure that's a good idea?"

"Move over."

I tossed the bag containing my shotgun into the back seat, slid in, and took the wheel.

"You're soaking wet," she said.

"Yeah. I'll dry."

"Well, try not to hit any more deer," she said.

I zoomed along the wet pavement, extra alert for stray wildlife and slow-moving tractors. We splashed through puddles, passed fields and forests and one-story prefab houses with mowed lawns. Jessamine watched the tracker's blip and called out directions.

As we topped a steaming rise, she said, "We're getting close."

I pulled off the road onto muddy ground. Propping my elbows on the driver's window, I swept my binoculars over the land spreading before us. Off across the unplowed fields stood a ramshackle farmhouse and two rickety outbuildings. No grazing livestock or crops. Just shiny weeds. Seeing the rusty brown Suburban parked out front, I said, "Bingo."

But this was still a tricky proposition. They should have let Travis go by now, but as far as we knew, they hadn't. Did this mean they weren't going to? Or that they just hadn't gotten around to it yet?

"What do you want to do, Jessamine? Wait or go in?"

"I don't know which is worse. I'm afraid to wait any longer. I'm also afraid to go in."

"Me, too," I said. "We don't know if Travis is being held here. If he is and we try to take him out by force, it could become very dangerous for him. Not to mention us. On the other hand, we've already tried to negotiate his release and look where that has gotten us. If he isn't here, that probably shows that the kidnapper doesn't intend to release him, and every minute we delay could bring him closer to death."

She turned slowly and looked at me for a few seconds. "I'm grateful to you. For being here and for doing this." She pressed her lips together, her face tense, seeming determined not to cry. "We could go back and forth on this all day long. Meanwhile, Travis is tied up in some damned cellar waiting to be killed. Please. For God's sake. Let's do something."

I pondered this for a moment, weighing the odds, and finally took a deep breath and said, "All right, here we go."

A long, narrow strip of pitted gravel led up to the once white house, which had faded to a dull gray. I turned onto it and, ten feet behind the Suburban, stopped and shut off the motor. The air was still as if all sound had been vacuumed away. It was a two-story frame dwelling with a wide front porch and a screen door, with the front door open behind it.

I honked the horn three times. Got no response.

Between here and the house, not much cover or maneuvering room. I'd be a sitting duck if I tried to rush the place. But there didn't seem to be any other option.

"Stay in the car," I said.

"Like hell. I'm coming, too."

I reached over the seat for the shotgun. "No, you're not. It's too dangerous."

"Screw that. You work for me, Guthrie. No way you're leaving me behind."

Quite a change from what she'd said two minutes ago. But I was getting used to her mercurial temperament. And apart from shooting her, I couldn't think of any way to stop her. After making sure both barrels were loaded and ready to fire, I slipped out of the Mercedes, shut the door without slamming it, and squatted with my back against the door. I counted to three. Then I jumped up with my shotgun at port arms and ran toward the house in a crouch, with Jessamine about three steps behind me. It was a risk, but when nobody shot at us, it paid off. Reaching the porch alive, we hugged the wall on opposite sides of the screen door.

"Anybody there?" I banged on the door frame. "Travis Tilford? Are you in there?"

Nodding to Jessamine, I darted through the door into the ominous darkness of an entry hall. I side-stepped immediately to keep from being silhouetted and almost gagged at the unmistakable smell of death. I held my breath, stopped, and listened. I was still wet but now also streaming with sweat. Hearing nothing, I pressed on into the living room and moved along the wall very slowly. I stopped again as my eyes adjusted to the pitch blackness. I cocked the scattergun, and pointing it ahead of me, started toward the kitchen. The closer I came, the worse the slaughterhouse stink of warm blood and feces got. It was unbearable in the kitchen where the body lay.

I got a sickly feeling and held up my hand, trying to keep Jessamine back. But she plowed ahead until freezing in the doorway and crying out, "Is that him?"

In the dimness, it was hard to tell. The room was utterly

still. Keeping one hand on the shotgun, I pulled out a flashlight and shone it around the room. When I was sure we were alone, I lowered the gun and pointed the light at the body lying on the floor. In the tight white beam, I saw a dark pool on the linoleum. No need to lean down and touch his cheek or check for a pulse. There was a circular gunshot wound in the center of the victim's broad forehead. Blood and brain matter had also been splattered on the refrigerator door. The victim looked nothing at all like the photograph she had shown me.

"No, it's not Travis," I croaked, throat tight, mouth dry.

"Oh, thank God," Jessamine said.

This was someone I had never seen before, a heavily built man, in his thirties, with a full head of long brown hair and glazed blue eyes that reminded me of those of the deer I'd killed. The money and the briefcase were gone. But the tracker, no longer blinking, lay by the corpse.

"I'm guessing this is our kidnapper," I said. Whoever killed him was in no hurry, having taken the time to find and disable the tracker while the body was still warm at his feet. If I hadn't been delayed, the killer might still have been here when I arrived. Hell, he might be now.

"But where is Travis?" Jessamine said.

"I don't know. Stay here while I search the rest of the house."

The hairs on my arms and neck were standing on end as I went through every room on the first floor. Finding no sign of Travis or the killer, I proceeded with extreme caution on up the steps to the second floor. There were three bedrooms and a bath, all empty. And no signs of anyone having been held captive here. No heavily padlocked doors, no chains in the walls or other restraints, no human waste on the floor or in a bucket.

In the medicine cabinet, though, I found toothbrushes and cosmetics. There were also used towels on the racks, and in the closets hung both men and women's clothes. I guessed that the dead man had been living here with a female partner, who fortunately for her had not been at home at the time of the murder. So where was she?

After this fruitless search, I found Jessamine where I'd left her.

"Travis isn't here," I said. "But I still need to go check the barn and the shed now."

"Can I come outside now?"

"No, the killer might be out there. Stay inside by the front door until I get back."

She didn't like hearing this but saw the sense of it and agreed to wait there.

I approached the barn warily, nudging the door open with the shotgun. Once, this had been a stable, but no horses were in the stalls, and no hay in the loft. It was the same story in the shed, with any farming equipment long gone.

"Did you find Travis?" Jessamine asked, coming out on the porch as I returned.

I shook my head.

"They must be holding him somewhere else."

Jessamine sat down heavily on the top front porch step, crossed her arms and hugged herself tightly.

"Are you okay?" I asked, thinking that seeing a dead body could do strange things to anyone, especially a civilian unused to it.

"I think I may be sick," she said.

I waited for a moment or two. When she didn't faint or vomit, I said, "I need to go back inside."

"I'll come with you," she said.

"You don't have to."

"I want to."

We went back inside the house. I elbowed the kitchen wall switch, triggering a flood of harsh light. The scene looked just as gruesome as before.

"Do you recognize him?"

Jessamine shuddered. "No, I've never seen him before."

I looked around carefully, not wanting to move any more

than necessary.

"But if he kidnapped Travis, then who killed him?" Jessamine said.

I faced her. "Maybe somebody who wanted to hijack the ransom. The victim probably knew whoever shot him."

"How do you know?"

"No signs of a struggle."

"I see. But what's become of Travis? And where's our truck?"

"I don't know the answers, Jessamine. The truck could have been left somewhere else, like maybe where Travis is being held."

"You think he's still alive?"

What else could I say? "I do. Let's assume that after imprisoning Travis elsewhere the kidnapper switched vehicles and drove the Suburban to the pickup. When he came back here from collecting the ransome, he found his killer waiting for him. Maybe the killer was an accomplice who double-crossed him."

"What accomplice? I only spoke to one person," Jessamine said.

So many questions, so few answers.

"I wish I knew."

"What do we do now? We don't even know what they may have done to Travis."

"No, but we must proceed as if Travis is okay. He's too valuable to them to harm or kill." I checked my phone. "We have the other tracker and it's still blinking."

"But what if the man who was killed was the only one who knew where Travis was being held? That means we may never find him." A tear slid down her cheek.

"Right now, we have a more immediate problem. If we leave here without notifying the police about this body, we'll risk facing serious criminal charges. Like obstruction of justice or even being an accessory to murder. I'm not willing to do that, and you shouldn't, either."

"What about calling it in anonymously?"

"That wouldn't get us off the hook. Calls can be traced."

"There must be something else."

"There is. Phone your father. Tell him what's happened. Ask him to use his influence to get the local officials to cooperate."

"I told you no cops."

"It's time for you to reconsider."

We went back and forth. In the end, she made the call. I stowed all the firearms in the trunk and called nine-one-one.

"What is your emergency?" the operator asked.

I responded in my professional cop voice, a flat monotone, to explain that I had found a gunshot victim. I gave her the usual information, got the usual instructions. Then, while waiting for the cops to arrive, got our stories straight. We'd tell the whole truth, keeping only the first ransom drop back. That way, we still had the upper hand in the investigation. Then we had a brief heart-to-heart on how to behave with cops.

"I know you're worried about Travis," I said. "And you've been through a lot today. But we don't want any trouble with the police. We need a non-inflammatory approach."

"What? Like not calling them fascist pigs?"

"That would be a good start."

"Relax, Jim. I'm not a complete fool."

"I know that."

"Well, you just be cool and so will I."

"Okay. But understand this. We've just reported finding a dead body. That is guaranteed to raise a suspicion that we did it. We're also from Louisville. You drive a Mercedes Benz. I'm a private investigator. That's enough red flags to get a caution lap at the Indy 500."

"But we've reported finding the body. That's in our favor, right?"

"As far as that goes, yeah. Doesn't mean they'll accept our account at face value, though. And that could really complicate our efforts to find Travis."

"But it's the truth."

"We look and sound different. Police always profile suspects, no matter how well-trained they are. It's human nature. They're going to doubt us. We need to come across to them in a convincing manner. An obvious question is what we're doing here in the middle of nowhere."

Jessamine sat quietly for a moment. "What do you suggest?"

"Like I said, tell them the truth, but leave out the tracker in the garbage truck. Hopefully, the phone call to your father will carry some weight and smooth our pathway. But remember, remain courteous and cooperative. Let them do the talking. And don't argue. You want to soothe an anxious cop, not put him more on edge."

"Is that all?"

"Stay calm. Control our emotions. The main reason for a cop to be suspicious is your behavior. They watch for fidgeting and other signs of nervousness that suggest guilt. Remember, their work is routinely dangerous, especially in a lonely location like this. Their most perilous moment is at the first approach. That's when cops get killed. Any furtive movement could provoke them and get us killed, too. Stand still. Keep your hands in plain sight, okay?"

"Okay."

We waited.

Chapter 8

We heard the siren coming and were out of the Mercedes and leaning against the hood, hands in plain sight, when a black and white with its red and blue light bar flashing slewed up the rocks toward us. A deputy wearing a khaki uniform lumbered out of the gleaming patrol car, which had "SHERIFF" stenciled in gold on the front fender. His nametag read "METCALFE." There were dark perspiration stains under his arms. He wore a broad-brimmed Smokey the Bear hat and was built like a bear himself.

"You find a dead body?" he asked.

"On the kitchen floor," I said.

"I'll take a look. Wait here."

"We're not going anywhere," I said.

We waited. He was inside a few minutes, then came out talking on his radio. "Looks like I've got a murder," he said. Finishing the call, he stuck the radio back in its slot on his duty belt, which also held a handgun and handcuffs.

"He's dead, all right. You know him?"

"No, we didn't know him," I said.

"Then what are you doing here and how'd you come to find him?"

"It's a long story."

The big deputy frowned and tugged on his belt. "Oh, we've got lots of time."

I sighed, knowing this was not the last time I'd have to go through it. "He was a kidnapper. We followed him here."

"Kidnapper?" Metcalfe said. "Okay, hold on. Let's go back to the beginning. Who are you?"

"I'm a private investigator." I told him my name.

"Let's see your ID."

I got my wallet out of my pants pocket slowly and showed him my P.I. license. He took, looked at, and kept it.

When the deputy turned toward Jessamine, she said, "You don't even need to ask. I'm Mrs. Travis Tilford." She took her time getting her driver's license out of her purse and handing it to him.

He kept it, too.

"Stay here."

"Like I said, we're not going anywhere."

"Are we in trouble?" Jessamine said.

I watched the deputy go to his car, presumably to confirm who we were. When he came back, he said, "Who got kidnapped?"

"My husband got kidnapped. Travis Tilford."

"So, where is Mr. Tilford now?" the deputy asked.

"I wish we knew," I said. "We were here to rescue him."

"You were going to rescue him. Why didn't you call the police?"

"I'd rather explain that to the detectives," I said. "Meanwhile, it's vital that this be kept confidential. Tilford's life depends upon it."

"Oh, I suppose that means I can't put it out on Twitter then." Face flushed, Metcalfe's lips turned up into a snarl. "Are either of you carrying?"

"Two handguns and a shotgun are in the trunk," I said. "That's not illegal."

"No shit, Sherlock." Metcalfe ordered the keys handed over

and told us to stay where we were. He opened the trunk and fished out the .45 with a ballpoint pen in the trigger guard. After sniffing the muzzle, he said, "This one's been fired recently."

"I used it to put a deer I'd hit out of his misery."

Metcalfe put the gun back where he'd found it. Closing the trunk, he went around and looked at the front of the Benz. "You say you hit a deer, but I don't see any damage."

"I was in my Mustang."

"Where's that now?"

"Beside the deer out on Highway 41."

"Are you sure it wasn't the guy in the house that you shot?" He looked at me expectantly.

"Pretty sure," I said, and couldn't resist grinning a little just to piss him off.

It worked.

"I need you both in the back seat of my squad car."

"What for?" Jessamine said. "We haven't done anything wrong."

"Just a precaution, ma'am."

"Why? Do you think we're going to flee the scene? We're the ones who called it in, remember?"

"Would you rather wait in handcuffs?" Metcalfe glowered.

Jessamine gazed at me. I shook my head, upset by my failure to follow my own advice. Metcalfe led us to the cruiser and put us behind the prisoner partition.

"This is ridiculous," Jessamine said.

"Take it easy," I said.

"Take it easy? I'm in a hurry to find my husband before somebody kills him."

"I know," I whispered. "But if we kick up a fuss, the cops are only going to keep us longer. The good news is that once they test fire my gun, they'll see that it's not the one that killed the victim."

"And then they'll let us go?"

"Maybe not right away."

"Aw, shit."

"Depends on how fast they want results. And how quick your father responds to your call for help."

"You don't know how much I hated doing that, do you?"

"I think I have some idea," I said. I leaned back to wait for the homicide boys.

A plain wrapper arrived—the kind of unmarked car detectives normally used. Police detectives ordinarily work in pairs and plain clothes. But only one man in uniform got out of the dark blue four-door sedan. His khakis were a shade lighter than his complexion. He had a neat little mustache and short black hair, thinning at the crown and receding at the hairline. After exchanging a few words with Metcalfe, this new guy put on some latex gloves and went into the house.

When he came back out a few minutes later, he got the car key from Metcalfe and used it to open the Mercedes' trunk. After bagging the firearms, he gave them to the deputy and took off his gloves. He stared at us briefly through the window glass before letting us out.

"I'm Detective Sanchez," he said, sweat popping from his pores. "I'd like to know what you were doing here today when you reported finding the body."

"Are we under arrest?" I asked.

"No, you're witnesses."

"Well, if that's how you treat law-abiding citizens who are only doing their civic duty, I'd sure hate to see how you treat violent criminals," Jessamine said.

"My apologies," Sanchez said easily. "I'm sure you can understand why a lone deputy would take precautions to prevent out of towners from possibly leaving the scene prematurely. After all, a man was shot to death and three guns found in your trunk."

"Nobody got shot with them," I said.

He watched my eyes as if they would reveal what he needed to know. "We need to make sure of that. I heard about this business with the deer. I'm sending someone to check it out."

"Good. While you're at it, ask them to have it towed somewhere for repairs."

"I'll see what I can do," Sanchez said. "So, your gun was only used to shoot a deer. That right?"

I just stared at him.

"Don't feel like talking?" He turned to Jessamine. "How about you, ma'am? Want to tell me about this kidnapping? Your husband was taken, I understand?"

"Yes, that's right, and the longer we stand here talking, the less chance he has of surviving."

"Noted," Sanchez said. "Did you report the kidnapping to the police?"

"No."

"May I ask why not?"

"I felt Travis had a better chance if I handled it myself," she said.

"But you asked for Mr. Guthrie's help?"

"That's right. He's worked for my family before. I trust him to help me get Travis back safely."

"And just how were you planning to do that?" he asked me.

"Mrs. Tilford decided to pay the ransom. She hired me to see that it went smoothly."

"But it didn't go smoothly, did it?"

"Obviously not. Knowing that was possible, I'd suggested putting a mini tracker in with the ransom. When the kidnapped didn't release Travis, we followed its signal here. But by that time, the money was gone and so was whoever killed the man in the house."

"Any idea who the killer is?" Sanchez narrowed his eyes, suggesting he suspected I was not telling him everything I knew. And he was right.

"I'd say someone who already knew what was going on."

"Who would that be?"

"Beats me. But how else would he know where to come and

hijack the ransom?"

"An interesting question to be explored further," Sanchez said, as two more county vehicles arrived. He looked at Jessamine. "For your husband's sake, I think we should all go downtown and sort this out in air conditioning."

"Do we have a choice?" Jessamine said.

"Of course," Sanchez smiled. "But you're going to need us now to find your husband. We have more resources and personnel, and we've been trained to do it."

Jessamine looked at him uncertainly.

"You can follow me in your car," he said.

That's what we did, with Jessamine driving. As soon as we were alone, I whipped out my phone and checked the tracker.

"Still blinking, but not moving."

"Where is it?" she said.

"Looks like it's at the landfill." I was relieved. "The driver could have stopped the truck and found the money while we weren't monitoring the tracker, but I don't think he did. I think we've been lucky."

"Why?"

"Remember, the kidnapper's probable reason for wanting two separate drop-offs was to make sure he wasn't being followed. There wouldn't be any opportunity to tamper with the load before it got to the landfill—not unless the truck stopped somewhere along the way and dumped out all the garbage. That would have required a place where it wouldn't be seen. Unlikely. At the landfill, the load would be dumped out, too, leaving the money buried under tons of trash."

"Shouldn't we go out there right now before it's too late and they make off with it?" Jessamine asked.

"We can't without tipping off the cops, which you don't want. Right? Or have you changed your mind?"

"No, I haven't," she said slowly. "What's the plan?"

"Wait and hope that I'm right."

"That's it? Doesn't sound like much of a plan to me."

"Think it through with me. First, we know the guy we think was the kidnapper is dead, so he won't be picking up anything. Second, if there's an accomplice—probably the garbage man—he won't risk digging through a tremendous volume of trash while others are around. He's going to wait until tonight when it's good and dark to hunt for that briefcase."

"Okay, I see. But what if you're wrong?"

"That's the risk we take without alerting the cops."

"So, for now, we just go on to the sheriff's office?"

"Yeah. It's our best bet. We need to keep our stories straight. The instant Sanchez finds a discrepancy in our statements, he'll be all over us."

"Then we'd better make sure he doesn't find any."

"One more thing. If they leave you alone in an interrogation room, assume it's bugged and that they may be videotaping you."

"Got it," Jessamine said.

"And watch your speed."

"Yes, Mother," Jessamine chirped.

I continued monitoring the tracker while she followed Sanchez to the sheriff's department on West Seventh. He showed us down a hallway to a small interrogation room.

"Why don't you have a seat, Mrs. Tilford?" Sanchez said. "Guthrie, you come with me."

"I don't think so," I said. "Not if we're witnesses."

"That's right, we'd prefer not to be separated," Jessamine said.

Sanchez's face was expressionless. Still trying to keep it cordial, he said, "That's fine. Can I get you something? Coffee? A soft drink?"

"No thanks. Let's just get on with it," Jessamine said. I didn't want any, either.

"I'll be right back," Sanchez said.

Interrogation rooms are all alike. They may look basic, but they're carefully designed to get results. This one was just big enough for three people, chairs, and a table. Maybe eight by ten feet with no unnecessary open space. It was kept a little dark to create stress. And more than cool. Cold, in fact, another old cop trick to increase our anxiety. We sat down at the table in a corner, with the detective's chair between us and the door. A way to make us feel like we couldn't leave anytime we liked, even though that's what we'd been told.

I wanted to check the tracker again but didn't dare get out my phone.

Sanchez returned carrying a notepad and file folder.

"Sorry, I know it's tough for you," he said in a sympathetic tone. "But let's talk more about the circumstances of your husband's disappearance."

"I already told the deputy everything," Jessamine said.

"But now I need you to tell me," Sanchez said.

Sighing impatiently, she said, "All right. Let's start with this," and played a video on her phone. It was the YouTube version of what she and Travis had shot the night before last. A publicity stunt, she explained, to promote their in-progress documentary film and attract new investment. Then she played a second version of the first video, except in this one you could see them on screen while making it.

Along with this second video was a phone call made to their motel room demanding fifty thousand dollars *not* to release the second video. Travis had laughed it off, telling the caller to go ahead, that releasing it would only benefit them even more.

"Shortly after Travis disappeared yesterday afternoon, I got another call from the same guy," Jessamine said, "only this time on Travis's phone."

She played the call and accompanying video, which showed Travis bound and gagged on a cellar floor. The kidnapper demanded a million dollars' ransom, but Jessamine said she couldn't raise that much. Ten minutes later, the kidnapper called again, this time to cut the amount in half.

"My father agreed to pay the ransom. On the drive home to

collect it, I hired Mr. Guthrie by phone. He met me. We placed a tracker in with the money and drove down here to wait for further instructions. Today, we left the money in a church bin, then followed the tracker to the farmhouse where we found the dead man. We don't know who he was, but think he may be the kidnapper, and was ripped off by an accomplice. That's all I know."

"Quite a tale," Sanchez said, placing his knobby hands on the table as if to keep it from shifting along with Jessamine's narrative. "You say the first call was to your motel phone? Who knew where you were staying?"

Jessamine shook her head. "No one."

"Did you go anywhere else after shooting the video?"

"No, we went straight back to the motel."

"So, the only way the caller could have known where to reach you was if he'd followed you there."

"That's what Jim said, too."

Sanchez looked at me and lifted his eyebrows.

I nodded.

"It seems the caller could only have found out what you were doing by accident. That makes the extortion attempt a crime of opportunity. But kidnapping required planning," Sanchez said.

I told him I agreed. "But not very good planning."

"No," Sanchez said, and turned his attention to Jessamine. "The interviews you were conducting. What were they about? You don't believe in UFOs or aliens, do you?"

"Says the man whose whole town does," Jessamine said.

"Maybe not the whole town," Sanchez smiled. "Are you and your husband UFO enthusiasts, then?"

"No, we're monolith enthusiasts."

"Like the one in the video." Sanchez sat back and folded his hands behind his head. "Look, I'm just a simple officer of the law. I don't understand your motivation. What's the point of all this?"

She told him the point was to document for history

the monolith craze of 2020, when over a hundred of them mysteriously appeared and disappeared all over the world.

"It was unique. Nothing remotely like this ever happened before. Think about it. A monolith was discovered by accident in a remote desert canyon in Utah five years after it was put there. Nobody knows who did it, or why. But the minute a video of it appears online, it sets off a chain reaction. For the next month and a half or so, more monoliths pop up mysteriously all over the world. Why?"

Sanchez smiled and lifted his hands in a search me gesture.

"Because it was inspiring, detective. Remember, we were in the middle of the pandemic when this happened. Everyone was afraid to go out for fear of catching a bug and dying. It was a dark time politically, too. We were all afraid of each other and miserable, when along came this amazing phenomenon that brought us together in spirit. I like to think of it as an epic poem—a tribute to humanity, hope, and happiness."

"That's quite a claim," Sanchez said.

"Travis and I wanted to document what happened so it wouldn't be forgotten. Our monolith's appearance was a publicity stunt to stir up interest in the project. The Little Green Men Festival was in the right place at the right time with the right audience. People who'd come before had expressed a belief in UFOs and aliens. We wanted to capture their reaction to finding a monolith had landed in their own backyard."

"What was their reaction?" Sanchez asked.

"Unfortunately, we didn't get to find out because of technical problems that sent Travis off for the replacement mic. I still want to know. Other people all over the world read into it whatever they wanted. Some believed the first monolith was put there by aliens, kind of like in *2001: A Space Odyssey*. Ever see that movie?"

"No, I'm not much into science fiction."

"The 2020 monoliths looked a lot like the ones in *2001*, only silver and more pyramid shaped. At the beginning of the movie, one appears on earth. It's the most interesting part. Audiences had a hard time understanding it because there's no dialogue for the first half hour, just music. Nothing is explained, except that it's millions of years ago. These animals are peacefully gathered around a water hole when suddenly a big shiny black slab shaped like a domino appears. It's a monolith. An ape man who touches it figures out how to use a bone to kill a rival. Then he hurls the bone up in triumph, and it soars end over end to become an orbiting space station."

"So, what does all that mean?" Sanchez asked.

"Let me tell you the rest of it first."

"Go ahead."

Jessamine was clearly warming to the task. Maybe it helped take her mind off her kidnapped husband. She did go to film school, after all.

"Astronauts discover a monolith on the moon. It's in contact with another one on Jupiter. A mission is sent there to find out what's going on. But on the way, their HAL computer decides to kill the astronauts to save the mission."

"Artificial intelligence," Sanchez says, shaking his head.

"The one surviving astronaut unplugs HAL. He apparently enters another dimension during a ten-minute light show and is reborn. Then he returns to earth as an infant in a bubble."

"Thanks for clearing that up for me," Sanchez said.

"In the novel, the first monolith was sent by aliens to speed up human evolution. The other two were an early warning system to let the aliens know when earthlings could reach Jupiter, where we'd fulfill our ultimate destiny."

"Whatever that means. No wonder people had a hard time understanding the movie," Sanchez said, shaking his head again.

"Documenting the monoliths was such a beautiful idea," Jessamine said. Then her mood darkened. "But now it's all gone wrong."

Checking his notes, Sanchez said, "You say your monolith was a way to encourage investment in the film. Didn't you already have enough investors?"

"You can never have too many investors, detective. We'd already spent all of our funding on the project when the kidnapper made his ransom demand."

Sanchez frowned, pinching the bridge of his nose. "You were instructed to leave the money at a church. Tell me about that."

Jessamine went through the details.

"Then you followed the kidnapper, Guthrie?"

Sanchez made me go through it again. I told him everything, starting with the tracker, hitting the deer, and being picked up by Jessamine, and ending with tracking the money to the farmhouse where we found the body. He poked at my account, cross-checking, verifying. Asking the same question in different ways. The cop method. Having established the facts of the case, he then raised the possibility of other bad actors being involved. But we had nothing to offer him there—unless you counted my early suspicions that Travis Tilford could have faked the whole thing. I still hadn't ruled that out, but saw no point in bringing it up.

Sanchez paused, as if considering all the possibilities. "You've spun an amazing story. I only have one more question: Why should I believe you?"

"Because it's all true," I said, "and because we are reputable. Call Lieutenant Leo Brownfield at Louisville Metro homicide. He'll vouch for me. You can also phone her father."

"Who is your father?" Sanchez asked.

"State Senator Shelby Barrett," Jessamine said.

That got his attention. "You're telling me this could be political?"

"Only in the sense that a powerful, wealthy man's son-in-law has been kidnapped and any failure to help get him back would probably reflect badly on you and your department," Jessamine said.

"Sit tight. I'll get back to you." Sanchez shoved his chair away and left the room.

Chapter 9

The minute Sanchez left us alone, I pulled out my phone to check on the tracker. Jessamine looked at me with a question in her eyes, and I nodded. No change. Still blinking in the same place. We didn't speak. Shoving the phone back in my pocket, I asked myself what was coming next. Whatever Sanchez interrogated us about, it would surely include Travis's character. That made me realize how little I knew about him.

"Jess, can you tell me more about your husband and his background?"

She masked her fears with a cheerful expression.

"Not to be too shallow, but he's really good looking. You saw his photo, so you know."

She began telling me how charming Travis was, how he focused only on you with an utterly reassuring smile and he was silver tongued, too. "He once told me I was such a pretty girl to say such wise things."

"Flattering."

"Yeah, I told him to make up his own bullshit instead of stealing F. Scott Fitzgerald's."

"I didn't realize you were so literary," I said, just to see what she'd do with it.

"There's probably a lot you don't know about me."

I was sure that was true.

"Travis is full of … allusions. He also once told me that if my life ever began to bore me, I should risk it."

"Who said that first? Was it Hemingway?"

She smiled. "James Dickey. I've heard my dad quote it before. He's a big Dickey fan."

"Sounds like something he might say. How do your father and Travis get along?"

"Pretty well for two such type-A males. Trav is like my father in some ways—bold, confident—but different, too. When I was growing up, my father could be a sort of charismatic bully, acting annoyed and short-tempered if I didn't measure up to his lofty standards. He often was dismissive of my ideas—especially about being a vegetarian. I think that's why I got into trouble so much. Then I turned around and married a man who treated me in much the same way."

"You were married before Travis?"

"Yeah, to Albert Jennings, who I met at college. I married him when I was twenty-three. See a pattern there?"

"I've heard it said that women who marry men like their fathers may be subconsciously seeking their father's approval," I said.

"Got it in one, Guthrie. Of course, I divorced Albert two years later. Dad loves me in his own way. He means well, but he's a control freak. Even when I became an adult, Dad acted as if I was still ten years old and he got to boss me. After my divorce, I traveled around Europe, trying to figure out who I was. After years of therapy, I realized it was simply a matter of establishing boundaries."

"You've set some boundaries now—like standing up to him about hiring me."

She nodded.

After sneaking another look at the tracker, I said, "You don't think your first husband could be involved in the kidnapping, do you?"

"Albert? No way. He's remarried, a big investment banker now. I can't see him doing this at all."

"When was the last time you talked to him?"

"It's been years. Forget about Albert."

"All right. Tell more about how Travis and your father are alike."

"Trav's strong like Dad, but positive. He helped me gain self-confidence when I was trying to re-start my life at UCLA."

"Self-confidence is not something I've ever noticed you lacking."

"Being self-destructive is not the same as being self-confident. I was so crazy back then. I can't believe some stunts I pulled. Before I met Travis, I dabbled in various careers—from art to fashion design. None was the right fit. I was still lost. But Travis seemed to know exactly what he wanted, and how to get it. He was always so supportive, too, saying all the right things."

"A silver-tongued devil, you said."

"Not a devil. You said that. Travis has always been there for me when I needed him. Now he needs me, so it's my turn."

"How did he help you develop more confidence?"

"Partly by just being there, partly by setting a good example. As I've told you, he had some professional credits before we met. For a while, he was drawn to the filmmaker lifestyle, being rich and famous. But then he re-discovered his original passion, wanting most to tell stories he really cared about."

"Did he ever share anything about his early struggles?" I asked.

"Coming from a one-parent household where money was a problem. Travis said he used his father's old Super 8 until it fell apart. Then he needed another cam, but had no money. In desperation, he pilfered one from a pawnshop in Inglewood."

I gave Jessamine a cautionary look.

Not that the Hopkinsville police were likely to charge Travis Tilford with a decades-old theft in California. But when it comes to crime, the boys in blue generally prefer black and white distinctions to shades of gray. Knowing Tilford had broken the law could undermine their resolve to help find him.

"Travis wasn't proud of what he'd done," Jessamine continued, ignoring my warning. "But he also wasn't the first filmmaker to steal a camera. He told me that when Werner Herzog was young, he'd swiped a 35 millimeter from the Munich Film School."

This revelation reminded me that Travis claimed he would do whatever it took to capture his one true subject on film. I wondered if that included staging his own kidnapping.

A few minutes later, Sanchez was back, clutching a file folder in his thick, hairy fingers. He was accompanied by two men, one in uniform, the other wearing a suit and tie.

"Mayor Logsdon," Sanchez said, "this is Jessamine Tilford, Senator Barrett's daughter."

"Pleased to meet you, Mrs. Tilford. I'm Theo Logsdon," the suit said.

He was short, lean, fortyish and, surprisingly, African American. In Kentucky, black mayors were few and far between. And Hopkinsville was the birthplace of Jefferson Davis. Mayor Logsdon nodded to the uniform, who was a medium-sized, middle-aged man with a gray buzz-cut.

"And this is Sheriff Wendell Elliott."

"Ma'am," said the sheriff, whose job title was spelled out in gold capitalized letters on his chest.

When Sanchez introduced me, the mayor shook my hand. The sheriff did not. Cops often despised private eyes—especially former cops like me—whom they considered turncoats who helped crooked lawyers get their guilty clients off.

"Why don't we all sit down," the mayor suggested.

With five of us in there, the little room seemed cramped now.

"Your credentials checked out," Logsdon began. "Lieutenant Brownfield in the Louisville department vouched for you,

Guthrie. And I just spoke to your father on the phone, Mrs. Tilford. He confirmed that you and Guthrie were here in connection with his son-in-law's kidnapping. Senator Barrett asked that you be extended every courtesy, and we intend to do just that. Right, Sheriff?"

"That's right," Elliott said.

Who you know matters.

"Now, how else can we help you?" the mayor asked.

"I'd like to know whose body we found," I said.

"Ed?" Sheriff Elliott asked, with a nod in Sanchez's direction.

"The victim is Sean aka 'Snuffy' McGinnis."

Sanchez shoved the open file folder across the table our way. The figure in the black-and-white photo was in his early thirties, a big, rakish looking guy with well-muscled arms and broad sloping shoulders. His dark hair was cropped short except for thick sideburns and his nose was crooked from being broken.

"He's a local, unemployed auto mechanic, lay-about, and ne'er do well," Sanchez said.

A small-time crook suspected of dealing marijuana, McGinnis was wanted on three warrants ranging from theft to receiving stolen property, assault, and battery, and probation violation. He'd also been charged with two counts of contempt of court for failing to provide child support.

"Are you surprised?" the mayor asked.

"I don't know what I expected," Jessamine said. "A monster, I suppose."

"He's about what I expected," I said. "Did he live in the place where we found him?"

"Yes."

"How about that old SUV?"

"That belonged to Snuffy."

So, the killer must've come in another vehicle.

"You mentioned drugs. Who was he affiliated with?" I asked.

"Hold on," Elliott interrupted. "This is sheriff's department business. I'm not sure you need to know, Guthrie. As I understand it, you've done what you were hired for, so your job should be over. Just leave the rest to us."

"I'll decide when his job's over," Jessamine said, "and that will be when we have Travis back, not before."

Now that sounded like the self-confident Jessamine I knew.

"Hold on, Mrs. Tilford," Logsdon said. "Let's not get excited. We're all on the same side here."

"You sure about that?" she asked.

Sheriff Elliott said, "C'mon, Mr. Mayor. You know we can't have some private eye sticking his nose in where it doesn't belong, compromising our investigations."

"We've discussed this, Sheriff." The mayor sounded a bit testy. "Obviously, there's some overlap here between our other investigations and this kidnapping. But we agreed to cooperate with Mrs. Tilford and her family in trying to find her husband. If they want to keep Guthrie involved, there's no law preventing that as far as I know."

The sheriff's face reddened.

The mayor turned to me. "While you may have legitimate reasons to want more information related to the kidnapping, there are also limits that must be respected. Do I make myself clear?"

"Not to me," Jessamine broke in. "We don't care about your limits or other cases and have no interest in mucking them up. All we want is to get my husband back. Anything you know, whether it's dealing drugs or rustling cattle, we need to know. Do I make myself clear?"

"Why don't we try to lower the temperature?" Logsdon said. "We understand that you've been on an emotional roller coaster, Mrs. Tilford. We can offer counseling and victim assistance. I understand that Mr. Tilford doesn't have any family?"

"Just me," Jessamine said.

"I see. Well, we'll provide the media with information about the kidnapping and ask the public for their cooperation."

"No," Jessamine said. Everyone looked at her. "I don't want

that."

"Why not?" Logsdon asked.

"Because it might get Travis killed. That's why I didn't report this to the police in the first place. If the kidnapper hears that you're involved—"

"But the kidnapper's dead now," the sheriff said.

Jessamine gave him a withering look.

"McGinnis is dead. But whoever killed him might be an accomplice. Travis's life is still in danger."

"You know that time is running out, Mrs. Tilford," said the mayor.

"Believe me, I'm well aware of that," Jessamine snapped.

"McGinnis's killer knows that when the victim's body is found, we'll get involved."

"But that doesn't necessarily mean he'll assume we've reported the connection to Travis. There's still hope. We've got to take any and all chances to save my husband," Jessamine argued.

"And that's what we're trying to do, ma'am," Sheriff Elliott said. "We need to ask the public for their cooperation."

"We can't," Jessamine said.

Mayor Logsdon held up his hand for quiet. "All right, we don't have to link the kidnapping with the McGinnis shooting, at least not until we have a better idea of what's going on. Right, Sheriff?"

Elliott scowled. "I don't think that's wise. But he's your husband. We're going to investigate the murder, though, no matter what. And that means calling a press conference. The killer will know that it's just a matter of time before we connect McGinnis's death to Tilford."

"Yes, but that time could make all the difference," Jessamine said.

"All right then," Mayor Logsdon said. "We'll provide the media with information about the murder, but not about the kidnapping angle. We don't want a media frenzy, anyway."

I could imagine Logsdon envisioning a blitz of journalists and TV news reporters bearing cameras and microphones descending upon the area. But not to good-naturedly cover the Little Green Men Festival or talk about how progressive his city was. Oh no, this would be an onslaught of negative publicity for him, for Hopkinsville, and for law enforcement. Reporters would ambush him about how Hoptown was suddenly a crime capital. They would spread strange rumors and unflattering gossip. He could become a laughingstock.

"No, let's keep this under wraps," Jessamine said.

At her words, Mayor Logsdon seemed to relax. "At the same time, rest assured, we'll do everything in our power to find your husband. Isn't that right, Sheriff?"

"That's right, Mr. Mayor. We'll do everything we can. But we're seriously short of manpower this weekend due to the big festival. We'll call in the FBI, state police, and every other law enforcement agency in the region. We'll need all the help we can get."

"Including mine?" I asked.

"Yes," the mayor said, glancing at Sheriff Elliott, who glowered at me.

"What else can you tell us about McGinnis?" Jessamine said.

"Sheriff?" the mayor said.

"Deputy?" Sheriff Elliott said, putting Sanchez on the spot.

"This needs to go no further," Sanchez said.

We nodded.

"We think McGinnis was a member of the Divine Tabernacle of Joy. It's either a UFO cult that dabbles in dope, or a dope ring masquerading as a religion. Either way, we suspect them of distributing not only marijuana but also speed and ecstasy to finance their activities. They've occupied some abandoned land way out in an isolated part of the county. There's an old church on the property, which they may use to move drugs. We've been watching them for a couple months but have not been able to gather any evidence."

"Who is the leader of this group?" I asked.

"Brother Bartholomew—real name Bart Proctor—is their self-professed prophet. He's done time for trafficking."

"Are they violent?"

"Haven't been up to now. Of course, that could change."

"How big is the drug trade here?" I asked.

The sheriff and the mayor looked uncomfortable.

Choosing his words carefully, Sanchez answered, "I wouldn't say huge. It's a way to make some spending money in a depressed economy. We haven't spotted much fentanyl yet, but it's probably just a matter of time."

"That's only speculation," the mayor said.

Sanchez nodded.

"What else do you know about Proctor?" I asked.

Tapping on the folder in front of him, Sanchez said, "He's a bit of a nutcase. He and his followers believe that aliens live among us and are plotting to take over the world."

"And do what?"

"Unclear. You can make up your own answer. That's what they do, I think. They also believe in Armageddon. Back in 2017, Proctor went around telling people to gather at his compound to await the solar eclipse because that would signal the end of the world."

"What made him think that?"

"I can't really say. Mumbo-jumbo about some ancient Mayan prophecy."

"What did he say when the world didn't end?"

"That he'd misread the signs. But not to worry—the end of times is still at hand."

"Must be convincing and charismatic."

"I think that's fair to say," Sanchez agreed.

"I'd like to know more about this compound," I said.

"It's on an isolated piece of land about twenty miles northwest of Hopkinsville. Beside the old church, there's a cluster of ramshackle buildings, tents, and dilapidated house trailers. Some cult members who sold their worldly possessions occupied it in 2017."

"How many are living there now?"

"Not sure. Fifty, maybe."

"Do all of Proctor's followers live there?"

"McGinnis obviously didn't. Some have jobs and live on their own."

"Could they be holding Travis at the compound?" Jessamine said.

"It's a possibility. But he could be anywhere."

"We should find out," she said.

She was right. But I had a feeling that it wasn't going to happen if left up to the sheriff's department.

"I'm afraid we can't raid the compound without a search warrant," Sanchez said.

"Then get one," Jessamine said.

"We can't, not unless we find more evidence," Sanchez explained.

"What kind of evidence? The murdered man—who kidnapped my husband—was a cult member, you said. How much more evidence do you need?"

"More than that," Sanchez said.

I signaled Jessamine to let it go. And surprisingly, she did. Sanchez asked for a photograph of Travis Tilford. From her large handbag, Jessamine pulled out one similar to what she'd given me.

"Travis was wearing this same shirt the day he disappeared," she said.

"Thank you. That will help when we send in the search-and-rescue dogs and handlers."

"Send them in where?" Jessamine asked.

"We'll start around Kelly Station Park. We'll be looking for Mr. Tilford, naturally, but also for forensic evidence and witnesses who can furnish information. We'll try to cover any secluded places where a kidnapper might keep someone prisoner. Like wooded or uninhabited areas, bodies of water, vacant buildings."

"Bodies of water?" Jessamine said.

"Lakes, ponds, streams."

"Travis doesn't have gills, you know."

Sanchez looked away.

"When will all this happen?" she asked.

"Right now, as we speak," the sheriff said. "The FBI will probably want to talk to you. They can't get involved officially unless state lines have been crossed, but they can share their expertise and resources. If anybody can find your husband, it's them."

"G-men always get their man. Or was that the Mounties?" Jessamine asked.

I cleared my throat loudly and changed the subject. "How about my guns?"

"You'll get them back. Ballistics compared the slug from the deer you shot with the one in McGinnis. They didn't match, which means you're off the hook for the murder charge. All in record time, I might add," Sanchez said.

"Great. That restores my faith as a public-spirited witness who came forward to do his civic duty."

"I think that covers everything," Mayor Logsdon said. "Sheriff Elliott and I have a press conference to attend."

"One more thing," I said, testing the spirit of cooperation. "Detective Sanchez, you said you'd have my car towed for repairs?"

He named a body shop where I could find the Mustang. With that, the top brass left. We started to follow, but Sanchez said, "Mrs. Tilford, Guthrie, hold on a minute."

"What now?" Jessamine said.

"Look, I know you're upset, and you have every right. But the situation is time critical, and we need to throw in everything we can to find your husband. If you want our assistance, we need you to answer a couple more questions."

Rejecting official help at this point was not a viable option. Besides, I was curious about what Sanchez was after. I nodded for her to cooperate. And once again, she did, saying, "Ask them."

"How well do you two really know each other?"

"I don't like your tone. We met fifteen years ago and didn't see each other again until yesterday."

"Guthrie helped your family in the past, you say. How did he help?"

"You have heard that he's a detective, yes? He found my mother's very expensive missing dog and solved several murders at the same time."

"Several." Sanchez brushed away some wrinkles in his uniform shirt. "Okay, we can talk more about that later. That's all I need from you for now. Guthrie, I need you to wait here."

"I'll meet you at the car," I told Jessamine, as she was leaving.

While I waited, telephones rang. Police work continued. People looked curiously at me through the door glass. But I hardly noticed. I was pleased with how well the interrogation went. We stuck together and followed the plan. While concealing what must be concealed, we also retained as much control over the situation as possible. We headed off some dangerous publicity, established our *Bona fides*, and secured the mayor's backing despite the sheriff's misgivings. Agencies with vast resources would soon join the search for Travis. Our relationship with Sanchez had gone from adversarial to cooperative. We could now move forward without too much police interference. Most importantly, we could continue to rely on our most potent weapon—the remaining tracker—to help us find Travis Tilford.

I was musing about Snuffy McGinnis and his ties with the UFO cult when Sanchez returned a few minutes later. He was carrying my tote bag. When he handed it over, the weight told me my ammunition and weapons were inside. I set the bag on the floor without opening it.

"Was that the straight dope on you and her?" Sanchez

asked, his somber eyes steady.

"What do you mean?"

"You know what I mean."

"Nothing's going on between us, if that's what you mean."

"Where did you say you slept last night?"

"I didn't say. Are you trying to trip me up? I thought I was in the clear."

"Why would I do that? Incidentally, where did you spend last night?"

I studied the dust motes swirling in the light. "In my car, if you must know. Why?"

"Can anyone confirm that?"

"The desk clerk at the Red Nebula Inn woke me up this morning by tapping on my window. And before you ask, I didn't get a room because there weren't any vacancies."

"Why not stay with Mrs. Tilford?"

"I was going to, originally, but we had a disagreement and she kicked me out. What are you insinuating?"

Crossed his arms, Sanchez leaned back and said amiably, "Nothing."

But he was.

"Jessamine loves her husband, okay? Our relationship is purely professional. All right?"

"Sure."

"Even if it wasn't, why would you care?"

"I wouldn't. None of my business. I'm just trying to get a handle on the case."

There was a knock on the door and a woman stuck her head in. "Detective?" she asked.

Sanchez stepped out. I could see them talking but not hear what they said. Sanchez returned a moment later and said, "I have some news."

After hearing it, I picked up the tote bag and went to find my client.

Chapter 10

She was waiting for me at the curb with the engine running and the air conditioning blasting. Staying cool. I felt anything but. I had a powerful urge to turn around and run back through those double glass doors. Anything to avoid having to tell Jessamine this foreboding news. But I couldn't, of course, and when she leaned over to unlock the door, I got in.

"What did Sanchez want to tell you that he didn't want me to hear?" she asked right away.

"Basically, he insinuated that you and I murdered your husband so we could run away together with all the money."

Jessamine jerked her head at me so hard I was afraid she'd sprain her neck.

"What? What did you say about that?"

"That he was crazy."

"The man's an idiot."

I cleared my throat. I hated it when people beat around the bush or tried to sugarcoat the unpleasant truth. It was best—and kinder—to just say it. So, I did.

"Something else has come up. They think they've found your van. It was burned."

"What? Was Travis—" She choked back the rest.

"We don't know whether a body was in the vehicle."

A ghastly look appeared on her face. "Do you think he's alive?"

"Yes," I said.

I knew if I was wrong, it wouldn't make any difference. To go on, she needed to believe Travis was still with us.

"Oh god, I hope you're right. Where's the truck?"

"Out in the county, about thirty minutes northwest of here. I'm going out there now to check it out. Want to come along?"

"Wild horses couldn't keep me away."

"Sanchez will be here any minute. We can follow him to the site. I think I should drive."

"I can do it," she said.

But I was worried about her state of mind. And given her penchant for unsafe speed even under normal circumstance, I felt I should insist on driving us myself. "I'll drive," I said.

"But it will distract me from my worries," she said.

"Your worries will distract you from driving. One accident is one too many; two would be disastrous."

"But you're the one who hit the deer."

"Move over. I'm driving."

When Sanchez pulled up, followed by Deputy Metcalfe, I was behind the wheel and fell in line behind them. For once the Mercedes obeyed the speed limit. Despite our grim mission, it was a brutally beautiful summer day. The sun bore down on the landscape, making it shimmer with heat. We left the city behind, humming along on molten black top whose edges were threatening to curl up.

Jessamine was quiet. "I can't stop worrying that the only way we'll find Travis alive is if the killer knows where he's being held. Do you think he knows?"

"I do. It's more likely than not, for several reasons. One—The killer would know if he was in cahoots with McGinnis from the start. Two—The killer would know if McGinnis told him where Travis was being held before being shot. Three—The killer would know if he had an accomplice who knows where Travis is."

"I like the way you're thinking. But what if he doesn't know where to find Travis?"

"We'll proceed as if he does, Jessamine. After all, he knew enough to grab half the money, and so far, he's gotten away with it."

"What about the other half?" she said. "If the killer doesn't know about the second payment, he'd have no reason to keep Travis alive. Safer for him if Travis died."

"I think the odds are in our favor."

"Why?"

Because I needed them to be, but I didn't say that, not while her face was frozen with all the animation of a tombstone.

"For the same reasons. So far, the killer's only gotten half the money. Knowing about the other half gives him two hundred fifty thousand incentives to keep Travis alive."

"Who is this guy?" she said.

"I don't know, but we'll find out." Before she could ask me how I knew that, I hurried on. "This whole thing has felt unplanned from the start. Haphazard, as if thrown together. McGinnis stumbles over you and Travis making your video. He takes advantage of the opportunity. But his scheme fails when you laugh at him."

"Travis did that," she said.

"So, what does Snuffy do next? Ups the ante from twenty-five thousand to a million, and from extortion to kidnapping—a capital offense and way beyond any crime he's ever attempted before. And he screws that up, too, cutting his demand in half just because you say you can't get that much, which is a lie. Then he has this cockamamie plan—probably found on an internet chat room—for two drops instead of one, thinking that is going to keep him from being followed. Of course, he is followed— and fails to find the tracker. What an idiot. And don't forget that this is a guy who believes in UFOs. He doesn't plan well or think things through. In the end, he gets himself killed. All that screwing up and yet you're still out half a million bucks and one kidnapped husband. How is that possible? The answer is that Snuffy had help. He must have. He was simply incapable of pulling this off himself. So, he had a smarter partner."

"I remember that he got in trouble for not paying his child support. Maybe he had a wife or girlfriend who was his accomplice," Jessamine said.

"Or a friend."

"Or fellow cult member," she said.

"Right. We need to find out more about Snuffy's associates. I wonder if there's a known connection with the garbage trucker driver."

I got out my phone and checked the tracker. Still blinking.

"It strains credibility to believe that his truck was chosen at random," I said. "I think the driver must be in on it. So, maybe he knows about the other half of the loot—"

"And where Travis is," Jessamine said.

"We're going to find Travis. And we're going to keep demanding proof of life until we get him back."

"Yes," Jessamine said. "Yes."

As inspirational messages go, it was not up to Saint Bernard rallying the Crusaders. But better than telling her to snap out of it or pull herself together. And, by God, it worked. She was now focused on the situation again instead of her fears about it. Did I really believe all this conjecture? Let's just say I like to keep an open mind. At this stage, almost anything seemed possible.

After twenty minutes of smooth highway driving, Sanchez slowed and made a right onto a narrow county lane. I turned and bumped along on it for a while without meeting any oncoming traffic. Not much to see but empty brush land and derelict farmhouses. At the edge of a big field speckled with stunted pines, Sanchez slowed and pulled off the road. A sheriff's car had beaten us here, along with a forensics van. Sanchez parked alongside them, and I parked beside him.

In the field, we could see the scorched and blackened remains of an old white GMC van.

"Oh my God," Jessamine said, splaying her fingers against her chest. She shook her head slowly, then faster, doubtless realizing that no one could have survived such a blaze. If Travis Tilford had been in that van, he was almost certainly dead.

I tasted ashes in my mouth, whether from knowing I couldn't protect Jessamine—or literally from the air—I couldn't say. Although numb from seeing many such terrible sights, I nevertheless felt a familiar pressure building in my chest and a sudden weakness in my legs. I couldn't imagine how devastated Jessamine must be.

"We don't know Travis was in there," I said, and threw myself at the task, showing Jessamine by example how to cope with her overwhelming grief, if only temporarily. When Sanchez and Metcalfe climbed out of their cars, I joined them. More deputies were working to secure the scene with yellow emergency tape. Other personnel examined the charred shell. They must've all just gotten there.

I took Jessamine's arm, and we walked toward them. When we got close, Metcalfe told us to stay back while Sanchez spoke to the fire investigator, who was poking around in the scorched ruins. Following their brief conversation, Sanchez brought the investigator over to speak with us. He was tall and thin, garbed in a full-sleeved surgical gown, cap, gloves, and shoe covers. He took off his face shield and introduced himself as Gavin Hendrix.

Sanchez said he had told Hendrix who we were and what we were doing here.

Hendrix said that firefighters had responded to a vehicle fire reported by a passing motorist.

"We have identified the vehicle from its VIN tag as registered to Travis Tilford, who I understand was kidnapped," he said.

"Oh, no," Jessamine groaned, and sagged against me. I put my arm around her to keep her from falling.

"I'm sorry, ma'am. I didn't mean to scare you. We didn't find a body in the van," Hendrix said.

Jessamine squared her shoulders, took a deep breath, and said, "Well, scare me you did."

Hendrix again apologized.

Encouraged by this excellent news, I said, "That's great. But we're on a ticking clock. What else can you tell us?"

"The flames toasted it," Hendrix said, staring at the van's spent frame, "making the tires explode and completely gutting the vehicle."

He pointed toward a red gas can on the ground.

"It's too early to say definitively what may have caused the fire, but that was found nearby, raising suspicions that the fire was set. Possibly by lighting a newspaper and throwing it into the doused front seat."

"Anything else, Gavin?" Sanchez asked.

"When I examined the grass for glass fragments, I found very few. But inside the vehicle, the floor was covered with windshield glass. It means the fire started inside, causing the windshield to fail and fall inward."

"Why bother to set the van on fire? Why not just dump it?" Jessamine demanded, stepping into the arson investigator's personal space.

Hendrix took a pace backward. "To destroy evidence, I suppose. Arsonists assume that everything will burn up. But when it comes to determining the cause and origin of a vehicle fire, there's a lot more evidence available than one might think— if you know where to look and what to look for."

"What evidence?" Jessamine persisted.

"Burn patterns. Sometimes fingerprints are identifiable."

"Find any here?" Sanchez said.

"Not yet."

"What about the monolith?" Jessamine said.

"The what?" Hendrix looked perplexed.

Jessamine explained that the monolith was a movie prop. Then she had to explain what it had been used for.

"My gosh, what a tangled web," Hendrix said. "And you think it was in the van?"

"It was—unless somebody moved it."

"Why would they do that?" Hendrix asked.

This struck me as an apt question. Maybe the killer was planning to use it again somehow. But for what?

"I don't know," Jessamine said. "I'm asking because it *was* in there."

"What was this prop made of?"

"Lightweight materials—easy to carry, except for the steel rod that held it all together."

"If there was a steel rod, it should still be in there. But I haven't seen anything like that."

"Then they must have moved it before setting the fire," Jessamine said.

"I guess all the DNA was burned up," Sanchez said.

"It usually melts away at extreme heat. These older vehicles are heavier and contain more metal than newer models, so they take longer to burn. It must have been quite an inferno," Hendrix said, shaking his head in awe.

"Fascinating," Jessamine said, in an acid tone. "But how does this help us find Travis?"

"I don't know what to tell you. I'm sorry. I hope you can get your husband back," Hendrix said.

"At least we know that Travis wasn't immolated and might still be alive," I said.

"Yes," Jessamine said. "That's a great relief. But I'm disappointed that we haven't found him."

"I share your disappointment. We have more help, more resources. But we're still running around in circles," I said.

"We know this much," Hendrix said, and pointed out a line of little colored flags marking off a nearby section of ground. "When I was looking for glass fragments in the grass, I also found more than one set of tire tracks."

"Indicating a possible getaway car," Sanchez explained.

Hendrix nodded. "We'll make a cast for identification purposes."

I was standing outside the crime scene tape. Leaning over the barrier, I used my phone to photograph the tire impressions from a ninety-degree angle, which I knew was considered best.

"I don't understand how this works." Jessamine looked perplexed. "I get that you compare the photo with actual tires to find a match. But most tires look a lot alike, and there are so many of them. It seems like looking for a needle in a haystack."

"Not quite," Hendrix said. "There are experts—people like former tire design engineers—who help police all over the country by analyzing photos of tire tread impressions. They can tell the type, size, and brand of the tire that made the impression."

"I guess that helps, but it still doesn't seem like enough," she said.

The arson investigator nodded and asked to see the photos I'd taken, so I pulled them up. After studying them, he said, "While no expert, I am familiar with the three main tire tread pattern types. This one is *asymmetric*, meaning the tread on the outside edge has large blocks designed to grip the road in wet conditions. It's a more expensive tire, which helps narrow it down a bit."

Hendrix explained that every tire shows not only different tread wear but also damage from tiny cuts and nicks. All those unique characteristics would show up on the tire track.

"See these grooves and wear bars in the tire's tread pattern? They're called 'anomalies.' The broken lines here, for instance, show something was wedged into the tire. Stones maybe."

"So, we really might be able to match the tire with the tracks?" Jessamine said.

"Yes, and these anomalies are as good as fingerprints when it comes to identifying the tire that made the tracks. It will take time, though."

"Thanks for the explanation, Gavin," Sanchez said. "Send

me a report."

"Will do," Hendrix said.

After returning my phone, Hendrix went back to the torched van with Sanchez and Metcalfe in tow. We waited for them to return. They weren't long.

When Sanchez stepped over the tape, he announced, "There's something else of interest that we know."

"What's that?" I asked.

"The Divine Tabernacle of Joy's compound is only a few miles away. Could be significant, since nobody else seems to live around here."

"But why dump the van near your own place? Doesn't make sense," I said.

"Criminals are not always bright," Metcalfe said sarcastically, clearly miffed at being left out of the conversation.

Criminals were not always dumb, either.

We headed for our cars. "This could be a convenient way to cast suspicion on someone else," I pointed out.

"Who do you have in mind?" Sanchez said.

"Someone you don't like. A convenient fall guy. I wonder if we'd see any matching tire tracks at the compound."

"One way to find out," Jessamine said. "What are we waiting for?"

"Can't do it," Sanchez said.

"Why not?"

"First, we need a search warrant, and that might be hard to get."

"Why?" Jessamine asked.

"We need evidence."

"But if these cultists are squatters, can't you just evict them?" Jessamine said.

"Not exactly a soft-hearted approach," Sanchez said.

"Was the kidnapper being soft-hearted when he took Travis? Was the murderer when he shot Snuffy McGinnis?"

"I'm with you," Sanchez said. "They are there illegally. But the county is satisfied for now just to keep them bottled up out of sight. When we get something solid, we'll swoop down on them like screaming eagles."

"But that might be too late," Jessamine said.

She was right. Now was the time for us to move. "What if we go there anyway and ask for their permission to search the compound?"

"Why would they agree to that voluntarily?" Sanchez said.

"They won't if they're holding Travis, but allowing the search might indicate their innocence."

"No harm in asking, I guess," Sanchez said.

My sentiments exactly. Maybe we'd find some matching tire tracks.

Chapter 11

We caravanned as before through the countryside, but this time we were sandwiched between Sanchez's car and Metcalfe's. Sanchez turned left onto a back road and continued onward through wooded areas. At the top of a rise, Sanchez stopped, got out, and grabbed a pair of field glasses from his trunk. We got out, too, and watched Sanchez steady himself with his elbows on the hood of the car while scanning the area below.

"Notice anything interesting?" Jessamine asked.

"See for yourself," Sanchez answered, and passed her the binoculars.

A half mile away in the trees rose a shantytown of tents, dilapidated trailers, and shacks. The ramshackle structures were made of scrap lumber and repurposed pallets, crates, and plastic bags. There was also an old church standing off to one side of the property.

"Is this the compound? It looks more like a homeless encampment," Jessamine said.

"That's what it is, in a way, since the occupants voluntarily gave up most of their earthly possessions to wait here for the end," Sanchez said.

Metcalfe reached for the binoculars, but reddened when Jessamine handed them to me instead.

"How many you figure are living there, Sanchez?" I passed the glasses on to Metcalfe. He was obviously peeved by his current position in the pecking order.

"Fifty, more or less," Sanchez said.

"Gawd almighty, what an eyesore. They need to be rousted," Metcalfe said.

"But not today," Sanchez said. "Let's go down and ask nicely to be let in, see what they say."

Metcalfe snorted at that.

Sunlight filtered through the leaves onto the car's hood as we slowly eased downhill. A four-strand barbwire fence was strung around the property, which included a padlocked gate. Sanchez climbed out of his car and approached the gate. Metcalfe followed him, appearing happier now that he was in action.

The front entrance of the church was about ten yards away and seemed abandoned, although a notice board near the door said, "The end is near. Are you ready?" To the left was a graveyard with a dozen rows of weathered headstones. The architectural style was early settlement—limestone foundation, weatherboard walls, steep roof with a gable and belfry.

A jowly fiftyish man wearing a gray hooded kaftan and flip-flops came out of the church.

"Yes? What can I do for you?" he asked.

Sanchez flashed his badge. "What's your name?"

"Hiram Jones," said the man, who had a fringe of grizzled hair around his large ears.

"Do you know a man named Sean McGinnis?" Sanchez asked.

"Yes, of course. He's a member of the Divine Tabernacle of Joy. Why do you ask?"

"Has he been here recently?"

Jones shook his head. "No, he hasn't. Sean has his own

place. What's this about?"

"McGinnis kidnapped this man." Sanchez showed him Travis Tilford's photograph.

"Snuffy a kidnapper? I don't believe it."

"Believe it," Sanchez said.

"When was this supposed to have happened?"

"Yesterday afternoon. Look at the picture again." Sanchez held it up once more. "Has Travis Tilford been here?"

"No, he hasn't. I'm the gatekeeper, so I would know."

"This is my husband we're talking about," Jessamine said. "Are you sure you haven't seen him? Or heard anything about him? How about an old white GMC van? Seen one of them?"

"No. I'm sorry," Jones said.

"We're here to search the compound," Sanchez said.

"Fine, if you have a warrant. Do you?"

"No, but we have Bart Proctor's permission."

"You're joking. Why would Brother Bartholomew approve this?"

"Because he knows that we suspect Travis Tilford is being held here. Phone Proctor for confirmation. We'll wait. But not for long."

Jones stepped away and used his phone. After a quick whispered conversation, he returned, saying, "You can search. Brother Bartholomew says we have nothing to hide."

Jones unlocked the gate.

"Let's start with the church," Sanchez said, and stepped into the building.

Natural light streamed through the windows of the one-room church. But there wasn't much to see. White plastered walls. Pews arranged in rows. An outline of a large cross on the wall above the altar. And the pulpit, where I suspected a different kind of sermon was now preached. The interior wasn't particularly neat or clean. A few backpacks and sleeping bags were stashed under the pews. We searched, but that was all we could find. Nothing to suggest that Travis Tilford had ever set foot in this place.

With a gloating smile, Hiram Jones watched us leave the building. Rather than return to what he'd been doing before we arrived—and who knew what *that* was—he stayed with us, saying it was a condition Brother Bartholomew had insisted on for permitting the search. We didn't care. Jones didn't seem like much of a threat.

As we trod the compound's unpaved road, I kept an eye out for tire tracks, especially treads with large blocks on their outside edge. But spotting them in anything other than sand, mud, or snow was a long shot.

Since we didn't have backup, we stuck together as we visited shacks, house trailers, and tents. Sites were irregular—straight, angled, or L-shaped—and positioned haphazardly. Usually, there was room per space for only one shelter and one vehicle parking, but not all spaces were occupied. After a while, we came to an area of tall bushy weeds where cars bearing Little Green Men Festival bumper stickers were parked. Five teenagers were leaning against the cars, drinking beer and staring at us with open hostility.

"Howdy, boys," Sanchez said.

He got nothing in return but stony silence and more sullen looks from the young men, who resembled tall bushy weeds themselves. Then the biggest one, whose ball cap was tugged down nearly to his eyebrows, said, "You can't come in here. This is private property."

"Brother Bartholomew gave them permission," Jones said.

The kid swigged his beer and gave Hiram one of those infuriating looks that only an insolent teenager can manage. The older man looked away.

"What's your name, son?" Sanchez asked.

"What's yours?" came the defiant reply.

Metcalfe started to respond, but Sanchez stopped him. "I'm Detective Sanchez, with the sheriff's department. Now what's your name?"

"Lance Young."

"Legal drinking age is twenty-one," Sanchez nodded at the beer can in his hand.

"Nobody cares. World's over soon, so what's the difference?" Lance said.

"You really believe that?" Sanchez said. "How about marijuana? Any of you growing it or smoking it? What would I find if I came back with a drug sniffing police dog?"

"What do you want, man?" Lance said.

"I'm looking for a missing person. His name is Travis Tilford."

"He's my husband," Jessamine said.

"Who cares?" Lance said.

She slapped the beer can out of his hand.

"Hey, you can't do that," Lance said.

"You're lucky I didn't slap your face," Jessamine told him.

"Listen, bitch—"

She slapped his face.

Lance backed far enough away to yell, "That's assault."

"I didn't see anything," said Sanchez. "Did you?"

"No, nothing," Metcalfe said.

I was expecting a possibly violent reaction, but nobody said or did anything else. Jones seemed ready to protest, but I don't think he liked Lance much and decided to let it go. Maybe he thought we were aliens. We watched with ill-disguised glee as Jessamine backed Lance up until he could go no further. She didn't need our help to deal with this one.

"You'd better start caring, kid," she said, pointing her finger in his face. "Now pay attention." She held up a photo. "This is Travis. Have you seen him? He's been kidnapped."

Lance shook his head.

"How about the rest of you?" Jessamine showed them the photo. "Any of you recognize him? Or know where he is?"

Four mutes.

"Are you sure?" She held up Tilford's photo again. "Take

another look."

"How about a white van? Or Snuffy McGinnis? Any of you seen him around in the last day or so?" Sanchez asked. Again, no response. "If you're holding back something and anything happens to this man, you won't need to wait for the end of the world. Understand? Now pour out the beer."

They didn't like it, but they did it.

"Thanks, gentlemen. Carry on," Sanchez said, and we walked toward the cluster of temporary housing.

"You're a little bit of a loose cannon, aren't you?" Metcalfe asked.

Jessamine didn't smile. "Sorry, I shouldn't have done that."

"Ever think of being a cop?" Metcalfe grinned.

Sanchez looked thoughtful. "What did you make of it, Guthrie?"

"They probably don't know anything," I said.

"I agree. They don't seem too fond of government officials, either."

"Who could blame them?" Hiram Jones said, quietly getting his two cents' worth in as we moved on to the next stop on our tour of the compound. "More jackbooted government agents abusing their authority."

"We're not from the government," I said, with a nod at Jessamine.

"Those two are." Jones gestured toward Christian County's finest.

"Look, no real harm's been done. You know the kid had it coming," I said.

"Doesn't give you a right to do it, though. We let you in voluntarily, and you do this." Jones shook his head, as if to say he should have known better. Or Brother Bartholomew should have.

"You can't tweak the nose of the law and expect to get off scot-free," I said.

"You just said she wasn't the law."

"Good one, Hiram. Were you a debater in high school? Or did that come after?"

He frowned as if about to continue fulminating.

To prevent this, I said, "You did the right thing letting us search—unless we eventually find something. Either way, to your credit, you did your duty as a law-abiding citizen. If the world's going to end soon, what's the difference, anyway?"

"Ha," Hiram grinned, flashing yellowed teeth. "You mock us now, but you wait and see. Your time's coming. And when it does, you'll wish you were with Noah on his ark rather than out there drowning."

Sanchez and Metcalfe began knocking on doors. There was little response. As we trekked on, Hiram and I slipped farther behind the others.

"I didn't realize the world was going to end by flood again, like in the Bible."

"I speak metaphorically." Hiram gave me a beady-eyed look. "Are you human?"

"What?"

"You heard me. Identify yourself," he said.

"I already did that. I'm as human and flawed as you are. What the hell do you think I am, an alien?"

Jones did not answer.

"What's your deal, Hiram? You act like you really believe in this Martian mumbo-jumbo. Do you?"

"It's neither Martian nor mumbo-jumbo, as you're about to find out."

"C'mon, tell me. What was your life like before you joined the Divine Tabernacle? Do you have a family? A job?"

"Why should I tell you anything?" he said.

"Maybe I'm interested in more than the case. Maybe I feel empty inside and sad. Maybe I'm looking for a new way, too."

"I don't believe you," he said.

It wasn't total bullshit. But I didn't blame him. "What have you got to lose by telling me something about yourself?"

Jones remained silent as he seemed to be think it over.

We caught up with Sanchez. "How about letting me take the next one?"

Sanchez shrugged. as if the say *why not*?

The next one was a house trailer. It seemed slightly more well-maintained than the others we'd visited so far. A small Kawasaki motorcycle was parked beside it. Both bike and trailer appeared in good repair. No rust or other apparent neglect. That was different from what I'd seen so far. It made me especially curious about the middle-aged man and woman who were sitting on metal frame lawn chairs under a canvas awning swatting at flies.

The man, dark and lean with short brown hair flecked with gray, was lighting a cigarette. But as we approached, he stopped with the match still burning in his fingers.

"Afternoon," I said, halting three paces away.

The man finished lighting his cigarette and addressed Jones. "What's going on, Hiram?"

"Brother Bartholomew wishes for us to cooperate with these people," Jones said.

"Oh," the man said. As Jones faded into the background, the main asked me what I wanted.

"Gerald, that is not very neighborly," the woman said.

Gerald blew out the match and dropped it in an ashtray on the small mesh table positioned between them. I noticed that their table also held a candle and a pot of petunias. It made me wonder if they craved normalcy while bracing here for anticipated life-shattering changes.

"We don't get many visitors. I'm Christine. Welcome." The woman was tall and tanned, had shining black hair and dark brown eyes. She was wearing a faded cotton dress with an orange floral print.

"Thanks," I said. "We're looking for someone. Maybe you can give us some help."

"Who are you looking for?" she asked.

"It's my husband." Jessamine stepped forward. "He's been kidnapped."

"Tell me about your husband in case I see him," Christine said.

"He's a wonderful man. And I'm so afraid I won't get him back."

"What does he look like?"

"Here's a picture." Jessamine showed her.

Running a hand through her hair, Christine said, "Well, he's pretty good looking. I can see why you want him back. I'll keep an eye out for him and get in touch if I see him."

"Thank you. How about you?" Jessamine said to the man, who shook his head.

"Haven't seen him."

"Would you mind letting me come inside and have a look around?" I asked, although it probably would be futile.

"We just told you we haven't seen anyone," Gerald barked, in a raspy smoker's voice, but shrugged his shoulders as if to say how can I stop you?

He seemed grouchy but unafraid. Maybe I was relying too much on appearances, but I found it hard to believe that a loony UFO cultist would dress like Gerald—in a button-down short-sleeve shirt, tan shorts, and running shoes without socks. Yet here we were in the compound of the Tabernacle of Divine Joy.

"Oh, let them search. We're not hiding anything." Christine nodded to me it was all right.

I went up the two steps to the door. The interior was surprisingly different, as if other people lived there. Everything seemed dusty and neglected. The floor, couch, and chair were covered with dirty clothes and dirty dishes. All the furnishings looked like ordinary, cheap stuff, which made sense. Why spend a fortune on possessions you're about to give up? When I flipped on a light switch, nothing happened. Same when I tried to turn on the water. No hookups, obviously.

The bedroom was mostly filled by a double bed covered with

a frayed bedspread. The dresser drawers contained underwear and socks. On a bookshelf, I found the King James Bible alongside novels by Stephen King and Anne Rice. I examined every space in the trailer big enough to contain a human body, found none.

I was growing frustrated. Everything about this couple, except for where they lived, seemed ordinary. Still, few serial killers look like we imagine them—or they'd have been caught long ago. I came out of the trailer shaking my head and thanked Christine and Gerald, who swatted flies.

We walked on through the hodgepodge of shacks and tents. When we caught up with Sanchez and Metcalfe once again, I said, "This could take hours. Why don't we just split up? We can cover the place twice as fast that way."

Sanchez considered it, then said, "All right. Metcalfe, why don't you and Guthrie pay a visit to that tent across the way, while Mrs. Tilford and I look over here?"

"Not a chance, chief," Jessamine said. "I'm staying with Guthrie."

Her determination swayed Sanchez. "Okay. But remember that I'm responsible for you two. Don't get in any trouble. But if you do, yell your head off."

"How could we possibly get into trouble?" Jessamine said.

Jones stayed with us as we talked to a few people with nothing much to say, and searched a few pitiful dwellings, finding nothing useful.

"You folks really don't have anything to hide, do you?" I said.

Jones smiled thinly. "Told you."

Although doctrinaire, Jones seemed educated. I quietly suggested that Jessamine take over the searching while I tried to get more out of Jones on my own. I'd try appealing to his core beliefs. She seemed eager to do so.

"I don't understand why The Divine Tabernacle holds that the end is near. Or that aliens somehow are part of it," I said.

"Would you like to know? Or is this just some government ploy to get in my good graces?" Jones asked.

"Why don't you enlighten me? I mean, what have you got to lose?"

He thought it over as Jessamine entered a shack. "Are you familiar with the Doomsday Clock?"

I was aware of the clock, albeit dimly. "Something to do with Armageddon, right?"

With a superior smile, Hiram explained that the clock was a symbolic timepiece, showing how close the world was to ending.

"So, what time is it?" I asked.

"It's now ninety seconds to midnight," he said, "midnight being the theoretical point of human annihilation."

"Scary."

"You could say that."

"According to whom?"

"The Bulletin of the Atomic Scientists."

"And who are they exactly?"

"You're a very skeptical person, aren't you, Mr. Guthrie?" Jones asked with a smile. "You pride yourself on it."

"Well, I don't know about priding myself, but you are talking about the end of everything. A healthy dose of skepticism seems appropriate."

He snorted. "The Bulletin is a nonprofit media organization."

"Not a scientific institution?"

"No, a communication tool that posts free articles about the perils we face from nuclear weapons, technology, political tensions. Scientists created the clock in 1947 and since then, the minute hand has been reset twenty-seven times. This is the closest we've ever come to the end."

I nodded at this sobering fact—at least it seemed factual. "It might interest you to know that I believe that climate change is an apocalyptic threat."

Jessamine came back out, shaking her head. We moved on to another trailer. As Jessamine talked her way inside, Jones told me, "Maybe you're not a total lost cause, after all."

"what's the Bulletin's position on aliens?" I asked, wondering if I had convinced him to trust me a little.

"They haven't taken one, as far as I know." Jones frowned. "Scientists can be a very wishy-washy bunch at times. They're not happy until they've done exhausting amounts of research."

"So, no position on aliens? That seems like a serious omission."

"Indeed. You believe in climate change. Let me ask you this. We are aware of the catastrophic risks—extended droughts, changing growing seasons, rising sea levels. Why aren't we, as a planet, doing anything about it?"

"We are," I said, "just not near enough."

"The threat of worldwide calamity should be enough motivation."

"I agree."

"Then why do we fiddle while Rome burns?" Jones said.

"Let me guess. Aliens?"

"Still skeptical," Jones said. "Have you considered the possibility of Tilford being abducted by extraterrestrials?"

"Not unless Snuffy McGinnis was an alien," I said.

"What if he was merely their tool—programmed to carry out this task?"

"Now why didn't I think of that?"

"You are blinded by the media. You asked me what my life was like before I joined the Divine Tabernacle of Joy. I'll tell you."

I perked up a bit at that.

"All my life, I have been seeking to know what happens after we die. And why we are here. I've also looked at the sky and the stars, imagining people living on other planets. Then, five years ago, I began receiving telepathic messages."

Oh, my.

"Telepathic? Meaning they could read your mind?"

"More like I was reading theirs," he said.

"What were they thinking?" I asked.

"That I should come to this area."

"Hopkinsville, Kentucky? From where?"

"Nashville, where I lived and worked as a postman."

As Jessamine came back out, wearily shaking her head, I was struck by the apparent and utter futility of this task. Nevertheless, we continued onward, stopping at each temporary dwelling. As we walked, Hiram Jones again picked up the thread of his story.

"Once I got to Hopkinsville, I immediately felt the presence of an invisible being from another planet."

"You mean like a sixth sense?"

"I suppose you could call it that. I just knew."

"What sort of being was this?"

"I can't remember."

Of course not. "Why not?"

"I think the alien somehow erased my memory before releasing me. Most researchers believe that's what happens."

Most researchers?

"They might have erased Snuffy's memory, as well."

Before he was shot in the head? Wait, did Jones know that McGinnis had been killed?

"I had a sense of time missing," he continued. "At the Little Green Men Festival, I wandered into a meditation seminar and sat down to meditate. I was expecting an old man with long gray hair and a white robe—not unlike what I'm wearing today. And that's who showed up, except his robe was yellow." He fingered the kaftan.

"Brother Bartholomew?"

Jones nodded with enthusiasm. "I closed my eyes to meditate and had this incredible experience. For the first time in my life, I felt at peace. Like I had found what I was searching for—maybe that's why the aliens had sent me here. When I went home to share my story and bring the others back with me, though, I lost my job and my family. I returned, joined the Tabernacle, and the *Ufologic* community became my home."

Whew. "Quite a transformation."

"A profound one, I assure you."

"There's something I'm wondering about. Why would aliens

tell Snuffy to kidnap Travis Tilford?"

"I don't know. They're often mysterious. You might ask Brother Bartholomew. He seems in closer touch than anyone else."

"Any idea where they'd tell Snuffy to hide his victim?"

"Not here," he said.

The next place was a miserable-looking tent pitched under a shade tree. Jessamine asked me to take over the search for a wile. Maybe she could get something else out of the gatekeeper.

Two bicycles were chained together beside the tent. Two men were sitting on low stools, waiting for the end of the world. I know because they said so. Both were in their fifties, unshaven, and smelled less than detergent fresh. They also struck me as bone tired, in body and mind.

I explained why we'd come. They said they didn't know or care about Travis.

"It's all right," the chubbier man said. "Bad news is good news. Nuclear war? Climate change? Kidnapped husband? The prophecies are now being fulfilled. Isn't that right, Deacon Hiram?"

"What prophecies?" Jessamine asked.

While Jones and the pair jabbered on about *multiple advanced extraterrestrials coming to conquer earth by unleashing a deadly virus,* I resisted the urge to inform them that the pandemic was over. Instead, I stuck my head inside their tent. It was dark with a sour whiff of sweat. I saw a couple of sleeping bags and a camp cot, a battery-powered lantern, and multiple cloth shopping bags filled with who knows what. I wasn't in there long. But when I pulled my head back out, Jessamine had disappeared.

Chapter 12

"Where's Jessamine?" I asked.

"She went that way." Jones pointed to his left.

There was no sign of her. She must have gone into one of the nearby temporary dwellings. But why she would go without me was puzzling.

"Jessamine," I yelled.

There was no answer.

Tingling with adrenaline, I hurried toward the closest one, a double-wide shaded by a maple three lots away. It was fancier than the others, with a concrete pad, wooden picnic table, portable charcoal grill, and a metal campfire ring. I slowed down as I got closer, approaching with the caution of experience. It was too hot to be indoors without air conditioning. Yet there were no power lines or hookups, and no generator sound. Maybe with the windows open and some battery-powered fans, it would be bearable.

With a fly buzzing near my eyes, I stepped up and peered through the door window. Glare made it hard to see, but a flash of motion reflected in the glass, and I ducked instinctively. Something with heft whipped past my head. I whirled around, raising my arm to ward off another blow. I caught it instead on my right elbow. This sent an electric shock wave up and down my entire arm and then numbed it. But lunging at me had thrown my attacker off-balance and given me an opening to counter. I clipped him under the chin with a stiff left uppercut, followed that with a jab, and then caught him leaning into a left hook that finished him off.

As he fell, he dropped a blackjack. I kicked it away, took a closer look at him. He was a lean, sharp-featured man, probably in his late twenties with short brown hair. He'd shaved his temples, revealing white skin like the sides of a whitewall tire. I'd never seen him before.

It was all over very quickly. As I tried to massage some feeling back into my numbed arm, Sanchez came around the corner, followed by Metcalfe.

"What the hell happened here, Guthrie?" the detective asked. "I leave you alone for two minutes and you get in a brawl?"

"It wasn't a very long one," I said, nodding at my assailant, who lay before us. "Why don't you cuff him while I go in there and find out what's happened to Jessamine?"

Without pausing for an answer, I gently pushed the door open and found my client waiting just inside.

"What's going on?" I asked.

She didn't answer but, while nodding down a hallway, squeezed my good arm hard enough to leave a red handprint. I halted, motionless, immediately beginning to sweat despite a large cordless fan pushing the overheated air around. The room looked more like a well-appointed apartment than a mobile home. The carpet was expresso gray, paintings hung on the beige walls, and there was a matching sofa and armchair in muted teal. But it smelled like lemon air-freshener and perspiration.

A barefoot young woman with stringy blond hair winding around her face appeared from the rear of the trailer. She was dressed in baggy cutoff jeans and an oversized, inside-out University of Tennessee T-shirt. Orange. Like her ball cap.

"Oh, I didn't know anyone was here," she said.

"We're working with detectives from the sheriff's department. Do you live here?"

"Sometimes."

"What times would those be?" I asked.

"When I need to. Brother Bartholomew lets me. I'm Zeta."

"Zeta who?"

"Rivers."

We told her our names.

"Sit down," Zeta offered.

She sank into the armchair, which seemed designed for someone bigger, positioning herself right in front of the fan.

"Love your cap. Can I see it?" Jessamine asked.

"Oh, this? Sure." She took the cap off. "I think it's a wonderful shade of orange, don't you?"

"Yes. Where did you get it?" Jessamine asked, turning the cap over in her hands.

"Found it along the road earlier today while I was jogging."

"Where?" I asked. "And how long ago?"

"Not far from here. About an hour, I guess. Why are you so interested in the cap?"

"I think it belongs to my husband," Jessamine said. "Look." She had pulled up a photo with Travis's cap.

"Let me see that," I said.

The cap in the photo and the cap in Jessamine's hands looked very much alike.

Zeta ran her hand over an armrest. "Really? Well, you can have the cap if you want. What's his name?"

"Travis Tilford." Jessamine switched to a photo of him.

"Why are you looking for him?" Zeta said.

"He's been kidnapped," I answered. "Do you know where we might find him?"

"Kidnapped?" Zeta sat up a little straighter. "Like I said, I just found the cap."

Sanchez came in. "What's going on?" he said.

"I think we've found my husband's ball cap," Jessamine

said, holding it up.

"Where was it?" Sanchez asked.

"This is Zeta Rivers," I said, as pinpricks of sensation returned to my arm. "She says she came across the ball cap while jogging in the area earlier today."

"Is that right, Ms. Rivers?" Sanchez asked.

Zeta said it was.

"It's too hot to talk in here. Why don't you all step outside while I look around?" Sanchez said.

It was a relief to get out of the sweltering trailer. We found Hiram Jones pacing in the shade, his flip-flops slapping on the trailer's concrete apron. Deputy Metcalfe and his manacled prisoner, who wouldn't look at me, were there, too. We waited with them in silence until Sanchez came out—empty-handed.

"You know this woman?" the detective asked the gatekeeper.

"Sure, that's Zeta," Jones said.

"And this man?" Sanchez gestured at the prisoner.

"Tim Murdock," Jones said. "He lives here. Tim, what were you thinking? Why did you attack Mr. Guthrie?"

"Found him snooping around and thought he was one of *Them*," Murdock said.

"Them?" Sanchez asked.

"Aliens," Murdock said. "You ought to know. You're probably one yourself."

"Do you know anything about the kidnapping of Travis Tilford?" Sanchez asked.

"Who's that?" Murdock said.

"How about the murder of Sean McGinnis?"

"Snuffy's dead? Who did it? Was it you?" Murdock asked.

Sanchez shook his head, as if saying this was a hopeless case. "We'll discuss the matter further downtown, Mr. Murdock. Meanwhile, you're under arrest for assault with a deadly weapon."

"Is that really necessary?" Jones asked. "After all, you were intruding."

"With your permission," Sanchez said, giving Jones an incredulous look. "Deputy Metcalfe, please move the prisoner to the squad car."

"Yes, sir," Metcalfe said with a smile.

"Does he have an automobile?" Sanchez asked.

"No, Tim rides a motorbike," Jones said.

So much for matching Metcalfe's tire tracks, Sanchez's frown seemed to say.

The deputy began questioning Zeta Rivers more specifically about the where and when she had found the ball cap. She said it was in a shallow ditch that Sanchez explained was on the same road we'd followed here. If the cap was indeed Travis Tilford's—no name or other identifying marks were found—and Zeta was telling the truth, it provided a tenuous link between him and this place. But that's all it did.

Sanchez went on interrogating Zeta, quickly ascertaining that she was a twenty-one-year-old college dropout who'd drifted into the cult's orbit a few months ago. Zeta described herself as "free-spirited" and said her relationship with the trailer's owner was "casual." She hadn't seen Brother Bartholomew today, but he could probably be found tonight at the Little Green Men Festival. Zeta claimed to know nothing of the Tilford kidnapping or the murder of McGinnis, whom she barely knew.

At this point, we'd covered most of the compound. Gathering our group back together once more, Sanchez led us through the rest of the search. We didn't find Travis Tilford or anything else connected to him, including tire tracks, ball caps, or aliens.

Chapter 13

"Well, what are we going to do now?" Jessamine asked as we headed back to town. "Sit around hoping to get another lead?"

"No, no sitting around—except when we're driving to our next point of investigation."

"Good, because I don't think I could bear that."

"As a matter of fact, we're on our way there right now."

"Where are we going?"

I was behind the wheel of the black Mercedes and took a moment to ponder. If Tim Murdock had kidnapped Travis, he wasn't saying, despite an emotional appeal from Jessamine. While law enforcement tried to get the truth out of him, we were free to pursue any other leads we could come up with on our own.

Discovering the burned van and searching the Divine Tabernacle of Joy's compound had proven bitterly disappointing, especially to Jessamine. We'd started with high hopes, but found nothing leading us closer to Travis. Plucky as she was, Jess wouldn't have been human if her fear and concern for her husband's welfare weren't weighing heavily on her.

She'd asked how an orange cap so much like Travis's had

found its way into the cult's hands. I'd expressed the suspicion that he had been there at some point but then been transported elsewhere. The cap could have been dropped while he was being moved from his van to the kidnapper's car. But Jess pointed out that didn't explain how it wound up in a ditch for Zeta Rivers to find. The young blonde could be lying, of course, but I didn't think so. Had Travis found a way to leave it behind as part of a trail? Unlikely, but possible. Suppose he had. Where did the trail lead? Not to the compound, apparently. And what of the tire tracks? Even if we found the tread that matched them, what would that prove? And how would it lead us to Travis?

Fortunately, there was still the tracker at the landfill. During the entire time we'd been searching with the sheriff's deputies, I had been periodically checking my phone to see if the device was still working and in the same place. It was. "We're going to the landfill," I said.

"Good," she sighed.

We found our way to Highway 41, then eastward to serpentine Latham Road, which ran through small brick starter homes. They were all unimaginative in design, but clean and well-maintained, as if their owners took pride in their property. After a mile or so of this, we came to the entrance of the Hopkinsville Solid Waste Enterprise.

We stopped across the road. The question now was how to get in without tipping off the remaining accessory to kidnapping.

Another bright new facility. This one had two large corrugated buildings, both painted brown and cream. The one marked "Office" had a few long narrow windows and a small visitor parking area in front. Displayed nearby, the landfill's permit and the names of the manager and the operator. Fees and hours of operation were listed. Old Glory flew on a pole out front. A very patriotic dump, I mused. The other building marked "Maintenance" was windowless and looked big enough to house garbage trucks.

Between these two structures lay a gravel employee

parking lot. A sign reading, "Enter scales slowly," was posted where vehicles pulled up to be weighed. The heaviness of each load would flash on a red digital readout. Yet another sign read, "No tailgate, no tarp, no dump. Enter at your own risk." Beyond the scales, garbage trucks entered the fenced landfill via a gate that slid open and shut on rollers attached to steel posts. The access road sloped into an immense bowl stretching seemingly to the horizon, but was hidden from most of the highway by a thick border of tall trees.

All government-run waste storage sites had bottom liners to contain liquid produced by degrading trash, but on such a hot summer evening as this one, a ripe smell wafted. Not as bad as I feared, but bad enough.

"We'll need to do a little shopping," I said, as I brought the Mercedes to a stop in front of the closed gate. According to a sign, the landfill had shut down at three p.m. The parking lot was now empty, the workers having gone home hours ago.

"Shopping for what?"

"Supplies we'll need to rescue Travis."

"Like what?"

"Neutrolene for blocking the smell from our noses, for one. And a few other items to help us when we break into this landfill."

No gatehouse, I noted. No night watchman. But when shut, the gate would effectively prevent illegal midnight dumping.

"Why in the world would we do that?" she said.

"Think it through with me. We start by measuring the kidnappers' intelligence by their harebrained, two-pronged ransom scheme. They obviously assumed that if we didn't tail them from the first pickup site, then we wouldn't from the second, either. That was dumb. One did not rule out the other. Still, as far as the kidnappers know—assuming at least one of them remains alive—their plan has worked. The money must still be in the landfill where they can pick it up at their leisure."

"Okay, but I still don't see how retrieving it gets Travis back,"

Jessamine said.

"We're not going to retrieve it, only watch and wait for the kidnappers to come for it." I held up the phone with the flashing tracker light. "Find it, find them, find him."

"I see." She mulled that over. "But how do we know the money is still in the case?"

"Has to be. The brief case was compacted and buried under a huge mound of trash in the garbage truck. No way the driver could have gotten it out of the hopper, found the tracker, and separated it from the money without making a lengthy stop—and he didn't make any such stop. I know because I monitored the tracker all the way here."

We sat quietly for a minute, each with our own thoughts. Mine concerned the keypad that controlled the gate electronically. It could be disabled with the right low-budget equipment. This was still a garbage dump, not a bank. Unfortunately, I didn't have the right equipment.

"You think the garbage man is our killer?" Jessamine asked.

"Possibly. We must act as if he is, in any case."

She gave me a weak smile, which quickly faded. "But what if he doesn't know where Travis is?"

"Then we're screwed, and it'll all be up to the FBI."

Looking the landfill over, I assumed there were also some specially designed remote cameras to further discourage unauthorized dumping here, so we'd need to keep our faces covered when we did our break-in later tonight. Getting inside this place was shaping up as difficult and dangerous—not least because of the real deterrent, which was spelled out on another sign: "Beware of dogs. They are faster than you."

I did not doubt this, though I hoped it was a bluff. But just in case it wasn't, we needed to come armed with pepper spray and tranquilizer darts.

I explained this to Jessamine while we reconnoitered the area around the landfill, including a dirt road that seemed to disappear into the forest. Thinking that might come in handy later, we drove back to town and entered the first big box store we came to. Shoppers were bustling around, buying everything from pharmaceuticals to pet supplies. We bought some pepper spray and a dart gun, which Jessamine put on her credit card.

The spray in the cannister we were buying was, as I explained, effective in repelling aggressive dogs without damaging them long term. A dart fired from the air pump tranquilizer pistol would put them out of commission for hours. It had a range of fifty feet, too.

"And you'll be glad to know that its *quiet propulsion* causes the animal less trauma."

"So, we'll shoot them, but we won't scare them?"

"That's it," I said, "though it sounds less impressive put like that."

"Hm," Jessamine said, looking at me askance, "that could be a plus, I suppose."

We picked up a few other items before checking out.

My next step was to phone the body shop recommended by the mayor.

"As I feared," I said, after completing the call, "it will take several days to repair the Mustang. By then, the case might well be over. But they think they can make it look like new again. Well, as new as a really old car can look."

"I'm glad," Jessamine smiled. "Will your insurance cover the cost?"

"I don't have comprehensive coverage, so it will be out of pocket."

"No, it won't," she said. "You wouldn't have hit that deer if it wasn't for me. It's my responsibility. Just include it on your bill."

"It might be expensive."

"Never mind that. My father has deep pockets."

"We'll need to get a rental car, too."

We located a vehicle rental place and were offered a dark blue Nissan Versa, a four-cylinder, one-hundred twenty-two horsepower subcompact sedan. It lacked the kind of muscle needed for a car chase, but the agent said it was the best they could come up with because there'd been a huge demand for rentals this week. Reluctantly driving the Versa, I followed Jessamine back to the motel.

Her phone began ringing as we walked in the door.

"It's my parents," she said.

"Don't tell them about the landfill," I mouthed, and went into the bathroom to give her some privacy.

Several moments later, she tapped on the door.

"They want to talk to you."

I took the phone. "Guthrie," I said.

"Jim, it's Cybil. What's the situation there?"

I hardly knew where to begin. I told her that the authorities were cooperating and we were planning our next move.

What was our next move, she asked?

I said that I didn't want to say over the phone. Truth was, I didn't want to say at all.

"Give me the phone," I heard Shelby Barrett say. "Guthrie. I want to know what's going on down there, and I mean right now."

"So do I, Senator. We're doing our best to find that out *and* bring Travis home safely. The authorities are looking for him now."

"Don't you dare try to play this close to the vest with me," Barrett snapped. "I want specifics. I'm paying good money for them."

He was right about that, but he wasn't my client. And, unlikely as it might seem, he could still be behind this whole scheme.

"As I told Mrs. Barrett just now, I can't talk about it over the phone. I'll let you know something as soon as I can. Until then, you'll have to be patient."

"Now, you listen to me," he began, but I was already returning the phone to Jessamine.

While she talked with her father and then showered, I was having a drink and checking the tracker, which was still in place and functioning. When Jessamine came back out a few minutes later wearing a robe, I told her that I'd been thinking more about the possible hijacking scenario and Snuffy McGinnis's death.

"The trouble with the theory is that you wouldn't blab about hatching something like that. Not when kidnapping is a capital offense. And only a lame-brained idiot would reveal where to pick up all the ransom money."

"Haven't you been saying all along that the kidnapper might be dumb?" Jessamine said.

"You're right. I have."

"Where does that leave us?"

"We need to find out who McGinnis was close to. Then we're on our way to who killed him, and that person may lead us to your husband."

Even as I made this statement, I didn't know if I believed it.

Chapter 14

We were leaving the Red Nebula Inn when we ran into the manager, Byron Hutchinson, who looked up at us with a smile. "Headed out for the evening?"

"We are," Jessamine said, matching his smile with a radiant one of her own. "Thank you for confirming what we told the cops about our stay here."

"No problem. Happy to be of help. But if you don't mind me asking, what's going on?"

"Byron, could we have a word somewhere quieter?" I asked.

"By all means. Come on into my office."

I knew it was a calculated risk to take him into our confidence. But the surest way to get something is to give something in return. With Byron, gossip and speculation might prove profitable. The motel office was in a small wood paneled room with a clear view of the parking lot. The front desk was a black box with an off-white laminated countertop. We went over and leaned against it.

"Byron," I said in a near whisper, nodding for him to come closer, "Can we trust you?"

"Absolutely. Part of the service."

"You seem like a solid citizen. Do we have your word that

what we're going to tell you will remain a secret?"

"You have my word," he said solemnly.

"Even from the police?"

He nodded.

Maybe he would, maybe he wouldn't. But that was as good as we were going to get. I told him about discovering Sean McGinnis's body, that we were here to rescue Jessamine's kidnapped husband, and what had gone wrong with the ransom payment. I left out the stuff we'd kept the cops in the dark about.

"Good grief," Byron said. "A murder. A kidnapping. Wow. That's crazy."

"Did you know Sean McGinnis?" Jessamine asked.

"Everybody knows everybody in Hopkinsville. I went to high school with Snuffy. But tell me more about this kidnapping."

"First, I need you to tell us everything you know about McGinnis," I said.

"Well, I know he is—was—a pretty no-account kind of fellah. But not no big-time desperado. He liked to work on cars mostly and get high."

"Police say he dealt dope," I said.

"I wouldn't know anything about that."

"C'mon, Byron," Jessamine urged. "This is Kentucky, the Bluegrass state."

Spock-ears gazed around his office, as if seeking answers in the wallpaper. "Well, not that *I* personally would ever engage in any illegalities, you understand, but I've heard that if you wanted to score, Snuffy's amigo Weedy Fowler was the man to see. Maybe he knows something."

Weedy. Snuffy. Slim. Did everyone in Hoptown have a colorful nickname?

"Where can we find this Weedy Fowler?" I asked.

"He hangs out at the C-Note Saloon. It's not far from here," he said, and gave me directions.

"Who does Weedy work for?"

"Whoa, that I definitely would not know," Byron said.

"Or maybe you just don't want to say?"

"Loose lips, you know." Byron looked at Jessamine. "'Course it could be aliens."

"Aliens?" she said.

"The kind from outer space, not Mexico. Maybe they took your husband."

"Little green men, you mean?" she asked.

"Could be green. Could be red Martians. I can't say for sure." He rubbed his chin. "But think about it. This town might be full of extraterrestrials right now, because of the festival."

Jessamine made the face you make while trying to apply logic to something inherently illogical. "Why on earth would aliens want to take Travis?"

"It's what they do," Byron said.

"Okay, but for what purpose?"

"Study us, eat us, breed with us? Prepare us to accept a mass takeover? That's what colonialists always do, isn't it?"

Byron smiled at our vexed expressions.

"Of course, not everyone in the UFO community believes that extraterrestrials are bad. Coming millions of light years from their own galaxy just to find us, I'd expect them to be curious about us. Maybe they've come to share their superior advanced technology."

"Why would they want to do that?" I asked.

"Because they're unimaginably intelligent and really nice guys." Byron said, with an arch smile.

"Is that what you honestly think?" I asked.

He scrunched up his face as if straining to come up with the very best answer. "I don't know," he said. "But it could be a game changer."

We both nodded solemnly, as if giving him the benefit of the doubt. But there was one hell of a lot of doubt.

"That monolith of yours could have something to do with what's going on," he said, "since it's a fake and all."

"Why are you calling it a fake? Because aliens didn't build

it?" Jessamine said.

"That's what you wanted people to believe, didn't you?"

"Maybe," Jessamine said.

"Okay, what if you were an extraterrestrial who had come all this way in peace to help us evolve and you were greeted by some bogus monolith? Wouldn't that make your alien blood boil? It would mine," Byron said.

"But it's no more bogus than any of them," Jessamine said.

"It looks cool. I'll give you that," Byron said.

"How many do you know personally, Bryon?" I asked.

"Well, none." Byron smiled at me indulgently. "But c'mon, man, they don't, you know, reveal themselves anymore like they done back in 1955. But they could be here among us, all right."

"And they've come to save us from ourselves. Not blow us up. Is that right?" I asked.

"I hope so. Some believe they want to drain our resources and wipe us out. But if that's what they wanted, they could have done that a long time ago. Killing people is easy. Blowing up stuff is easy. Fixing what's broken is harder."

I glanced at my watch. We needed to bring this to a close.

But Jessamine asked, "So, what's broken?"

"Everything. Look at climate change. We're all fixing to be toast soon."

That gave me pause. Although I believed in the existential threat posed by climate change, I wasn't expecting Byron to. For a moment, I was tempted to consider the farfetched notion that aliens really were here *and* trying to save the planet.

"Think about this," Bryon continued. "All the best ideas we've ever had about aliens come from the Golden Age of Science Fiction back in the fifties when Bradbury, Asimov, Heinlein, and Clark were writing their masterpieces. Where do you think those writers got those ideas all at the same time?"

"Surely not from aliens?" Jessamine said.

"You said it, not me," Byron winked.

"How many of those science fiction writers' books have you

read, Byron?" Jessamine asked.

"All of them. You want to see?" He led us into another room, where shelves bulging with paperbacks lined the walls. Jessamine ran her finger lightly along the spines of *Stranger In A Strange Land* and *The Martian Chronicles*.

When I asked if anyone else in town shared his beliefs, Byron said, "Oh, hell yeah. I'm not naming names. But you can learn a lot out there at the park—if you keep your ears open. Live long and prosper."

He didn't smile. That's not what Vulcans do.

Chapter 15

The C-Note Saloon was on the other side of town, but nothing in Hopkinsville was far from anywhere else. We drove through the central business district in the rental car. It was almost nine-thirty and getting dark in a hurry. Nearly everything was closed for the night.

"What did you make of Byron?" I asked.

"He seemed harmless and mostly rational," Jessamine replied.

"I agree. He struck me as delusional, but not dangerous. Doesn't mean that there aren't plenty of people around here who are dangerous and delusional, though."

"I think we've already met a few," Jessamine said. "What are you saying?"

We passed some boarded-up businesses, the plywood gray with age. "I'm worried about running into them," I said.

"You think that's likely?"

"We're asking for it, aren't we? By using irresistible bait to lure our victim. That's what this whole monolith scam is all about, too, isn't it? Trying to draw moths to a flame."

"Not that again. It's not a scam. I've told you before. Why is this so hard to understand?"

"Not hard to understand at all. You were trying to fool people, con them into believing something that wasn't true."

"Like what? That aliens made the monolith?"

"Perhaps. Sanchez and other cops take a dim view of misrepresentation or deception of any kind."

"I don't see any reason to think what we did was wrong."

"Sanchez thinks you did."

"What? That's ridiculous. Nobody accused the other monolith makers of wrong doing. I don't see how we're any different."

"I guess the difference would be if you were trying to make a profit," I said.

"So, you agree with Sanchez?"

"I didn't say that. In fact, I argued against the idea with him." I made a right onto a dark, grimy block, heading west, thinking we must be getting close to the bar.

"I'm glad to hear that," she said.

"At the time, I couldn't see how you would profit financially. But I'm starting to wonder about that."

"Why? If you think documentaries like ours are profitable, you are much mistaken. What a joke. Remember what I told you about how few indie films ever even get seen? We're only trying to raise enough money to fund it, not get rich."

I took a deep breath and let it out slowly. "I don't know whether documentary films make money. My sense of it, based on no proof, is that they probably don't. But some of them must. Right?"

"And you think ours will?" she asked with a scornful glare. "Thanks very much. I'm touched by your faith. Unfortunately, the truth is that it probably won't. I mean, how much money do you imagine our film will make when most people didn't even notice the monoliths when they were all over the planet? Most people still don't know about them. Curing their ignorance is part of what makes our project worth doing. But making money probably doesn't come into it."

"So, even if it won't be profitable, you'd still make it?"

"It's art, Guthrie. You paint. You're an artist, a painter. You ought to understand that. Do you always expect to make money on your work?"

"I haven't made any yet."

"Maybe you're just jealous."

"Maybe I'm just skeptical by profession."

"And suspicious by nature? Yeah, I get that. But look, art is art. Our film may not make a dime. So what?"

She said it earnestly, with conviction.

I could have pointed out that she was already rich, or would be someday, I assumed, when she inherited her parents' estate. But I didn't because her idealism seemed not only plausible but entirely consistent with what I knew about her more radical past.

"Only a few have ever come forward to claim credit for making a monolith. Most creators have remained steadfastly anonymous, never taking credit because—I believe—that would have ruined the whole thing. Instead, they let the monoliths speak for themselves, which is what makes them so wonderfully mysterious."

Wonderfully mysterious—an appealing phrase to a detective. But half a million bucks was appealing, too. And her husband was not rich. And I knew next to nothing about Tilford beyond what she had chosen to tell me.

We passed a lit-up gas station and a dark church and a row of old frame houses with vehicles parked out front. A quiet town on a Friday night. But I suspected there was plenty of action ahead.

"Why do you think the monolith craze happened when it did?" she asked.

"I don't know. Maybe it had to do with being in the depths of the pandemic when people were bored and depressed."

"See, you do understand. The monoliths provided unexpected inspiration when people needed it the most. That's why we took up this quest—"

"Is that what you call it—a quest?"

"You think I'm being too grandiose? A quest is nothing but a long, hard search for something. Ours is to document the monoliths before they vanish and are forgotten."

"Hasn't that already happened?"

"Unfortunately, yes. Or it soon will. But our documentary will revive their memory and preserve it as a testimonial to the universality of human hope."

Put like that, her quest really did sound grandiose. I'm not against being high-minded but hearing this jarred me because life is seldom that way. There is usually more lurking beneath the surface. Even if Jessamine's motives were pure, look at what already had happened to Travis Tilford and Snuffy McGinnis. And who knew what was next?

"Looks like we're here," I said.

The C-Note Saloon's neighborhood did not inspire much confidence in me. The bar was located in a rundown strip center next to three other storefronts. Two of them had "FOR RENT" signs in the windows. A third sign read, "Pawn, Buy, or Sell jewelry, gold, guns, electronics, musical instruments, tools, and much more."

Once traffic had whooshed by, I turned in and parked in the side lot. Before getting out, I looked the place over carefully. It was a one-story brick cube with a flat roof and neon beer signs in the tiny windows. What I saw of this crummy joint convinced me immediately that going in there at all was risky and would be even more so with Jessamine.

When I asked her to wait in the car, she said predictably, "Why? Do you think I need protection? Did I not just participate in searching the compound of a UFO cult?"

"Not the same. This looks like a dangerous place."

"More dangerous than kidnappers and murderers?"

"Kidnappers and murderers are exactly who we're here to find."

"Guthrie, I know your male brain feels an instinctive urge to protect me. But I am a strong, independent woman who can handle whatever I have to on my own."

"Look, you might *think* you can handle anything on your own. But this dive is probably full of rednecks intent on proving their masculinity by how much liquor they can hold. Do you understand?"

"I understand. I've been in a bar before, you know," she said.

"But maybe not like this one."

"I doubt that."

"When some of them see you, believe me, they are not going to leave you alone. I don't want to have to fight my way out of there."

"You won't have to," she said stubbornly. "Like I said, I can handle myself. I'm coming with you."

"What purpose will your presence serve? Are you going to question Weedy Fowler?"

"Maybe I just want a drink."

"Be reasonable," I said.

She rolled her eyes and flatly refused to wait in the car.

"At least let me go in alone first. I don't want to attract attention."

"Are you saying I will?"

"Have you been listening at all, Jessamine?"

I got out of the Nissan and went in.

Pushing open the frosted double glass front doors, I was greeted by a blast of hot air despite a huge wall unit air conditioner. There was also a stench of stale beer, plus deafening country music and drunken shouts. Friday night at the C-Note Saloon. Even dirtier, darker, and more crowded than I'd feared.

I paused in the dimness to let my eyes adjust. More beer signs hung on the walls. Christmas lights dotted the ceiling. Each pool table was lit by three-light bars suspended on metal chains over the green felt surface. The bar itself was in back. I wove toward it through a maze of dart enthusiasts, pool shooters, and red-faced men drinking shots and domestic beer right out of the bottle. Four rows of liquor were shelved on a vinyl-topped back bar. Cold storage cases held beer and there were wall racks full of bagged pork rinds, popcorn, and jerky. As I was starving, I grabbed a bag of snacks, plus a can of beer, and got in line at the cash register.

"Looks like business is booming," I observed in a friendly way.

The bartender who took my money was a chunky woman with pendulous breasts barely contained by an unflattering tank top.

"Yeah, I'm busier than a one-legged cat in a sandbox." When I didn't move on immediately, she added, "Get you something else?"

"Actually, I'm looking for somebody." My eyes swept over the room.

"And who might that be?"

"Guy named Weedy Fowler. I hear he hangs out here."

"What do you want with him?"

"Conversation. Is he here?"

"No, he's not." She started wiping off the bar with a wet cloth.

"Do you know where I can find him?"

"Probably in here, if you wait a while."

I laid an Andrew Jackson on the countertop. "When he comes in, will you point him out to me?"

She scooped it up and tucked it into her bra. "Sure."

I took a seat at the far end of the bar, near a table occupied by a pair of loudly cursing young hoodlums—fit, inked, boisterous, aggressive. The wiry one was sandy-haired with a long narrow face and close-set blue eyes. The other was barrel-chested and bull-necked with a jutting jaw and a cauliflower ear. Maybe a wrestler. I ignored them, nursing my beer and scarfing down beef jerky.

Jessamine swept into the saloon like a fresh summer breeze

and threaded her way to a stool in the middle of the bar. The noisy pair sitting near me reacted to the sight of Jessamine and her thin-strap dress with loud wolf whistles. Like me, she ignored them. She ordered a drink. While the bartender was pouring it, the rowdy whose long sandy hair was shaved close on the sides went over and stood close to Jessamine, talking to her. She looked back at him and shook her head no. He tried again, and she turned away from him.

Precisely the problem I had anticipated. I was about to get up. But the bartender handled it.

"Stop hittin' on this lady like a big-mouth bass on a flutter lure," she said. "Can't you see she doesn't want you? Now leave her alone or just leave. Your choice."

Sandy shrugged and surprised me by returning to his table grinning and muttering something about *what a stuck-up bitch.*

I continued to sit there, a solitary drinker swigging his beer and munching on beef jerky, which while not exactly beef tips and gravy had quieted the rumble in my stomach.

As the bartender added a slice a lime to Jessamine's drink and set it in front of her, I heard Jessamine say, "Sorry, didn't mean to disturb the wildlife."

"Where you from, honey?" she asked.

"Louisville."

"Didn't think I'd seen you before. What brings you to Hopkinsville?"

"Actually, I'm here for the Little Green Men Festival."

"You believe in UFOs?" The bartender seemed surprised.

"Don't you?"

"Why, yes. We consider them a tourist attraction."

Jessamine laughed.

A short, thin man came in and joined Sandy and Bull at their table. The new arrival had a jagged scar on one cheek and a thick, black droopy mustache. Rolled up in one sleeve of the death metal T-shirt glued to his skin was a cigarette—or a joint. The bartender caught my eye and shot a meaningful glance at him. Weedy Fowler, drug dealer, I presumed. I waited for him and the other two to finish their macho posturing. Once they settled down, I picked up my beer and wandered over and sat down in the last empty chair at their table.

"How's it hanging, Weedy?" I asked.

The man with the scar stared at me intently and I stared back. The silence at the table grew as neither of us blinked. When Weedy realized that he was not going to win the staring contest, he cocked his head and grinned at me as if I was crazy.

"Do I know you, dude?"

"No need to stand on ceremony just because we haven't been properly introduced, Weedy. The name's Guthrie and I want to talk to you. Just you."

What I said made the other two restless, I could tell. But they kept waiting to take their cues from Weedy, and he wasn't giving any. I could see him assessing me, a big, tough-acting stranger with a cop look and wondering whether to be afraid of me. He must have decided he should be because he jerked his head for his two companions to leave, and they did without a word.

"You a cop?" Weedy asked once we were alone.

"Private."

He seemed to relax a little. "What can I do for you?"

"I need some information about one of your former business associates."

"Why should I tell you anything?"

"Because if you don't, you could easily go down for murder, kidnapping, and extortion."

"What the hell are you talking about?"

"Your *former* associate, Sean McGinnis. Remember him? He was killed today."

Weedy turned his head. "That's sad. But it's got nothing to do with me."

"I say it does."

"You're crazy, man." He started to get up.

I grabbed his arm and clenched it tightly. "Stick around."

He tried to yank his arm away but found he couldn't do it. My grip was too strong. Instead, he gave me a grin that was oddly menacing.

"Be smart for once, Weedy. Tell me what I want to know. Maybe then I won't have to mention you to the FBI."

"FBI?"

At the mere mention of those three letters, Fowler's resistance seemed to melt. I let go of him. Suddenly he was slick with sweat and a vinegar-like smell of fear came rolling off him.

"Are you shitting me?" he said, sitting back down. "Oh, Jesus."

"That's right. They're going to take a real interest in you once I tell them what I know."

"What do you know?"

"That you're up to your neck in this."

"No, you got it wrong."

Leaning forward on my elbows, I said, "Somebody killed Snuffy and ripped him off. I think it was you."

"No, hell no. I don't know anything about a murder or that other stuff."

"You disappoint me, Weedy—and I don't handle disappointment well." I sat back, getting into the role. "Now is the time to get on the right side of this before it's too late. Tell me who killed McGinnis."

"I tell you I don't know. I swear."

"Sorry to hear that." I made as if to leave.

"Where are you going?" Weedy asked desperately.

"Where do you think?"

"Look, I'd tell you if I knew, but I don't. I just deal a little weed. That's all."

"I'd like to believe you, Weedy. But I can't leave empty-handed. You've got to give me something."

"What? What do you want?"

Seeing how eager he now was to cooperate, I said, "I want to know who else was close to McGinnis."

"There's his girlfriend, Bonita Atkinson. They live together out on the farm. I can tell you where it is."

"I already know. It's a crime scene now. Where would Bonita go to stay for a while?"

"How should I know?" He rubbed his sweaty palms on his jeans.

"Think harder. Unless you want to wind up being charged as an accessory."

"You can't do that."

"You sure?" I gave him a look that strongly suggested I could.

He put his face in his hands. "Well, Bonita might be staying with Doobie. But I don't know where she lives."

"Who's Doobie?"

"Darlene Dooley. She runs The Cut-Up Hair Salon where Bonita works. It's closed, but you'll probably find her there tomorrow."

"You better hope I do, Weedy."

As I escorted Jessamine out of the C-Note to the parking lot, I heard footsteps crunching on the gravel and two figures emerged from the shadows. Their faces were neon red from the bar lights. But there was no doubt about who they were: Weedy Fowler's two associates. Sandy was carrying something by his side that might have been a sawed-off pool cue, and Bull held a knife with the blade pointed at the ground.

"Hey, big man," Sandy said. "Don't run off now. The party is just starting."

They started toward us at a slow walk, not so docile anymore, and I wondered if Fowler, who had caved with surprising ease, had sent them as payback. I regretted leaving my gun in the car, but I would never get to it in time now. I would have to deal with this armed pair using only my fists. Never a great idea in a street fight despite what you see in the movies. When they fanned out, I told Jessamine to get in the car and lock the doors.

"That won't help," Sandy said, a faint smile playing on his

lips. "After we fuck you up, we're still going to have some fun with your little bitch girlfriend."

They kept coming, taking long strides, heads held up and eyes focused on their target. Sandy headed straight toward me while Bull peeled off leftward in a flanking movement. I figured if I were them, I would first try to knock me off my feet. Once I was down, it would be much easier to finish me off. I couldn't let that happen, so I continued moving and keeping them in front of me. When they were only a few paces away, they slowed down and slid further apart as if to coordinate their attack. Sandy would go high with the stick while Bull aimed lower with the knife. This was a mistake. They had done me a favor by making it easier to take them on one at a time instead of having to deal with both at once.

I never stopped, just went straight at Sandy, picking up momentum. Before he could swing the cue-stick and slam it against the side of my skull, I leaned forward in full stride and head-butted him. It knocked him back and off balance, and while he staggered and struggled to regain his footing, I turned to face Bull. He came roaring in, waving the blade back and forth like an amateur instead of immediately going for the kill. This allowed me to bicycle backward out of his reach. And when he swung again, I dropped under it this time and launched myself up at him, spearing him in the chest and knocking him off his feet. As he fell, he dropped the knife, which skidded away from him across the rock. Bull tried to scramble over and grab it. But I took one long step and kicked him in the head. It knocked him flat. He immediately tried to get up again, so I kicked him again and he stayed down.

Which was good because by this time, Sandy had recovered and was once more trying to turn my brains into mush. As he swung the cue, I screamed with all my lung power, hoping to throw off his aim and dodge the blow. As the stick whistled harmlessly past my ear, I poked him in the eye with my thumb. Not very gentlemanly, but effective. As he clutched his eye, I punched him in the solar plexus, knocking the wind out of him, and he fell to the ground.

Breathing slowly, I wiped the sweat out of my eyes, leaned over him, and said, "Did Weedy put you up to this?"

He answered with a muffled curse.

I slapped his forehead with my open palm. "I asked you a question."

"Weedy didn't say shit to us," he grunted.

"Does this have anything to do with Bonita Atkinson?"

"Who cares about her?" he winced. "Look man, I'm hurt bad. Call an ambulance."

At that moment, ironically, as I stood there with my lungs heaving and my pulse pounding, a screaming siren approached. But it soon veered off and faded away. I was becoming aware of other street noises—whizzing traffic, slamming doors, music spilling from the saloon—when I heard Jessamine yell, "Jim."

She had finally found my gun and was standing beside the car, pointing at the ground. I wanted to scold her for not shooting our attackers. Or maybe for having the gun out at all. I wasn't sure which. I tucked in my shirt and brushed the dirt from my jeans.

"You drive," I said.

And she did.

Maybe Weedy would find his pals and call EMS.

Chapter 16

"Are you okay?" she said, as she spun the rental out of the lot and steered a course for the landfill. "You don't look so good."

"You should see the other guys."

"I did. You really kicked their asses."

"They had it coming."

Her eyes widened in admiration. At least, I hoped it was admiration.

"Seriously, are you okay?" she asked.

The answer was that I was still riding a wave of adrenaline, which dulled the aching in my head.

"Yeah," I said, through gritted teeth.

"Maybe you should go to the hospital and get checked."

"Thank you for your concern. But aside from being stiff and sore tomorrow, I'll be all right."

"If you say so," she said, though obviously skeptical.

The sun was long gone as I rolled down my window, and the temperature had dropped from scorching to simmering.

"I thought drug dealers were supposed to be tough. Weedy Fowler folded up like a paper Chinese hand fan, and you whipped the other two with ease. Do you think they belong to a gang or cartel?"

I laughed and explained that most low-level dealers only start a life of crime when they figure out that working at Wal-Mart will never get them where they want to go. Most don't get very far that way, either.

"I guess we all work for somebody farther up the food chain, don't we?" I asked.

"Now *that's* a cynical attitude, Guthrie."

"You say cynical, I say realistic."

"I'm assuming you don't believe those ruffians had anything to do with kidnapping Travis."

"Fair assumption, but who knows?"

"Are you always this bleak?"

"Usually bleaker."

She looked at me with those big eyes of hers and smiled. A deep silence fell between us.

At ten-thirty by my watch, we came to the entrance to the landfill. It was full dark by now, except for some gleaming moonlight. We hid the Nissan across the road in the trees, away from the prying patrols or nosy parkers. Gathering up our gear, which included a heavy carpet remnant for protection against barbwire, we hiked back to the gate.

When no guard dogs appeared, I scaled the fence. Jessamine followed, exhibiting impressive athleticism. Once inside, we followed the tracker's green blip along a snaking stretch of bumpy dirt road barely wide enough for two-way traffic. It led us through some sections that had been graded over and flattened. Eventually, we came to knolls and hummocks created by heaped up trash. Near where a gigantic yellow bulldozer was parked on the shoulder, the tracker indicated the briefcase was nearby.

We hid behind the bulldozer and bided our time, listening for a discordant sound in the night's thrumming or a telltale flash of headlights. After a few minutes, I heard something. I looked back the way we had come and glimpsed movement. Was it a guard dog? Or maybe two? Why hadn't they shown up sooner? Well, it was a big landfill, and they probably roamed freely.

Suddenly, perspiration was running down my face and soaking through my clothing. Not due to the temperature, either. If dogs were coming, our best refuge would be up on the dozer looming above. There was a ladder, but the rungs were in an *up* position and out of reach. To boost Jessamine over the tall treads and into the cab, I struggled to find solid footing because the ground was thick with fleshy slime. But before I could get myself up there to safety with her, the two large dogs arrived,

They came bounding toward us marked by their cropped, erect ears as Doberman Pinschers. It was a breed that inspired fear. The dogs were usually well-trained and not easily subdued or outrun. These two did not growl, which meant they were trained to attack with no warning.

And they ran right at me, slavering, their glistening fangs bared, ready to gnaw on me like a juicy pink pork chop. Having dealt with their ilk before, I assumed one dog would leap to knock me off my feet while the other lunged at my heels to bring my throat down within jaw reach. In this respect, they were remarkably similar to Sandy and Bull, but quicker, stronger, and more ferocious.

To avoid being ripped to pieces, I waited till they were ten feet away and I couldn't miss. I hit them both with multiple bursts of pepper spray. It stopped them, stinging their eyes and sensitive noses. As they sneezed comically and uncontrollably, I fired hypodermic tipped darts from an air gun into each dog, making only a hollow pop and *phufftt* sound. In seconds, the Dobermans stopped their thrashing and dropped to the ground, unconscious.

"That was close," Jessamine called down from the cab. "I'm glad you didn't have to hurt them permanently."

"I'm glad they didn't have to hurt *me* permanently," I said.

The dogs would be out of commission for hours. But it

wouldn't do for them to be seen by the kidnapper when he came for the ransom money. I dragged them out of sight behind the dozer's huge U-shaped blade. I lingered there beside them with sweat running into my eyes. I batted mosquitoes away and forced myself to endure the landfill's fetid odor for what seemed like an eternity.

This was real detective work, I thought sourly. I wished I could be methodically pondering clues and making sudden intuitive leaps while seated in a comfy armchair in air conditioning instead of down-in-the-trenches here. But as soon as headlights appeared, I forgot all about that in my excitement and called for Jessamine to start recording everything on her phone.

Edging silently into thicker shadow as the moon drifted behind the clouds, I waited like a wolf ready to pounce on the oncoming vehicle, a pickup truck. It stopped close by and the driver's door groaned open. A bulky figure got out encased in highly visible and reflective Hazmat gear. He wore a hood with a clear face panel. But I could not see his features clearly enough to hope to identify him. I'd have to get it off him.

He grabbed a rake and a shovel from the truck bed and set off between two steep man-made foothills.

As he vanished behind the dunes, I ran over to his truck and crouched behind the passenger side, waiting with great anticipation to see the tracker's green blip to begin moving on my phone. When it did, I would know that Senator Barrett's briefcase was returning at last. My plan was simple—subdue Hazmat Man, take the case away from him, and make him take me to Travis Tilford.

When he came close, I stood up and let him see me. Instead of surrendering sensibly, he threw the rake and shovel at me and took off with the money. He wasn't heading toward the gate, so I didn't know where he was going, but if he worked here, he might know another way out. That meant I had better run him down. It was a slow, exhausting slog across the uneven, mucky ground.

Nevertheless, I kept after him. His too cumbersome gait and the Hazmat suit slowed him down. Before he got fifty yards, I dove at him, crashing into him knee high. He lurched forward and fell, dropping the briefcase, but was back up on his feet with astonishing agility for a man wearing a spacesuit. Maybe he was an alien.

But he knew what a gun was, and he understood English because when I pointed my gun at him and said, "Hands up, Hazmat. Surrender peaceably and I might not have to shoot you," he obeyed my instructions.

Jessamine, who had filmed the whole thing with her phone, gave it to me while she went to retrieve the briefcase. "Money's still here," she said.

"Great." I gave her the phone back. "Now take off that Halloween mask."

Hazmat Man slowly complied, lifting the hood over his head and cradling it. I didn't recognize him. He didn't recognize me, either.

"Who the hell are you?" he said. "You're not a cop. I know all of them."

"That's right, I'm not. Know what that means as far as you're concerned? It means you have no rights. Now turn around and put your hands on the truck and spread your legs.

I patted him down. He wasn't armed. Under the suit, he wore street clothes. In his pants pockets, I found a wallet, car keys, and a phone—all of which I kept. I couldn't read his ID in the dark, so I made him shuffle around in front of his own headlights, which Jessamine switched on.

"What do you want with me?" he said, hands covering his eyes from the beams' glare.

"I want you to lose the rest of that costume."

He started to protest, but I cut him off. "Shut up. Just do it."

He was sweating like a pig. Under all that protective gear, he wore long khaki work pants and a green short-sleeved work shirt. There was a sanitation department logo on the shirt pocket. He seemed smaller now, maybe five-eight with a medium build and he was muscular, doubtless from hefting garbage cans all day.

"What's your name?" I asked.

"Clawson. Skeets Clawson."

It matched the name on his driver's license.

"Turn around and put your hands behind you, Skeets."

"What for?"

When I moved the gun barrel in a circle, he turned around, proving that sometimes pictures are better than words. I gave Jessamine my gun while I was binding his wrists tightly together with plastic ties. He had workman's hands. Big, callused, hairy. I grabbed his shoulders and rotated him around to face me.

"Okay, Skeets, so you a sanitation worker."

"No, I'm a garbage man."

"Is there a difference?" I smiled. "All right, garbage man, get in the back of the truck."

"Where are we going? Who are you? What do you want with me?"

"I'm the one who, if you cooperate, may save you from being put away for the rest of your life."

He kept blabbing until I told him to shut up. I helped steady him as he climbed into the truck bed and sat down with his back against the cab.

"I'm talking about the kidnapping of Travis Tilford and the murder of Snuffy McGinnis," I said.

"What? I ain't kidnapped or murdered nobody."

"You're boring me, Skeets."

"I'm telling you the truth. I don't know what you're talking about. Really. I don't."

"Save it. You'll find out soon enough. We need to move him, Jessamine," I said, worrying that a sheriff's patrol might happen by.

Jessamine drove us out of the landfill and across Latham Road, where over his strenuous protests we transferred him to the rental car's trunk. Then she followed a lonely track deeper into the woods. After tussling with Clawson, scuffling with Weedy's thugs, and knocking out two Doberman before they could eat me, I could have used some rest. But that would have to wait until after we finished interrogating our prisoner and hopefully got a line on where Travis Tilford was being held captive.

At the entrance to a narrow trail, Jessamine pulled the car off the dirt road and stopped. Using a Mag Lite I'd transferred to the rental car, I shepherded Clawson over the ground, carpeted with shredded leaves, decomposing stems, and bark. At a huge fallen oak that blocked us from going any further, we sat down to talk.

"How did you know about the briefcase?" Jessamine asked.

"I didn't."

"Liar. Then who paid you to collect it?"

"Who says anybody paid me? Salvaging's not illegal. I do it all the time."

"We don't care if it's legal or not," I said.

Clawson's eyebrows went up. "Then why bust me? I'm just trying to make a buck. All day long, I'm breathing and touching all kinds of dangerous shit. I will salvage anything that could be valuable, whether it's a fancy purse or a fur coat."

The damp air was thick with the earthy sweetness of pine needles. Taking a big breath, I said, "How about a bag full of cash? Many of them turn up?"

"Cash? Are you saying that briefcase was full of cash?"

"You know, I don't believe you're grasping the seriousness of the situation," I said. "You might've gotten away with loading the money into your garbage truck. But by coming back for it, you have made yourself vulnerable to being charged an accomplice to the kidnapping of Travis Tilford."

"Bullshit. You can't prove that."

"Keep on lying yourself into ten to life," I said.

The forest mumbled ominously. After hearing the faint screams and squeals, grunts, and growls of predators and prey,

Clawson said finally, "How much is in there?"

"Two-hundred and fifty grand."

"Two-fifty!"

"As if you didn't know."

"I didn't."

"How much did they promise you to pick up the briefcase?"

Clawson's face was crosshatched in the flashlight's beam. "What if I said—hypothetically speaking—a thousand bucks?"

"I'd say that was a poor return on a quarter of a million dollars."

"Those cheap, miserable bastards."

"Was Snuffy McGinnis supposed to pay you? That would be convenient with him dead now and unable to contradict your story. Did you kill him?"

"No. How could I when I was still on my route when it came on the news that he'd got shot? Anyway, why would I kill somebody who owed me money?"

"I've heard that one before, Skeets. We don't care about anything right now except finding Travis Tilford. Do you know where he's being held?"

Clawson shook his head in vigorous denial. "No. How could I?"

"Well, you knew where the money was hidden. That's going to be tough on you because by the time I'm done, you will go down for this," I said.

"The hell I will."

After making a dramatic gesture out of turning off her phone, Jessamine bared her teeth and said, "Listen to me, garbage man. If you don't help us and Travis winds up dead, I swear I will kill you myself. Do you understand?"

"I can't tell you what I don't know," Clawson said, cringing under Jess's wrath.

We kept at him, trying to trip him up. By the time I decided that was all we were going to get out of him, stars were shimmering in the coal-black sky.

"All right, back to the car, you," I barked.

"What are you doing?" Jessamine said.

"This is not working. We need to try something different."

"Such as?"

"For now, let's just get him into the trunk."

"No way," Clawson said. "I'm claustrophobic."

"Would you rather get dead?" I jabbed him in the nose with the pistol. He looked at it cross-eyed and got in. I slammed the trunk shut.

"Don't leave me in here," he yelled, and began kicking at the lid.

Jessamine and I stepped out of earshot. "Do you believe him?" she asked.

"About being claustrophobic?"

"About not knowing where Travis is."

"I don't know."

She closed her eyes and took a deep breath, like a condemned prisoner hearing her sentence pronounced. "What are we going to do?"

She wasn't going to like this part. I didn't like it much myself. But a course correction seemed needed. "Let's turn him loose."

"What? When we've got him dead to rights, and you want to let him go?"

"He's made it clear that he won't talk. What do you want to do, torture him?"

"If that's what it takes," she said, meaning it, I thought.

"No, I won't do that." Looking at her, I said slowly, "There's no guarantee that he even knows anything else. We're not the police, Jessamine. We can't hold him without becoming kidnappers ourselves."

"He's in this up to his neck. He's basically admitted it."

"But only hypothetically."

"We've got him and the money, and a video showing him with the briefcase in his hand, and you're just going to let him go?"

She threw up her hands and dropped them heavily to her side.

"It's all circumstantial evidence and illegally obtained. It won't stand up in court. Even if it did, that wouldn't save Travis. We can't prove that Clawson wasn't just doing his usual landfill diving. If we turn him in, we'll have to tell the sheriff about the second ransom drop, which means they'll take the money. Besides, you didn't want to involve them in the first place."

Jessamine buried her face in her hands. "Then we're no better off now than before."

"You could argue that we're even worse off."

"Is that your idea of a pep talk?" Jess grabbed fistfuls of her hair and pulled.

"You could also say we're better off now. What are the possibilities? One, Clawson was in on the kidnapping from the start and was picking up the ransom payment now because it seemed safe to do so. Two, Clawson was not in on the kidnapping, but was being paid to show them where the money was buried. Three, the kidnappers contacted Clawson *after* the McGinnis's murder to fetch the brief case and deliver it to them. Or four, after McGinnis's murder, Clawson decided to get the briefcase out on his own."

"How does that make us better off?"

"Now we know that somebody is still trying to get their hands on the money. It could just be Clawson, but his bitterness at being underpaid rang true. I believe he was hired to deliver the money. But now that he's failed, they'll try again. When they do, they'll have to come to us."

With raised eyebrows, Jessamine said, "Are you sure about all this?"

"Pretty sure."

We drove back to the landfill entrance and opened the trunk. I cut Clawson loose.

"You're letting me go?" he said, looking confused while rubbing his wrists. "Can I have my thousand bucks?"

"Not a chance in hell," I said.

We took off and waited down the road for him to lead us to Travis. Instead, he drove to a shabby little clapboard house in Hopkinsville. The address matched the one on his driver's license. We weren't ready to give up yet and decided to sit on his house for a while, see if he went back out. While we watched from down the street, Jessamine started talking about the guard dogs we'd tranquilized.

"Do you think they're okay?"

"Sure," I said. "Dogcatchers use darts to bring animals under control all the time. They'll be out for another couple of hours. When they wake up, and they'll be fine."

"What if they're not fine? What if we used too much of the drug? We should go back and check on them."

Saying this suggestion was unwelcome would have been an understatement. Especially with somebody pounding an insistent bass line on my forehead. Note to myself—ixnay on the head butting.

"Bad idea," I said. "I used the correct amount of tranquilizer. The dogs are fine. If we go back, they'll try to attack us again."

"What's happened to you, Jim?" Jessamine asked in a softer tone.

"What do you mean?"

"I don't recall you being so cold-hearted when you were trying to find Cybil's dog. What sticks in my memory is how appalled you were when you told me about finding that abandoned truck load of dogs."

We headed back to the landfill, where the endangered Dobermans met us by growling furiously and hurling themselves against the gate.

"They seem okay to me," I said.

"Yeah," Jessamine said. "But I remember when you weren't so hard-boiled about the suffering of animals."

"Maybe it's because I've seen more dead people over the years than dead dogs," I said.

She looked at me with sad eyes.

When we got back to her motel room, we were both stinking so badly that we couldn't stand ourselves. Jessamine headed straight for the bathroom. She tossed her dirty clothes out the door. I added them to the garbage bag containing mine and took it out and dropped it in a dumpster. When Jessamine was finished showering, I took my turn under the hot water until it ran out, scrubbing away every trace of the landfill.

I came out of the bathroom to find the atmosphere of our room much improved. She was waiting for me with a plastic motel cup of bourbon. We sipped the bourbon neat, savoring the burn.

She'd asked about my daughter. "Sarah? That's her name, right? By now she must be, what, twenty?"

Not really wanting to talk about it, but not wanting to seem bad humored, either, I said, "Twenty, yeah."

"It's all right if you don't want to talk about it."

"There's not much to talk about. She's a college student now. Lives in Vegas near her mother."

"Are you close?"

"As close as you can be with someone you see two weeks out of every fifty-two,"

"Sorry."

Holding up my hand, I said, "It's okay. I've tried to be part of her life, but it's not easy when you're two-thousand miles away."

Jessamine nodded.

Finishing her drink, she said wearily, "I'm tired. I'm going to bed," and crawled between the queen-sized sheets.

I had another drink. By the time it was gone, she was asleep. Two minutes later, so was I. Maybe I dreamed, but I really couldn't say.

Chapter 17

At 7:30 Saturday morning, I opened my eyes after sleeping without waking through the night. I made the mistake of pressing my thumbs against my forehead to see if it would hurt. It did. A lot. In fact, my breath caught in my throat as I tried not to cry out from the pain throbbing deep inside. I realized it had to be from doing the head butt wrong. Instead of butting the thickest part of my skull only into the guy's nose or cheekbone, I'd also caught part of his skull.

It throbbed when I squinted, so I tried not to do that. When the pain subsided a bit, I pushed myself out of bed, but now felt a little nauseated. I grabbed my kit and went into the bathroom and laboriously removed the plastic covering from a plastic drinking glass. I filled it with tap water and downed three tabs of ibuprofen.

I turned on the squeaky faucet in the shower and waited, testing the water temperature until it was right. Stepping inside, I inhaled the steamy air for a long time before lathering up. The spray rinsed my body and drained the suds away. I turned the water off. Carefully toweled dry. I wiped off the steamy mirror. The face in it looked better than I felt.

By the time I put on my clothes, Jessamine was already fully dressed in a white summer blouse and khaki shorts. She had combed her auburn hair back and tied it.

"Good morning," she said. "I'm starving."

No wonder. We hadn't eaten since lunch yesterday. My nausea was gone, my head ached less than before, and the tight muscles in my arm had loosened up. I decided there would be no fast food this morning. We were going to have a proper breakfast in a restaurant. As we left the room, the breeze mentioned on the weather forecast hadn't arrived yet. Instead, the air was warm and sticky. I questioned my decision to wear long pants to look more professional instead of shorts.

Down the highway, we found a café with a big neon sign. "BREAKFAST," it read. When I opened the door, the scent of sizzling bacon and freshly brewed coffee wafted over me. Another good sign was how busy and noisy the place seemed. As soon as we had seated ourselves in a booth near the back, a curly-headed server came over and poured steaming mugs of coffee for us without even being asked.

"Figured you'd want it," said the server, whose nametag read Sally. "Everybody does."

I nodded and blew on mine while reading the one-sheet menu. "*Casual, cozy, and family friendly*," it read at the top. As if that wasn't enough, it added, "*Hometown atmosphere, locals, and a good place to sit and talk.*"

"They had me at casual," I said.

Jessamine merely nodded.

I drank some coffee. It was strong the way I like it and seemed to settle my stomach. I asked Jessamine what sounded good. She complained there was no mention of healthy choices on the menu. No yogurt. No cereal.

"How about this?" I said, pointing out the Belgian waffles and French Toast.

"Not healthy choices. High in fat and carbs, with little nutritional value."

"Guess you don't want the All-day Breakfast Special either, then."

The special was two eggs, three strips of bacon, grits, with biscuits and gravy for $5.75. A genuine deal.

"I haven't seen prices like that in years," I said.

"Yeah, it's cheap, all right." Jessamine sounded grumpy.

When our server returned, I ordered two scrambled eggs and toast. Jessamine got oatmeal.

"You want anything on that, honey?" Sally asked her. "Brown sugar? Honey? Nuts? Apple butter?"

"Do you have any fruit?" Jessamine asked in a condescending tone.

"I think we might have some," Sally said, and went off to see.

"Funny. Didn't we both have pizza and beer the other night?" I asked.

"Oatmeal is why I occasionally get to have pizza and beer." Jessamine looked thoughtful while sipping her morning coffee. "Ever wish for a second chance?"

"At what? Life?"

She nodded.

"I hate philosophical questions first thing in the morning."

"Come on," she said.

I stared into my coffee cup. "Not really."

"No regrets?"

"Sure, plenty."

"If you got a second chance—"

"I'd probably keep right on making the same mistakes, or even worse ones."

"You don't believe that people learn from experience and can change?"

"Well, I've seen *Groundhog Day*, if that's what you mean."

She gave me a sour look, which I deserved.

"Do I believe people can change? You mean adults, I presume."

She nodded.

"I guess I'd have to say no. We are who we are."

"I think you're wrong," Jessamine said.

"Wouldn't be the first time."

"Well, I'd like a second chance. If I got one, Travis would be here now because we'd never have done what we did."

"Stage the monolith sighting?"

"I was thinking more about how we blew off the kidnappers' original demand. We should have been smarter and gone for help immediately. Underestimating them made this much worse. I just pray Travis is all right," she said, with a catch in her voice.

I felt sorry for her then in a new way. Patting her hand, I said, "Don't worry. We're going to get him back."

"You're not just saying that?" Hope filled her eyes.

"I'm not just saying it," I said.

But I was.

Our food, including a banana, arrived along with the check, which Sally laid on a wet ring left by my coffee mug.

We ate quietly.

Eventually, Jessamine looked at me and said, "Sorry about last night. I spoke out of turn."

"Forget it. I've heard it said that the surest way of getting to know someone is by being cooped up with them on a small boat. But I think a small room at the Red Nebula Inn will do just as well. Don't you?"

By ten o'clock, we were parked in front of The Cut-Up Hair Salon, which was housed in a small white frame building on a street lined with other small businesses and apartments.

"We need a plan," Jessamine said.

"We have one."

"We're just going to walk in and say, 'We're here to talk about your boyfriend, Snuffy McGinnis, who was murdered after he kidnapped my husband.' Is that your plan?"

"Something like that."

"What if she doesn't want to talk to us?"

"Then we'll have to persuade her."

"How are we going to do that? Stretch her over an anthill?"

"We'd have to lure her outdoors for that. And find an anthill."

Jessamine shook her head.

We walked up to the front door and stepped inside. Three women were in the shop, two customers—one in a salon chair, one under a beehive shaped hair dryer—and the stylist dressed in an all-black uniform like a martial arts instructor or assassin. Pretty and blonde, she was in her mid-twenties with shoulder-length hair.

She greeted us with five words I'd never heard from a barber:

"Do you have an appointment?"

Not surprisingly, I had never spent much time in beauty parlors—a passé expression I preferred—let alone *salons*. My idea of a hair care professional was a barber clad in a short sleeve beige jacket. Since there was no old pedestal barber's chair with armrests and footrests here, I felt out of my comfort zone.

"I understand Bonita Atkinson works here. We're looking for her," I said.

"Sorry, but Bonita's out today. Can I help?" the stylist asked in a deep, breathy voice.

"Thanks, but this is a pressing business matter, and we really need to talk to Bonita. Do you know where she can be found?"

"No, but if you'll leave your number when she checks in, I'll have her call you."

I wrote down my phone number on a notepad. "Any idea when that might be?"

"Not really. Now I have clients waiting, so if that's all?"

Clients. Not customers.

"Jim," Jessamine said to me, "as long as we're here, I need about half an inch trimmed off the bottom."

"Really?" My voice was filled with doubt.

She turned to the stylist. "Hi, I'm Jessamine."

The hairdresser, who had resumed combing and de-tangling her client's ends, said, "Nice to meet y'all. I'm Darlene."

"We're away from home, and I can't stand my hair like this

for another day. Could you fit me in?"

"Well, we're a little short-handed today, as you can see. Where y'all from?"

"Louisville."

"Mm. On vacation?"

"Not exactly," Jessamine said.

Darlene continued trimming the hair of the woman in her chair. "How do you know Bonita?"

"As Jim said, we have a business connection. Oh, by the way, I have heard good things about you and this shop."

"Oh? Like what?"

"I read several online reviews. One person said when she came in, her eyebrows were really messed up—way too thin, the arch destroyed. But after you waxed them, she said they were gorgeous."

Darlene chuckled. "I love your hair color. It's natural, too, isn't it?"

Jessamine nodded. "Lots of redheads in my family."

"I thought so. Thanks for telling me about that review. You know, I think we can work you in—if Jim doesn't mind."

"He doesn't," Jessamine said.

"I don't mind," I said, being agreeable.

"All right then, take a seat until I finish up with this client," Darlene said.

"Okey doke," Jessamine said.

Okey doke?

We perched on a couch piled with pillows facing a television tuned to one of those Family Channel cooking shows where contestants quickly make something in front of the camera from surprise ingredients. Again, something I'd never experienced in a barber shop. I'd never heard of making ice cream out of sauerkraut, either, but that's what they were doing.

"Okay," Darlene called. "I'm ready for you now."

Jessamine walked over to the stylist's chair and took a seat.

"What was it you'd like me to do?" Darlene asked.

Coiling a strand of her auburn hair around one finger, Jessamine said, "The ends have gotten a little raggedy."

They looked fine to me, but Darlene nodded. "You want some off the bangs or just the bottom?"

"Just the bottom. About half an inch."

"I think we can manage that." Darlene brought over a trolley full of white towels, gowns, gloves. While she draped a cape around Jessamine's neck, I studied the salon, which was stuffed with lighted mirrors and sinks and shelves of floral-scented shampoo.

"How long have you been a stylist?" Jessamine asked.

"A while now, but I don't plan on being one forever."

"What would you rather do?"

"Don't laugh, but my dream is to be in the movies someday." Darlene's face seemed to take on a rosy glow as she said this.

"Not a laughing matter. I could see it happening," Jessamine said.

"Well, aren't you sweet?" Darlene smiled. "You think so?"

"Sure. Do you have any acting experience?"

Darlene said she'd played some roles in the community theater, just trying it out. Jessamine kept her talking about that for a few minutes.

When there was a brief lull in the conversation, I said, "Say, Darlene, that's a funny cartoon." The reference was to a *Carpe Diem* comic strip taped to the mirror. A fleet of flying saucers was approaching Earth in the single panel strip. One alien was flipping a coin. "*OK, it's heads*," the extraterrestrial said. "*We come in peace.*"

Darlene smiled. "We certainly hope they do."

"I saw where a monolith was found here a couple days ago," Jessamine said. "What's the story on that?"

"Probably aliens," Darlene said nonchalantly.

As my eyes widened, Jessamine said, "Do you believe in people from other planets?"

"Uh-huh," Darlene said. "Some of them are my best

customers." She grinned. "Just kidding. But I do think there's just too many sightings for it not to be true."

A short roly-poly man stepped out of a back room, interrupting her. I recognized him immediately as the monk-like man I'd seen at yesterday's festival. This time he was dressed all in black except for gold-colored shoes—or rather slippers of quilted silk that whispered with each step across the vinyl floor.

"Got some new people here, Darlene?" he asked, in a high-pitched voice that didn't seem to go with the rest of him.

"Folks from Louisville, Brother," she said.

"Long way to come for a haircut," he smiled.

"Not why we came," I said. "She called you *Brother*. Are you related?"

"Well, I'm called Brother Bartholomew."

Brother Bartholomew, aka Bart Proctor, who, according to Sanchez, had done time for trafficking. The self-professed prophet of the Divine Tabernacle of Joy—a UFO cult that dabbled in dope, or a dope ring masquerading as a religion—whose compound we had visited. Why hadn't the sheriff's investigator mentioned Proctor was also a hair stylist?

"But we are all brothers and sisters in the eyes of God, of course."

"Are you a monk?" I asked.

"More of a lay preacher." Bartholomew smiled, showing big bright teeth. "Did you come here today for a haircut, too?"

I wondered if he already knew why we'd come.

"No, we heard about the festival and wanted to see it for ourselves," I said.

"What do you think so far?" he asked.

"Lots of fun. Didn't I see you out there?"

"You probably did. If you don't want a haircut, how about a shave?"

Was he on to us? Had Hiram Jones described us to him? If the prophet was aware of our interest in him, did I really want to risk him holding a straight razor to my throat? Maybe not, but it seemed the best way to engage him in meaningful dialogue. Besides, I doubted he would cut my throat here in front of witnesses.

I rubbed my two-day stubble. "I believe I could use a shave, at that."

"I do it the old-fashioned way," Bartholomew said. "Your face will look younger, cleaner, and smoother. I guarantee it. In fact, when I am done, you'll look and feel like a king."

"A king? Okay, sounds good."

Maybe we could discuss kidnapping and murder. Or at least monoliths.

His salon chair was at the other end of the shop. From there, the two women sounded as if they were conversing in whispers. That meant they wouldn't hear us, either.

"What's your take on this monolith showing up here in Hopkinsville?" I asked, as Bartholomew wrapped a white sheet around me.

"My take? Well, I wonder if we're being set up."

I wasn't expecting this from him. "Darlene said she thinks it's aliens."

"Aliens. Who knows?" Bartholomew doused a small white towel with hot tap water and scented oil, then wrapped it around my face. "Now, that will soften your whiskers and help you to enter a manly, Zen-like state."

"A Zen-like state. What exactly does that mean?" I asked.

"It means a state of calm attentiveness where one's actions are guided by intuition rather than by conscious effort."

"Intuition, eh?" My intuition was telling me to run away, run away. But I ignored it.

"You'll become one with the shave, lost in the rhythm of the task at hand," Bartholomew said.

"All that for the price of a shave? Sounds like a real bargain."

He smiled beatifically and began stropping a straight razor on a flexible strip of leather hooked to a drawer for tension. I wondered if the Zen-like state included the shrinking I suddenly felt in my scrotum.

"A bargain, yes."

"Your shaving hand will be guided by conscious effort, though, right?"

He smiled again. "My fingers do not make mistakes."

It wasn't his mistakes but his intentions that had me concerned. Still, there seemed nothing to do but go through with it. Oddly, as soon as I did, my stiffness and soreness began to ebb. Maybe there was something to this after all.

"Getting back to what Darlene said about aliens, do you think she's right about men from outer space being responsible for the monolith's appearance?"

"She may be," Bartholomew said. "Darlene is wise."

"But?"

"It could've just fallen from the sky. But it could also be a hoax."

If you only knew. But then maybe he did. "You're saying somebody faked it? Why would anybody want to do that?"

"To get on YouTube, I suppose," Bartholomew said.

"You can get on YouTube by picking your nose."

He nodded and smiled. "There is not much that is not fair game these days. The world is full of charlatans, and we're an easy target here in Hopkinsville because of the Little Green Men Festival commemorating our history with flying saucers."

"Do you think spacemen really have been here before?"

"Perhaps it seems farfetched, I know. But if extraterrestrials could reach the earth seventy years ago, as many witnesses said, how farfetched would it be to think they could assume any form they chose?"

"I see what you mean," I said, as he set the razor aside. "Shape shifters like the skin-walkers in Navajo culture."

He removed the towel from my face. "New Mexico has a rich history of alien visitation. Who is to say they cannot take on the appearance of an earthling? In fact, who is to say they are not impersonating us now?"

"Whoa, that's a scary thought," I said. From what little I knew of him, it was not unexpected.

"Indeed." Bartholomew began brushing on a thick layer of lather. His hands were blue-veined, his fingers full of jeweled rings.

"You said you're a lay preacher." Unlike Jessamine, I couldn't bring myself to call him *Brother*. "What church do you belong to?"

He set the soap aside and handed me a card.

"The Tabernacle of Divine Joy," I read aloud. An address and website were also printed on it. The address matched the compound.

"You are welcome to visit us anytime," he said.

No hint of irony in his voice or face. If he knew we'd already been there, he was a damn good actor.

"Never heard of that one. What do y'all believe?"

Bartholomew smiled. It struck me that he smiled too often, and too inscrutably.

"We believe that we are not alone in the universe." He drew my skin upward with his fingers to make a smooth shaving surface. "We believe that aliens are real and have been visiting Earth in UFOs throughout history."

"That's a lot to believe," I said.

He tightened his grip on my head and began shaving me, using slow, even strokes.

"We also believe that both good and evil aliens live among us."

"Excuse me for asking, but why?"

"Because it's been prophesied, and the signs are all around us."

"Prophesied by whom? And what signs?"

He wiped off dabs of foam. "You are right to be skeptical. Letting go of our illusions is not easy."

He could say that again.

"There is too much to tell you during a shave. It's a much

longer conversation. Come by and see us."

He splashed on bay rum aftershave.

"Seems like we should be doing something about this threat."

"Oh, we are," Bartholomew said. "We are unlocking our spiritual potential to survive. Doesn't matter who you are, or your age, wealth, nationality, language."

Profession?

"The Joy will be universal."

"The Joy?"

"Come to a service."

He brushed talcum powder on my face and whipped off the sheet.

"What about Bonita? Does she believe this, too?" I asked.

"How do you know Bonita?" he said, suddenly very still.

"I don't. Jessamine does some business with her. That's why we're here. We understand she didn't come in today."

"Thought you were here for the festival," Bartholomew said.

"We are combining business with pleasure," I said.

"I see. Yes, Bonita believes."

By now, Jessamine's styling had been completed. I wanted to confront Bartholomew with some direct questions, but something told me to hold back, and maybe the Zen-like state had taught me to trust my intuition more. With nothing else to say, we paid up and left the shop.

Chapter 18

Outside the Cut-Up Salon, wreathes of exhaust fumes rose from the pavement while pedestrians trudged through the heat like desert travelers. Jessamine slid behind the wheel. I mopped the sweat off my forehead and cranked up the AC.

"Did we blow our cover in there?" Jessamine asked.

"Maybe. I'm not sure it matters."

"Do you think they know anything about Travis's whereabouts?"

"Hard to say. They might know, but it's still only a suspicion. We have no evidence directly linking them or the cult to Travis's kidnapping."

"So what? I don't care if we put them in jail. All I want is Travis back in one piece."

"Yes, I understand. The trick is how to do it. Bartholomew and Darlene were bound to be circumspect around strangers from the big city, especially ones asking questions."

"This is so discouraging," Jessamine said with a sigh.

"It may seem so, but take heart. Look at what we've already learned. The leader of the UFO cult works with Travis's kidnapper's girlfriend, who is conveniently absent. Your van was found near their compound. We're pretty sure the cap that turned up there belonged to Travis. Everything seems to point back to the Divine Tabernacle of Joy."

"What's our next move?"

Jessamine's favorite question.

"Find Bonita Atkinson and get her to spill her guts."

Just then Jessamine's phone rang, sving me from having to explain how, which was fortunate, because I needed time to think. "Who is it?"

"Detective Sanchez."

"Put him on speaker."

"Have you found Travis?" Jessamine demanded immediately.

"I'm afraid not," Sanchez replied. "I'm calling because we need to see you at the sheriff's office."

"Why?"

"I'll explain when you get here."

"I'd prefer that you explain now," Jessamine said.

"I need your statements. As for the rest, best not to discuss it over the phone."

I spoke up. "Here's something we need for you to do, Sanchez. Find out if Bonita Atkinson or Darlene Dooley have criminal records. Atkinson was McGinnis's girlfriend. She works at the Cut-Up hair salon with the other woman and— guess who—Brother Bartholomew. I assume you didn't know, since you didn't mention it."

"I didn't make the connection," the detective said.

"Seems worth following up." I hung up.

"I wonder what that was all about," Jessamine said as she shifted into drive and set out for the sheriff's department, only a short | distance away.

"I guess we'll soon find out."

"You know, Jim, sometimes I just can't bear to think any more about what's happening to Travis."

"That's understandable. It must be unimaginably hard."

"It is."

She drove on in silence for a couple of blocks, then she said:

"I wonder if Brother Bartholomew thinks we're aliens."

"It wouldn't surprise me," I said.

At the sheriff's department, Sanchez met us and showed us to a conference room. The door was shut, the blinds drawn.

Elliott came in soon after. "How are you holding up, Mrs. Tilford? I know this has been stressful for you."

Before Jessamine could answer, in strolled her parents.

"How are you feeling?" Cybil asked, giving her a hug.

"Worried, I guess."

"Of course you are."

"Dad, what are you doing here?" Jessamine said. "Why didn't you tell me they were coming, Sheriff?"

"I asked the sheriff not to," Barrett said, sounding agitated. "You haven't been answering my calls, and I was afraid you might not come if you knew we were here."

I hadn't heard about the calls.

"I stopped answering because I was tired of your meddling. And tired of arguing with you," Jessamine said.

"I've learned virtually nothing new since this began. You're my daughter. I care about you. It's also my money. I have a right to know what is going on."

The senator talking about money made me feel edgy. To keep him from mentioning the other $250,000 in front of the cops, I said, "Could we have the room for a moment, Sheriff?"

Elliott's expression told me he didn't like this. But his boss, the mayor, had already rolled out the red carpet.

"Of course," he said.

Once the sheriff and Sanchez stepped out, I closed the door.

"Look, the sheriff's going to come back in a minute with questions. Before he does, let's all try to get on the same page, shall we?"

"That would be a first." Barrett scowled. "I want to know everything that's happened so far. And I mean everything. Start with this McGinnis who got killed and tell me what's happened since."

"You explain," Jessamine said to me.

I quickly outlined the kidnapper's two-step ransom scheme and what went wrong.

"Why the hell would he want to do it like that?" Barrett asked.

"Apparently he thought he would be safer that way—"

"Who killed him?" Barrett interrupted.

"We don't know who killed McGinnis." I tried to keep my tone and body language neutral.

"And my money?"

"Gone, apparently stolen from the kidnapper by his murderer."

"Great," Barrett said. "Who else knew about the ransom arrangements?"

"Only McGinnis and whoever he may have told. We certainly didn't tell anyone. McGinnis might have confided in his live-in girlfriend, Bonita Atkinson. We've been trying to contact her."

"Could they have done it together?" Barrett asked.

"It's possible," I said, and described our attempt to contact Bonita at the Cut-Up.

"Now tell me how the ransom money wound up in a landfill," the senator said.

I explained that we'd followed the kidnapper's instructions, then recovered half the ransom.

"What about the garbage man?" Barrett asked.

"Skeets Clawson? I kicked him loose in the hope he'd lead us somewhere useful."

"Did he?"

"No, not yet."

"You've made a hash of this, Guthrie," the senator said. "I don't know why we ever listened to you."

"I listened to Jim because he usually knows what he's talking about, Dad," Jessamine said, "which is more than I can say for the rest of us."

"Jessamine!" Barrett's face turned a light shade of purple.

"You need to keep on listening to Guthrie."

Taking that as my cue, I said, "If this gets out, Senator, it will stir up a shit storm of publicity, and probably create a wildly chaotic, unmanageable situation. Once we reveal the second ransom payment's existence and what's already happened, Senator, that will outweigh your influence with the mayor. We're in his city. Local authorities like him are going to do what they perceive is in their best interest. If you tell him about the money, we'll lose the only leverage we have over any future negotiations."

"You think there will be any future negotiations?" Cybil asked.

"Whoever is holding Travis only has half the cash. They've already tried to snag the other half but failed. I think they'll try again. So yes, I expect more negotiations."

"Now wait just a goddamn minute," Barrett said. "Sounds like you're still spinning your wheels, Guthrie. We're no damn closer to finding my son-in-law than we were at the outset. I say it's time to turn this over to the authorities while there's still some hope of a rescue."

"No, Dad," Jessamine said, in a tone that defied argument. "Nobody could have tried harder than Jim. I know because I've been right there beside him every step of the way."

"Maybe your father's right," I said. "Maybe the sheriff and the others could do better."

"Exactly," Barrett said.

"Now hold on, Shelby," Cybil said. "Don't be so quick to write Mr. Guthrie off. Don't forget that he saved me and my dog back when nobody else could."

Barrett frowned. "Ancient history."

"Not that ancient." After staring him down, Cybil turned to me. "What if the kidnappers do try again?"

The moment of decision.

"It will be an instant replay, but with one major difference."

"And that is?" she asked.

"We insist on exchanging the money for Travis at the same time."

"But they wouldn't go for that before. What makes you think they will now?" Barrett said.

"Greed. We're not dealing with McGinnis anymore. Whoever this is really wants the cash. They'll do it if they think this is the only way they're going to get it."

"Are you sure of that?" Barrett said.

"No. But I believe this is Travis Tilford's best, and possibly only, way of surviving. The choice is yours."

With the matter still unresolved, the sheriff and his deputy came back in.

"I just got off the phone with the FBI," Elliott said. "I'm sorry that Travis has not been found. The bureau says that the more time passes, the better his chances of being released alive."

"Do you think Travis is still alive, Sheriff?" Jessamine asked.

"We're operating on that assumption, yes."

"Then tell us what you're doing to find him," Barrett said.

The sheriff looked at Sanchez, who was carrying a file. He explained that the K-9 Unit had searched the area where Travis Tilford was last seen—Kelly Station Park—and had expanded the search to include the entire county.

"We're still looking hard," Sanchez said.

"If you catch McGinnis's murderer, you could ask him where Travis is," Jessamine said. "Right? How close are you to doing that, Sheriff?"

"I remain hopeful. Unfortunately, we don't have a crystal ball."

The Barrett family members exchanged meaningful looks. When nothing further was said about the extra $250,000, I assumed they had made up their minds individually to keep that information to themselves and proceed independently, as I'd outlined.

"What can we do?" Cybil asked.

"Go home, Mrs. Barrett," the sheriff said.

"That's not going to happen," Barrett said.

"There's really nothing for you to do here, Senator. We're already doing everything possible. We'll find him."

"We're here and we're staying here until my son-in-law is safe, Sheriff. I expect to be kept in the loop from now on. You can reach us at our hotel."

"Would you like to come and stay with us, Jessamine?" Cybil asked. "We've got plenty of room."

"How did you find any accommodations? Every room was sold out because of the festival," Jessamine said.

"Connections. You should collect your stuff and come over. Guthrie can keep your room," Barrett said, giving me a withering look.

I didn't blame him. Me sharing a motel room with his daughter wasn't a good look, as Sanchez's insinuations had already demonstrated. Appearances matter when you're a public figure, especially an elected official. It might get Jessamine out of my hair, though she had been surprisingly helpful so far.

"I'd prefer to discuss this with my parents privately."

The sheriff showed the rest of us out. After Eliot left us behind, Sanchez said, "You're not going to stop the lone wolf act, are you?"

"I was hired to do this job. I mean to see it through. What counts is saving Travis Tilford. You have the resources for a proper search, so make one. I'll try to stay out of your way."

Sanchez drew his eyebrows together, tightened his facial muscles.

Seeing that he was unconvinced, I changed the subject.

"What did you find out about Bonita Atkinson and Darlene Dooley?" I asked.

"Aside from working for Bartholomew? No arrests except for being a public nuisance. Bartholomew and his followers show up in groups in public places like a flash mob. They hand out leaflets about aliens among us taking over the world. It's bizarre."

"I met him this afternoon," I said.

After I reported what I'd learned, Sanchez tapped the file in his hand.

"I can tell you this much about Brother Bartholomew Logan. Twenty years ago, he was a soldier at Fort Campbell. While arrested for public intoxication, he apparently experienced paranoia and hallucinations. The army gave him a random drug test, which he failed. After that, Private Logan was diagnosed with paranoid schizophrenia and given a medical psych discharge."

"How do you know all that? Some of it must have been confidential information," I said.

Sanchez sat mute.

"Never mind," I said.

"While hospitalized, Logan received antipsychotic medication that controlled his symptoms until he stopped taking the drugs."

Sanchez said Bartholomew began behaving bizarrely, giving away his clothes, laughing for no reason, screaming gibberish, saying everyone was going to die. After being thrown in jail and the psych ward multiple times, Bartholomew dropped off the radar. Several years later, he resurfaced again in Hopkinsville.

"This was one of the best places on earth to view the total solar eclipse of 2017," Sanchez said. "Lots of zealots thought the eclipse meant Doomsday was at hand. Tens of thousands showed up here. When Doomsday didn't happen, most of them left. But not Bartholomew. He stayed on and became the leader of our local loons, who believe in all kinds of preposterous crap."

"I'd like to see that file," I said, nodding at it.

He handed it over just as Jessamine came out of the conference room alone.

"What's been happening in there?" I asked.

"Just telling my parents goodbye. That I'm a big girl and will continue handling the situation as I see fit."

"Did they give you a hard time?"

"My father asked what Travis would think of what we're doing. I told him that Travis would understand, and that he should, too."

"How about your mother?"

"She offered her unconditional support, which pissed off Dad."

"Detective Sanchez has been telling me more about our friendly local guru." I showed her his photograph.

While Sanchez quickly brought Jessamine up to date, I flipped through the rest of the file.

"What I don't understand is how a lunatic like Bartholomew became the leader of anything," she said.

Sanchez had no answer. As they shared tight-lipped grimaces, I made a stunning discovery.

"Holy shit, look at this." I held up the page so she could see the face of the man in the photograph.

In the fifteen years since I'd last seen John Drake, he had made some drastic changes to his appearance. People can't alter how they look by becoming shorter or younger. But with some effort, they can seem taller and older. Drake had cut off his long black hair, grown a scruffy beard, and started wearing tinted glasses. No wonder I hadn't recognized him standing beside Brother Bartholomew at the festival.

Jessamine didn't react at first. Then she paled, going from shock to disbelief to horror.

"Oh, my god," she said. "It can't be him. He's in prison for life."

"Apparently not," I said, though I'd put him there myself.

Chapter 19

"Who are you talking about?" Sanchez asked.

"John Drake, Mrs. Barrett's first husband," I said.

"Are you sure?" Sanchez asked.

"There's no doubt about it."

"Let me see," Sanchez said, taking the file back. "We need to talk to your mother."

"This will bring back terrible memories," Jessamine warned.

"There's no way around it. Her life may be in danger," I said.

Squeezing her eyes shut, Jessamine nodded. Sanchez opened the door.

"What's going on now?" Shelby Barrett demanded as we trooped back in.

"Recognize this man?" Sanchez showed them Drake's photo.

"Oh no," Cybil said. "This is impossible. Isn't it?"

"I'm afraid not," I said.

"John Drake. Alias Owen Pike. Age forty-six. Six feet two inches tall. Two hundred pounds. Black hair. Brown eyes. Convicted of attempted murder, and first-degree murder. Sentenced to life imprisonment. Released six months ago," Sanchez said.

Bringing a shaky hand to her forehead, Cybil said, "He tried to kill me fifteen years ago. How can be out when he was given a life sentence?"

I was wondering the same thing. Had Drake escaped? Been granted clemency? Kentucky's last governor had handed out a huge number of highly questionable pardons as he left office. Had Drake gotten one? If so, why hadn't we heard about it?

"In Kentucky and most of the U.S., a life sentence means being in prison for fifteen years with the chance for parole. Having served fifteen, Drake became eligible for parole earlier this year, and was released," Sanchez said.

"How could they let him go without informing us?" Cybil said.

"Somebody screwed up. We've heard about failures like this happening occasionally. It's likely a technological error," Sanchez said.

"Technological error?" Barrett was trembling with rage. "Our lives are at risk over a technological error?"

"Under the VINE alert system, registered victims are supposed to be contacted when an inmate is scheduled for release from custody or a parole hearing. You should have been told."

"But we weren't," Cybil said. "This is crazy. He's dangerous."

"According to this file, Drake and Brother Bartholomew did jail time together. That's the link between them.

"Do you think Drake and Bartholomew are both involved in Travis's kidnapping?" Jessamine asked.

"Seems possible. Drake is now a member of the Divine Tabernacle. He seems an unlikely UFO convert, but the drug trade connection makes a lot of sense." Turning toward Cybil, Sanchez said, "So, Mrs. Barrett, time for you to come clean. You've been holding back information that might help us rescue your son-in-law. Why?"

Cybil regarded her husband sadly, knowing he wouldn't like having the past raked up.

"Don't look so dejected, Shelby. I'd hoped that the truth

wouldn't have to come out. But it's unavoidable now, regardless of the consequences."

To Sanchez, she said, "I didn't tell you about Drake because I didn't know he was involved."

"Go on," Sanchez said.

"Not many people know that I'm originally from Hopkinsville. I've tried to keep that out of the public eye. This afternoon I drove by what used to be our house. A gas station stands on that property now. It was a happy home for a while, but when I was fourteen, my father died of a heart attack."

As she spoke, she seemed to grow more youthful.

"He was a good man. When Mom remarried two years later, my stepfather seemed all right at first and she was happy. Mom and Dad had always wanted me to finish high school and go on to college. That's what I wanted to do, too. But my stepfather said they didn't have the money. By then, I was physically mature. It seemed like every boy in town was after me. But after meeting a handsome young soldier named John Drake at a dance, I was only interested in him. John could have had any girl he wanted. But he wanted me. I remember spending my time brushing my hair and dreaming of the day we could finally be together."

Cybil cleared her throat.

"John was sweet but ferociously jealous. Any boy who looked twice at me could expect a beating. Foolishly, I believed it was a sign of his love. But John was only part of the problem. My stepfather had begun drinking heavily. And when he did, he abused Mom and found ways to touch me when she wasn't looking."

Cybil made a bleating sound in her throat. Jessamine looked horrified. Barrett stared down at the floor. But there was no going back now. The floodgates holding back Cybil's secrets had burst.

"I tried not to be alone with him, but he wouldn't stop. When he molested me, I couldn't tell her. But I had to tell somebody, and finally I let John know what was happening.

He said, 'I'll kill him,' and I believed him. To escape, as well as to keep John from killing my stepfather, I ran away with him. On the night we left town, Mom was in bed asleep when I went to collect my things. My stepfather had passed out in his easy chair. John and I sneaked away. Thirteen hours later, we were in Houston. We got married by a justice of the peace and John started working construction while I looked for a job. But John quickly tired of manual labor. Instead, he committed a string of armed robberies. Worse, he forced me to take part. We got caught and put in jail. That's when I found out what John had done on the night that I left home. He'd set fire to our house, killing my stepfather—and Mom."

Cybil shook her head, sighing deeply.

"I was grief stricken. I agreed to testify against John in exchange for leniency. There was no proof that he'd committed murder or arson, but he was given a stiff sentence anyway for the robberies. After serving a short time, I was given work release outside the jail. But when I heard that John had escaped, I ran away and became a fugitive, dyed my hair, and changed my name. I was waitressing at a truck-stop in eastern Kentucky and felt my life was over. Until Shelby Barrett came in one night and swept me off my feet. He wanted to marry me. I said if he knew me better, he wouldn't. But he said he'd already lost one wife to illness and couldn't care less about my past. He was relentless."

She gave Barrett a wan smile.

"He wore down my resistance. What can I say? I agreed to marry him, even though I was still John's wife. Crazy, I know. But my whole life was crazy. After that, we lived happily—until the day John Drake showed up again and stole my dog. That's when I hired Jim Guthrie."

"Oh, Mom," Jessamine said.

"It's all right, honey. Why don't you tell them what happened next, Jim?" Cybil said.

I took it from there.

Cybil hired me to find her dog, which had disappeared one

night while out on a walk with a trusted farm hand. I didn't want to take the case initially. But I had to when a lawyer friend of mine called in a favor. The dog was a champion Irish wolfhound, a huge dog bred by the Romans to kill wolves. A gentle breed now, but still a sight hound. Once a dog like that starts chasing a running animal, it won't stop, not even for a fence.

"Remember that."

I raised my eyebrows at Sanchez.

The first day, we found the old farm hand dead in a sinkhole on the horse farm. The violence of the act suggested that the motive was more than theft. After an investigation that uncovered several other murders, I traced the perp to a puppy mill, a place where stolen dogs are bred until they drop. The pups are sold to unsuspecting dog lovers in pet shops. This one was hidden in the knobs of southern Indiana. Cybil insisted on coming with me.

We drove up there and hiked through the forest to what appeared to be an abandoned farm. I told Cybil to wait for me and went down to check it out. The house was deserted. After passing a slimy, stump-filled pond, I came to a vine-choked barn with a slaughterhouse reek. I shoved the sagging doors open and flies swarmed out at me. After covering my nose and mouth with a handkerchief like a desperado, I went into the barn with my .45 in one hand and a powerful flashlight in the other. It was a grisly scene. Small skeletal corpses lay everywhere in the murk—in feed troughs, empty cages, on the dirt floor, even stacked like cordwood against the leaning walls. All dogs.

I shook my head at the foulness of the memory.

I heard a low growl and found a dog the size of a pony staked to the ground. When I went over to make friends with him, something caught me solidly on the back of my head. I woke up with my face in the dirt and my arms bent up behind my back and lashed together. Cybil was unconscious beside me. As I fought to control the panic, John Drake slashed my face with a cane fishing pole. Then he cut off the rope binding me and thrust a long-handled spade in my hands. I was to dig our grave while he covered me with my own gun.

Cybil awakened and began screaming her dog's name. Drake told her to go ahead, that nobody would hear her. He was wrong. Magoffin heard and suddenly appeared, dragging the chain and stake behind him. Drake panicked and began firing wildly as the 150-pound Irish wolfhound charged and crashed into him. Fortunately for Drake, Cybil called the dog off before it killed Drake by biting him behind the ears.

After that, with Drake back in jail, I advised Cybil to get a good lawyer and to stop trying to hide from her past. With a story as sympathetic as hers, I figured she'd get off with time served. Instead, Senator Barrett persuaded the prosecutor to take the death sentence off the table in return for Drake's silence. If he broke the agreement, other murder charges would be brought against him. By hushing it all up, the senator deprived his political opponents of a scandal that might have driven him from office. A quiet dissolution of one marriage was followed by a quiet ceremony for another, and all's well that ends well.

"A tidy solution," Sanchez said ironically.

Hands flat on the table, Barrett leaned forward and said, "Can we trust your discretion, Detective Sanchez?"

"Depends on what you mean by that," Sanchez said. "You can trust me to enforce the law. To cover up nothing. You can also trust me not to reveal confidential information just to ruin someone's life."

"I'm glad to hear that," Barrett nodded. "What about your bosses?"

"You'll have to talk to them," Sanchez said. "Maybe you folks should return to Oldham County now until this is sorted out."

"I'll go home when Travis is by my side again," Jessamine said.

Barrett scrubbed a hand over his face. "Enough. I'll get

my personal security detail down here to protect us."

Sanchez nodded.

Jessamine and her parents exchanged hugs. Then we parted ways with them.

Chapter 20

As we got into my rental car, Jessamine said, "That was quite a shock. I never dreamed that John Drake would turn up again."

"He makes the situation far more dangerous."

"I knew he was bad news, but not a monster."

After remaining silent for a couple of beats, I asked, "How do you feel about all this?"

"I respect my mother even more. Look at what she's had to go through in her life. I'm so lucky—or have been up to now. If I can get Travis back alive and whole, I'll never complain about anything again."

Her phone buzzed. The screen showed the caller's number was blocked. She put it on speaker.

"We have your husband," said a woman's voice—one that I had never heard before. Traffic sounds in the background suggested she was using a cell phone somewhere outdoors.

"Where is Travis? Is he all right?" Jessamine asked.

"You want him back?" The voice was cold.

"Yes, of course I do. Who is this? What do you want?"

"I want to do a deal. I'll trade your husband for the two-hundred and fifty grand."

Jessamine looked over at me.

Proof of life, I mouthed.

"I'll need proof of life," she said.

"I can't guarantee that."

I shook my head.

Jessamine closed her eyes and said, "Then no deal."

"I'll be honest with you," the caller said. "Your husband is probably still alive, but he could also be dead by now."

"No!"

"I'm sending a photo."

Opening an app, Jessamine scrolled down to messages. Her breath caught in her throat when a photo of Travis appeared. Same hair, stubble, and vest as in the previous photograph. He was sitting cross-legged with his wrists tied in front of him in a dimly lit place.

"Satisfied?"

"When was this taken?" Jessamine asked.

"An hour ago."

"Is he still okay?"

"He was when I took the picture."

"You're not with him now?"

"Enough talk," the kidnapper said. "We want the money in cash. No tricks, no trackers, or he's dead. Understand?"

Make the deal, I mouthed.

"I understand. Where are you?" Jessamine said.

Directions were given. Jessamine was to come alone to a motel parking lot on the west side of town and wait in her car. The kidnapper would do the rest.

"I'm on my way," Jessamine said.

Knowing they'd be looking for the tracker, we removed it. Severing our last link with Travis was not easy. Jessamine put a hand to her face and exhaled heavily as I started up the car and drove north to the rendezvous. It didn't take long to get there. The motel was permanently closed and the lot empty. The kidnapper made us wait twenty minutes before a silver Honda

Accord pulled up diagonally behind us. By then, we were both on edge and jittery. The driver watched us before slowly getting out. She left the motor running and the door open for a quick getaway.

She moved easily, like a young person. Other than that, all I could be sure of was her height, about five-eight, because she was wearing a red bandanna as a mask, dark sunglasses, a loose T-shirt, and baggy sweatpants. Her hair was hidden under a straw hat.

She approached the passenger's side. Jessamine rolled down the window. The kidnaper pointed a pistol—a small one, maybe .22 caliber—in her face.

"You were told to come alone, but you're not. From this moment on, any other failure to follow directions and you'll never see your husband alive again. Clear?"

I didn't recognize this woman, but I thought I did know her voice. It was breathy, like the voice of the blond stylist at the Cut-Up Salon, Darlene. But the directions had been given by a woman with a lower-pitched voice. So, two women kidnappers. Surprising.

"Yes, I understand."

"Where's the money?"

"In the back seat," Jessamine nodded.

"Get it."

She reached over the seat and grabbed the brown leather briefcase. It looked banged up after the last twenty-four hours. We probably did, too.

"Put the money out the window and drop it," the kidnapper said.

Instead, Jessamine rested the briefcase on the sill. "Where is my husband? You tell me and I'll pass you the cash."

"Uh-uh, that's not our deal. I've warned you twice. This is the last time. Now drop the case."

Jessamine obeyed reluctantly.

"Don't move."

The kidnapper backed away, still pointing the gun in our direction. She went down on one knee and thumbed the clasps open. When she dumped out the contents one-handed, bundles of hundred-dollar bills spilled across the rough, cracked pavement. She pawed through them, apparently searching for a tracker. Not finding one, she put the money back in the briefcase and stood up.

"I'm going now. Follow me."

"Where are we headed?" Jessamine demanded.

"To get your husband back."

"How do I know you aren't going to pull a fast one and just drive off?"

"Please, a car chase in this thing? Don't worry. I'll lead you to another vehicle and it will guide you to him."

"How will I know it's not just some random vehicle?" Jessamine said.

"It's a five-year-old dark blue Kia hatchback with an antennae topper shaped like a ball with an American flag. Okay? Believe me now? Let's go."

As I pulled out, I saw the Honda had no license plate.

"What if she tries to run?" Jessamine said.

"Then I'll follow her. But I don't think she will. This is all planned out. I'm guessing she wants to put some distance between the money and Travis, so we can't get both at the same time."

Keeping up with the Honda in light traffic on county roads was simple enough. Our hopes went up each time we passed an abandoned property. But the Honda kept going until we reached a fast-food joint that had been shut down, and the Honda pulled into another empty parking lot where a blue Kia hatchback with an antennae topper was waiting.

"This is it," Jessamine said.

No tags on the Kia. Another masked driver. As it slowly drove off, "Darlene" waved for us to follow it. Then she turned the Honda around and went the other way.

"I wonder if we're following Bonita Atkinson now," I said.

"I don't care who it is as long as they take us to Travis."

Five miles later, the Kia turned onto a one lane road with weeds growing between the tire ruts. We went over a hill to a 1950s style stone ranch house with a foreclosure sign staked out front. The Kia disappeared behind the house, dragging low-hanging tree limbs along with it over the windshield.

"Try to keep her here until we've seen Travis," I said, as I tailed the Kia around back.

"How am I supposed to do that?" Jessamine asked.

"With this." I handed her my .45.

The Kia had stopped at a two-car garage. I pulled up beside it and rolled down my window.

"Where's Travis?" I asked.

"In there." The driver pointed toward the cellar doors angled close to the ground. They appeared solid. A heavy looking concrete bird bath had been placed on top of them. Thinking there could only be one reason for that, I clambered out and rushed over.

"Travis Tilford? Are you in there?" I yelled, beating my fists on the doors.

No reply.

I rolled the pedestal and basin off the doors. The paint had worn off, leaving the doors weathered, warped, and rotted. But they were secured with a shiny new padlock.

"Do you have the key?" I yelled to the Kia driver, who shrugged.

With the right tools, I could easily crack the lock. Not having any, I studied the hasp that held the doors closed. The lock's installer had left the small wood screws exposed. I ran back to the rental car and popped the trunk. With the crowbar I found there, I pried up the hasp and pulled the creaking doors open. Another door was at the bottom of a dozen steps. I rushed down and opened it.

A musty, darkened, underground space yawned before

me. I hit the flashlight app on my phone. The beam pierced the dimness, revealing a body sprawled on the dirt. A man, I thought, and hoped it was Travis and that we weren't too late. I ducked through the cobwebs and, with my heart racing, found enough headroom to stand.

"Jessamine," I shouted, as I hustled over to the prone figure. "It's Travis."

But was he alive? He wasn't moving. I bent over and checked the thick artery below his left ear for a pulse. My own jumped when I found he had one. But Tilford's breathing was labored. I sawed nylon rope off his wrists with my Swiss Army knife and wrestled him into a sitting position with his back against the wall.

I called Jessamine again. But the hairs on the back of my neck bristled when I recognized John Drake's voice and heard him yelling, "Get down there, you goddamn bitches."

Seconds later, Jessamine half fell down the steps, closely followed by the Kia driver. I wanted to launch myself up there, but the others were in my way. By the time they weren't, the outer doors had been slammed shut. I rammed my shoulder against them, but they didn't give much. I heard a gunshot and wood splintered near my head. Instinctively, I dropped and slid back downstairs as more shots ricocheted off the steps and walls. When the shooting stopped, a few slivers of gray light leaked through the bullet holes in the doors.

"Where's my gun?" I asked Jessamine.

"He took it," she said.

Then Drake yelled, "Still breathing, Peeper? But not for long. When I saw you again after all these years, I couldn't believe it. You really haven't changed much—still butt ugly."

"And you're still a murdering bastard," I said, and slipped sideways in case he'd reloaded.

"That's harsh. Hey Bonita! Thanks for the memories."

Bonita. So, it was her driving the Kia.

When I heard no answer, I eased back into the depths of the

cellar where Jessamine was cradling her husband and Bonita Atkinson was trembling beside her.

"Anybody hit?" I asked.

They said no.

"How's Travis?" I asked.

"Semi-conscious. I'm worried about him," Jessamine said.

"Worry about yourself," Bonita said. "Pike's going to kill us all."

"Pike. We heard that's what he was calling himself. His real name is John Drake. You didn't know that?"

"No," Bonita said.

"You're in this up to your neck. So why does Drake want to kill you?" Jessamine said.

"Isn't it obvious?" Bonita said.

I swept the flashlight beam over the rest of the cellar, which measured about twelve-by-twelve. Two of the walls were bare, and two were lined with wooden shelves filled with empty canning jars. Damn it, there was no other way out. Spotting a gallon-sized plastic jug, possibly left for Travis by the kidnappers, I scooped it up. After giving it the smell and taste tests, I splashed some of the water in Travis's face.

He opened his eyes and croaked, "Jess?"

"Yes, Travis. I'm right here," she said.

After two days in this cellar, he was no doubt dehydrated. I handed Jessamine the jug, and she held it up to his lips.

"Small sips," I cautioned, as he drank greedily. "He'll vomit if he drinks too fast."

When he finished, I said, "How are you feeling, Mr. Tilford?"

"Who are you?" he asked.

"My name's Guthrie. I'm a private investigator trying to rescue you."

"Did you hire him, Jess?"

"Yes, Travis. I did."

"What's been happening?"

"Too much to tell right now," I interceded. "What can you

remember about being kidnapped?"

"Not much. It's all kind of a blur."

"You may have suffered a concussion."

I checked him over. He seemed exhausted, but otherwise unhurt. "Can you feel your fingers?"

He shook his head.

"Don't worry. They'll start hurting soon enough. Have you been down here the whole time?"

"As far as I know."

Something banged loudly on the cellar doors. "Hey, down there."

"What do you want, Drake?" I yelled back.

"Those fifteen years of freedom that you deprived me of, for a start."

"You deserved thirty. They never should have let you out."

"But they did, and that's too bad for you. When I left the pen, the world had changed so much it was like being on Mars. I panicked every time I went outdoors. You did that to me."

"Owen, let us out of here!" Bonita cried. "You can have all the money. Just let us go."

Drake laughed. "Thanks, but I've already got most of it, and I'll soon have the rest. You thought you and Darlene had it all figured out, didn't you? Get the other two hundred and fifty grand and cut me out. Bad idea. Well, Darlene has cut you out of it, all right, and I'm going to do the same for her. Then I'll have half a million bucks to go wherever I want and do whatever I please."

"You bastard," Bonita shrieked.

"The question is, what do I want to do with you?"

"Same as you did to Snuffy, I imagine." I was trying to provoke him into making a mistake.

"Let me tell you about old Snuffy," Drake said. "I go over there, pick the lock with an expired credit card, and pull out a chair to wait. When I hear tires on gravel, I cat foot it to the living room and look out the window. An old white van pulls up. Snuffy gets out wearing an orange ball cap and carrying a briefcase. He can't believe it when he comes in and sees me waiting for him.

"'Where's Bonita?' he says. I shrug and ask what he's got there. 'Oh, this?' he says, all innocent and holds up the briefcase. 'Let's see,' I tell him. He dilly dallies around and finally snaps it open. I look at all the money and wonder how this moron managed to get his hands on it. So, I ask him, and he claims he found it. That's when I show him my .357, which will stop a charging grizzly, and Snuffy knows he'll never outdraw me.

"He says he'll cut me in. That I can keep all the cash. He won't say a word. I say he doesn't have to do that. Just let me see that fine orange ball cap he's wearing. He tosses it on the table and I put two slugs into his forehead. He drops the briefcase, money flies everywhere. I pick up the bundles, check for blood and brain matter, and what do I find? A GPS tracker. Well, well. I toss it aside and shove the money in my gym bag. Then I wipe down the place and cruise away in the old van, a very rich man."

"Why'd you burn up the van and leave it near the Divine Tabernacle compound?" I wanted to keep him talking.

"Why do you think? Same reason I threw that cap out the window. It's called *misdirection,* in case you don't know. But what should I do with you? Starve you maybe? I was a level four prisoner, Guthrie, which means I got locked in my cell 24/7. I had to be handcuffed and have an escort with me, sometimes a three-man escort, just to shower, get medical, or have a visitor. Yard time meant spending an hour in a gorilla cage."

I heard something splash against the doors and smelled gasoline.

"It was like living underground in a bunker. That's why they call it *the tomb.* Now it's your turn. I can't give you the full fifteen-year experience, but I can give you a taste. How's that sound?"

"Like the pathetic creep you are. But I never figured you for a UFO believer, Drake."

"Crazy like a fox. Brother Bartholomew and I got to know each other when I was in prison. He told me all about little green men and flying saucers. I thought he was whacko, but he really believed in that shit. He said it would also be a great cover for dealing dope, and when I got out, if I wanted, I could be part of it. Unless the aliens had taken over by then, of course. I'm from Hoptown, you know? But I would never have come back here if it wasn't for old Bart and an opportunity that was too good to pass up."

"So, it's all about dealing drugs," I said.

"Maybe not *all*. I don't turn up my nose at a little kidnapping and extortion, either—especially when some fool like Snuffy had already done the heavy lifting for me. It was all perfect. And then *you* turned up again, trying to wreck everything. Well, not this time," he said, and I heard a *whoosh*.

"Oh god," Jessamine said, as smoke began pouring into the cellar.

"We've got to get out of here," Bonita said.

I couldn't have agreed more. A firefighter once told me that cellar fires burned very hot and smoky. And because they burned below ground, the ventilation was poor and there were lots of toxic vapors and gases. The dirt floor and concrete block walls wouldn't burn. The heavy ceiling joists would. We'd be dead of smoke inhalation long before they collapsed on top of us.

"Keep low," I said, coughing while I desperately looked everywhere for a way out of this deathtrap.

But there wasn't one.

Then I realized the back wall Travis was leaning against looked different from the others. I thumped it with the heel of my fist.

"What are you doing?" Jessamine gasped.

"It's not concrete," I said. "It's drywall painted to look like concrete. Get out of the way."

As the others scattered, I stood up and started mule kicking it with my heel, trying to make a hole big enough for us to fit through one at a time. Breaking through the surface, I felt a surge of energy. I knew I could do this. I kicked twice as hard. When turned around to see what I'd accomplished, I discovered a dirt wall behind the other one.

"Shit," I said.

"We're done for," Bonita sobbed.

I was so angry now that I elbowed the drywall chest high, and to my astonishment, broke through—because there was nothing behind it this far off the ground. It was a crawl space half as high as the ceiling, and it had to go somewhere. I couldn't kick it at this angle, which was bad news as arms are much weaker than legs. But you work with what you've got, and I was riding a huge wave of adrenaline as I smashed the drywall repeatedly with my elbows and fists. As a fissure opened, I clawed and tore and ripped to widen the hole and make it taller.

All this time, the flames were burning through the cellar doors, and we were blanketed with thick velvety smoke that made it very hard to breathe. It occurred to me that this crawl space might've been intended as an emergency exit in case of getting trapped by storm debris on the doors. I didn't care why, really. I just wanted out.

"Come on, Travis," I said, and hoisted him through the hole.

Shoving him forward, I squirmed into the crawl space and grabbed hold of him. In a crouch, I half pulled, half dragged him along. There was no other option, as I was the only one strong enough to get him out. Jessamine and Bonita would have to follow us as best they could while we inched along. It was slow going with blinding, choking smoke making it that much harder. I was almost exhausted when I saw the half-door with slivers of light showing at the edges.

I threw myself against it, but the door would not budge.

Brute force having failed, I tried to think my way through this obstacle. At first, nothing came to me, and Bonita's dire predictions seemed about to come true after all. But then my eyes fell upon the place where door met door jamb, and it gave me an idea. Leaving Travis aside, I swiveled around and lashed out with my heel. It took three attempts before the wood splintered. I ripped out the rest and dragged Travis into what turned out to be a space under the front porch. The final barrier, a lattice door, yielded easily compared to the others, and all of us found ourselves gasping and gagging on the front lawn.

After that, I passed out.

Chapter 21

When I regained consciousness, I was looking into the face of a burly, bespectacled, middle-aged man wearing green scrubs, gloves, and a surgical mask. A stethoscope hung around his thick neck.

"How are you doing?" the big man asked.

I was coughing and couldn't speak. Everything seemed hazy, but maybe that was just in my mind.

"It's common to cough for a few minutes after breathing in smoke or fumes from a fire. Your breathing should return to normal within a short period of time, about thirty minutes," he told me.

"What fire?" I mumbled.

"You don't remember?"

I didn't.

But I'd become aware of a cacophony of sounds—moaning, groaning, crying, distressed breathing, whispering. And I could smell a strong odor of antiseptic mingled with cleaning products. I was amazed that I could recognize these smells when I couldn't even think straight, but the mind is a strange and wonderful instrument.

"Another symptom of smoke inhalation is mental confusion.

Can you tell me who is President of the United States?"

"Obama?" I said, coughing and choking.

The man wearing the stethoscope smiled and placed it on my chest and listened to my breath sounds.

"Do you know what city you're in?"

The answer was no. All I knew was that I was lying in bed with metal arm rails digging into me. I was wearing nothing but a thin gown. My face was covered by an oxygen mask. I had an IV stuck in my arm. From all this, I used my Holmesian powers of reasoning to deduce that I must be in a curtained-off hospital emergency room.

"Louisville?"

"No, you're in the ER at the Jennie Stuart Medical Center in Hopkinsville," the big man said. "Mental confusion can impair your short-term memory, disorient you as to time and place."

Hearing the static of a police radio and someone popping open a canned drink, I rubbed my eyes and said, "I think I may be cured now, Doc."

"Good," he said.

"Why am I here? How did I get here?"

"Smoke inhalation. You don't have serious burns, but you swallowed a fair amount of smoke."

"How bad is it? I mean, am I going to live?" I was feeling cocky for no apparent reason.

"I don't want to alarm you unduly," the doctor said, "but the number one cause of death related to fires is smoke inhalation."

"Thanks, I think." I sat, twisting the plastic admittance band on my wrist.

The doc told me his name was Curry. A frizzy-haired, skinny woman in her thirties who told me her name was Mary said she was my nurse. Like him, she was wearing scrubs. They kept tag-teaming me, checking my vitals, assessing my condition. They asked for my doctor's contact info, but I told them I didn't have one. They drew blood from me for lab work and prepared for a chest X-ray. I was okay with all that, but rebelled at being slid into a compression chamber that clanked and groaned like a WWII Nazi U-boat. I likewise objected to being kept in the hospital overnight.

"I thought you guys sent everybody home right away these days."

"We do, but you need to stay longer for your own good."

"Sorry, no can do, doc."

"Why not?"

"I have important stuff that needs my attention."

"More important than breathing?"

I liked Dr. Curry's witty sense of humor. But when he was suddenly called away, I felt glad to be spared from answering him.

An orderly wheeled me to a small patient room with a private bath and a window. It was a typical hospital room painted in warm pastels—ochre and earthy brown. Besides my adjustable bed, it had a laminated over-bed table for food trays, an old-style table telephone, wall television, and recliner chair. Wall mounted racks held coiled electrical cords and other sinister looking medical equipment featuring rows of buttons and lighted greenish screens. Clear drip bags hung from metal posts.

I was still trying to get my bearings when someone in a wheelchair rolled in and moved his footrests out of the way.

"Hey, Mr. Guthrie. How are you doing?" he said.

I didn't recognize him at first.

"Listen, Jim—all right if I call you Jim?" he asked.

"Sure. What should I call you?"

"Are you kidding? Call me Travis. Look, I never got to thank you for saving my life. Without you, I wouldn't be here today. So, thank you. I've got to tell you—"

And it all started coming back. Travis. The fire. Jessamine.

"How is Jessamine?" I interrupted.

"She's fine. The doctors are checking her out. She'll be in to see you soon."

"And how are you, Travis?"

"Smoke inhalation," he coughed.

"Bad stuff."

"Better than burning to death, though," he said.

"Agreed."

"How about the other woman—Bonita Atkinson? Did she make it?" I asked.

"Yeah, she did."

"Have you or Jessamine talked to her?"

"No."

Our Q and A ended when Jessamine stepped in with phone in hand, wearing a hospital gown.

"How are you, Jim?"

She sounded genuinely concerned, which I liked.

"Lots of soot on my hands and arms, but not so much in my airway passages. Doc said my skin color looks good, too."

"You made up that last part, didn't you?" she asked.

"What gave me away?"

"You're a nice shade of gray." She smiled and took my hand. "I don't know how to thank you. Words seem inadequate. Travis and I owe our lives to you."

"Happy I could help," I said.

"Don't you dare give me that aw shucks," she said, and hugged me hard. Then she kissed me on the cheek.

These Barrett women knew how to get what they wanted and were generous in expressing their gratitude.

"We had quite a time, didn't we?" she smiled.

"Are you referring to the cute guard dogs or of being trapped in the burning cellar?" I asked.

"Both, also to Byron and his ears, and the Red Nebula Inn, and the little green men. It was hard to grasp it at the time, but we had an amazing adventure, didn't we? One I'll never forget."

Her phone rang. She let go of me to answer it. After a moment, she said, "My parents are here. I'm going to meet them."

"I'll wait here," Travis said.

Jessamine looked surprised. "Well, okay. See you in a few minutes."

"I wanted a word alone," Travis said. "Using the monolith for publicity was dangerous, obviously. If I hadn't dissed McGinnis, maybe none of this would have happened. But it worked out. While I was being held, we raised enough funding to go forward with the movie."

I chewed on that for a moment. Hard to learn from mistakes that you still benefitted from.

"I'm happy for you."

"We want to include the kidnapping in the documentary. I mean, how could we leave it out? We'd like to interview you for it."

I remained silent, letting the statement hang there a while.

"It's going to premiere at the Alhambra," Travis said. "We're going to donate the monolith to Kelly Station Park."

"I think they'd like that." When he hesitated, I asked, "Was there something else?"

He looked down at his feet. "In the cellar, I felt so afraid of death that I was paralyzed. Even now, the terror won't go away."

I nodded. "I understand. That's a normal reaction to a major trauma like you experienced. You'll start feeling better soon. Give it a few weeks."

"I wish I had killed Drake," he said.

"Killing is much more gruesome in real life than it is in the movies. And harder to get over. You, as a filmmaker, of all people, should know that."

"I know it intellectually."

"You need to know it in your gut. When you've taken someone's life, you've taken *everything* from them." I let that sink in. "Everything. Even when they're evil—and that includes a stone-cold killer like Drake—and you have no other choice, it's still a big-time trauma."

"That's good stuff," he said, brightening.

"I'm not trying to punch up your script, damn it. Do you

hear me?"

"Okay, I hear you."

"Good."

"If that's how you feel, how can you keep doing your job?" he asked.

I didn't have a pat answer. Fortunately, the Barretts entered the room, so I didn't need one.

"Jim, you've saved us again," Cybil said, and leaned over to hug me.

"You're welcome," I said, gently disengaging from her grasp.

Barrett came over and shook my hand.

"Thank you, Guthrie," he said. "You've proven me wrong—and I'm grateful for it. Now we need to talk in private."

He turned to the others.

"Could we have the room, please?"

Uh oh.

With the door closed, I said, "What's this about, Senator?"

"How's your health?" he asked. "Are you ready to go back to work?"

"In what capacity?"

"I want you to find John Drake and put him away. Permanently."

"Hold on. I don't think I heard you right. You meant put Drake back in prison, correct?"

"Interpret it any way you like. So long as he never menaces us again."

"This is a matter for the authorities. Let them handle it."

"Like they handled letting him out of prison? Those bunglers."

"I'm not happy about that, either."

"Not happy? I'd think you'd feel more strongly about it than that."

"They'll get Drake. It's just a matter of time."

"We are not safe while he remains at large. You get him, and I'll make it worth your while."

"This isn't the Old Wild West, and I am not a gun for hire. I don't kill people for money."

"No? Not even someone like Drake, who by my count has already tried to kill *you* three times? Don't you want revenge?"

How ironic, considering what I'd just told his son-in-law.

"Forget it, Senator. I don't want your blood money. We never had this conversation."

"Hold on," he said. "How about this instead? Drake apparently still has half a million dollars that belong to me. I'd like to get that money back. If you do that for me, I'll give you a ten percent finder's fee. How does that sound?"

"It sounds like twenty-five thousand dollars."

"So, you'll do it?"

I could use the cash. No doubt about that. And I had no qualms about returning stolen property. "I might give it a whirl."

"Good. And if Drake should get dead in the process, I'd double it."

That was a bad deal—a devil's bargain. But Drake was still out there, gunning for me. I had to take him off the board somehow.

"I'll try to get your money back, Senator. But I won't kill anybody to do it. So, like I said, we never had this conversation."

"What conversation?" Barrett walked out as Jessamine and Travis came back in.

"What did Dad want?"

"That's confidential. Are all of you going back to Oldham County now?"

"Well, the Little Green Men Festival ends tonight ..."

"Hold it right there. I can't believe what I'm hearing. Tell me you're *not* thinking about going back out there tonight."

"Well, if we don't, we'll probably never have another chance to capture this," she said.

"Jessamine, do you have a death wish? You know it's not safe with Drake at large. The festival is the last place you should go. Remember what Travis just went through and put this out of your mind."

"Jim's right," Travis said.

Jessamine's eyes widened in surprise.

"It's too dangerous, Jess. The film can wait. Besides, I'm nowhere near a hundred percent physically or mentally."

She looked at him for a moment. "No, of course, you're not. I don't know what I was thinking."

"Glad to hear that," I said. "You've made the right decision."

"What about you, Jim?" she asked. "What will you do now?"

"As soon as I get my Mustang back, I'll be on the road again, headed for home. This time, I'll be keeping a closer look out for deer."

But I wasn't telling the whole truth and nothing but. I had other plans before leaving town.

Chapter 22

When a nurse escorted Jessamine and Travis away, I slipped out of my room and traipsed through a hectic corridor to the nursing station, the boundary between bustling nurses and patients who needed attention. What I needed was Bonita Atkinson's room number. At the sleek neutral toned counter, I approached a nurse who was staring at a computer screen.

"Excuse me," I said.

"I'll be with you in just a minute," she said.

I noticed the multiple lights blinking on the telephone in front of her, possibly indicating someone on hold.

After another beat, I cleared my throat. "Can you tell me Bonita Atkinson's room number, please?"

The nurse glanced up at me, clearly annoyed. "What's the name again?"

I repeated it.

Tapping keys and looking at her screen, she said, "218-B," and returned to what she was doing when I interrupted her.

I found 218-B and quietly pushed the door open. The room had an antiseptic smell, like the ER. The lights were switched on. Bonita lay in front of the blank screen of the wall mounted television with her eyes closed. She was in a wheeled bed hooked up to an IV drip and cheeping monitoring devices. The side rails were in the up position.

"How are you doing, Bonita?"

Her brown eyes fluttered open, but she didn't answer. A plastic pitcher sat on her over-bed table. I asked if she wanted some water. No response. I picked it up anyway, poured some into a foam cup with ice cubes and a straw, and placed it within her reach. But she made no move to pick it up.

"Not thirsty, huh?"

"What do *you* want?" she scowled.

I wasn't sure what she'd seen in Snuffy McGinnis, but it was easy to tell what he saw in her. In a hospital gown without her disguise, Bonita Atkinson looked young, maybe twenty-five. Her pretty oval face was unlined, her hair chopped and layered, with brown with red undertones. It was a popular messy look she'd probably often done as a stylist at the Cut-Up Salon.

"A friendly chat."

"Bullshit."

"Okay, an unfriendly chat."

More silence.

"About what?"

"About how hard life will be for you during a long stretch in jail."

"You can't prove that I broke the law," she sneered.

"Sure I can."

I sat down in a padded chair facing her. Picking up the hand-held hospital bed controller without asking, I raised her to a sitting position. As she rested against the elevated mattress, she crossed her arms and looked at me as if to say, *You can fiddle with the bed, Bud, but you'll get nothing out of me.*

I pulled my chair up closer.

"Now listen, Bonita. John Drake, who you know as Owen Pike, was in prison for murder. Did you know that?"

Something in her eyes changed, and she shook her head.

"Well, it's true. Drake will literally do anything to avoid

going back to jail because he knows he'll never get out again. He's the one who killed your boyfriend, Sean McGinnis, and he just tried to do the same to you and me. When Drake learns that he failed, he'll try again. I probably won't be around to help you next time. You're also in deep trouble with the law. Did you tell Drake where the cellar was and when to be there? No? Then your accomplice, Darlene Dooley, must have told him as well as set you up to be murdered. When Darlene finds out that we survived the fire, she'll throw you under the bus. She and Drake will try to cop a plea by implicating you in murder and kidnapping."

"But I didn't kill anybody. I had nothing to do with Snuffy's death."

"Doesn't matter. If you're charged and found guilty as an accessory to murder, you'll face the same penalties as them. That means you could end up in prison for life without parole."

"But I didn't do it."

"I believe you."

"Can you help me?"

I nodded.

"I think so. I can't promise you a deal in return for your cooperation. But I can put in a good word for you with the prosecutor, provided you give up the others. My client's father, State Senator Shelby Barrett, is rich and powerful. His influence could make a big difference."

"What do you want to know?"

"Everything. Start at the beginning."

What Bonita told me about the kidnapping mostly matched my suppositions. McGinnis was passed out in the field and accidentally witnessed and recorded Jessamine and Travis shooting their monolith video. He followed them to room seven at the Red Nebula Inn, then called them to demand twenty-five thousand for his silence. Snuffy was furious when that failed, and they came up with another scheme.

Bonita told me the initial glamor of hair styling had worn off and she had begun to chafe at living in a town where everybody knew everybody else's business. She'd had it with the hard physical work of the salon. Every part of her body ached—wrists, elbows, shoulders, hips—from the daily grind. Despite doing hundreds of basic shampoo and haircut appointments last year, she'd only made twenty-seven thousand. And the hours were brutal—mostly early mornings, evenings, or weekends. She was sick, too, of clients who spilled their guts to her about their predictable infidelities and humdrum dramas. It was too much.

She just wanted a better life and was already imagining one.

It wasn't Snuffy's fault that he was shiftless. Computers had changed car engines so much that grease monkeys like him weren't needed anymore. What was he supposed to do? That's why he'd turned to crime. Being laughed at was the last straw. Bonita thought they might buy the old farmhouse and make it cozier. Repair the leaky roof. Update the old electrics and rusty pipes. Turn the weeds into a big vegetable garden. She wouldn't have to work anymore. Hopkinsville's cost of living was low, and you could see the stars at night.

"All it took was a little case of kidnapping," I said.

"Yes, but not murder."

Bonita had found the two-drop ransom demand scenario in an online chat room. She knew Snuffy would go for it because he *really* wanted to teach that arrogant city boy a lesson—and not to trifle with them. Snuffy's second cousin Merle's place was in foreclosure. That's where they stashed the moviemaker guy. Everything had gone perfectly—right up to when Snuffy was shot.

"By Drake?" I asked.

At the time, Bonita didn't know that. She hadn't told anyone else their plans. So, unless Snuffy had blabbed—he was always trying to impress Drake—she didn't know how the killer found out about the money. When Snuffy's body was discovered, Bonita panicked. She told Skeets Clawson to fetch the briefcase from the dump. He didn't know what was in it, and she promised him an extra thousand bucks if it hadn't been opened when he delivered it.

"After you took the money away from Skeets, I needed to confide in someone. I didn't really trust Darlene, who is gorgeous and knows it, and has a habit of making every conversation about herself. Also, by telling her I'd be admitting that I'd committed a crime. But there wasn't anyone else. Once I started talking, I couldn't stop," Bonita said.

Snuffy was dead and Bonita was in trouble with the law. She needed that money more than ever. Darlene was dissatisfied with her life, too. But instead of fixing up an old farmhouse, she wanted to go to Hollywood and get into the movies. Who didn't? But Darlene truly believed she could do it—if she could only get a break. After listening to Bonita, Darlene offered her help.

"How did Darlene find out about today's drop?" I asked as a wheelchair squeaked past the doorway. Machines continued to gurgle. I heard ring tones and a one-sided conversation out in the hall.

Against this background noise, Bonita said, "I told her. It was her idea to try the ransom gimmick a second time. She planned the whole thing."

It all seemed to fit. "How did Drake get involved?"

"Darlene must have told him. She and Drake were sleeping together. But they didn't know about the second two hundred and fifty thousand. Or where the movie guy was stashed—until I partnered up with Darlene. Now you know it all," Bonita said.

"Except how to find them before they get away," I said.

"They're still around. They won't leave before tonight. It's Darlene's big moment and she won't go anywhere until after it's over. See, she's going to introduce Brother Bartholomew as the keynote speaker at the Little Green Men Festival tonight. I know it sounds crazy, but that's Darlene for you."

"At what time?"

"Nine o'clock."

"What about Bartholomew? Is he involved?"

"He knows nothing about it," Bonita said.

"What if he finds out? How's he going to feel about being left out? I mean, he's a drug dealer who likes to make a profit."

"You don't understand. The man lives on another planet. He really thinks the Great Joy is close at hand."

"And you don't? But you belong to his cult."

"I'm more fallen away, you know?"

I believed her.

"So, you'll help me?" she said.

I said I would. After advising her not to repeat what she'd told me unless her lawyer was present, I went back to my room to put on my smoky clothes.

Chapter 23

I was standing in front of the closet about to get dressed when Detective Sanchez suddenly loomed in the doorway.

"Going somewhere, Guthrie?" he said.

"Just checking on my clothes."

"I can smell them from here." He wrinkled up his thick nose. "Forget about professional cleaning. I'd throw them away."

"Right now, they're all I've got."

He parted his lips in a smile. "You won't need them."

"How do you figure?"

Sanchez's black uniform shoes creaked as he stepped all the way into my room and shut the door behind him.

"I heard the medical staff wants to keep you overnight."

I nodded. "Yeah, that's what they said."

Despite the air conditioning, Sanchez was sweating in his rumpled khakis. He reached for a handkerchief and blotted his broad forehead and receding hairline.

"I understand you rescued Travis Tilford and some other folks, including yourself, from a house fire."

"That's right."

"Bravo. Want to sit down and tell me all about it?" He pointed at the bed.

I remained standing.

"I'll explain, but first you need to arrest Bonita Atkinson immediately for kidnapping and extortion. And make sure she can't get to a phone." I felt bad about this, but you do what's necessary. "You also need to impose a temporary media blackout about what's happened. John Drake—aka Owen Pike— still thinks he's in the clear after burning us all to death in the fire. His accomplice Darlene Dooley does, too. When they find out different, they'll run. Or try to kill us again."

Studying me as if making up his mind about something, Sanchez said, "Just a minute," and stepped out to confer with a uniformed young deputy stationed in the hallway.

From where I was sitting on the bed across from the window, I could look straight out to the parking lot. The mattress made a slight creaking sound whenever I moved. And the smell of smoke still permeated the room.

After a brief talk, the deputy went off and Sanchez came back in and closed the door. Sinking into the recliner chair in the corner, he said, "I put a man in her room. Tell me the rest."

By the time I had laid out Snuffy McGinnis's knuckle-headed, two-pronged extortion scheme, and how it played out, Sanchez was shaking his head. I added the short version of how half the ransom money wound up in the county landfill.

"Why in the hell didn't you tell us all this from the start?" Sanchez said.

"My client was afraid the authorities would get her husband killed. I think you can figure out why she might have felt that way. I did what I could while following her wishes."

"Look, is there anything else you haven't told me about this case? I need to know everything."

"There is something I didn't tell you, Detective."

"Spit it out."

I told him about the second round of ransom calls. How after giving the money to Darlene Dooley, we'd followed Bonita Atkinson to the cellar where Travis Tilford was being held. How

John Drake had trapped us all in the cellar and set the place on fire. How we'd escaped after finding another way out and woke up in an ambulance suffering from smoke inhalation.

Scratching the unshaven part of his skin where a dark, heavy stubble was beginning to show, Sanchez said, "You are damn lucky to be alive."

"Don't I know it? But I figured after so much bad luck, I was due some good."

"Maybe if you'd come clean in the beginning instead of withholding information, none of that would've had to happen. Maybe Sean McGinnis would be alive."

"I doubt it."

I told him as much as necessary to put him in the picture. He listened intently.

When I finished, he said, "All right, you got Tilford back. But his kidnappers are still on the loose, including Drake. Any indications as to where to find them?"

"My best guess would be that they're long gone by now. That is, unless they have some reason to stick around."

"What reason?"

"Darlene Dooley is supposed to introduce Brother Bartholomew to the crowd for the finale of the Little Green Men Festival."

"How do you know that?"

"I'm an investigator."

Sanchez frowned. "When's this happening?"

"Around nine o'clock."

He glanced at his wristwatch. "That doesn't leave us much time."

"So, we're going out there?"

Sanchez stood up. "By us, I didn't mean *you*. From here on, this is strictly a police matter. You're staying here."

"You can't make me," I said.

"Want to bet?" he said and grabbed the hospital bag that contained all my clothes.

Chapter 24

Stealing my clothes! What a low-down dirty trick, I thought in admiration.

Sanchez probably assumed he had me right where he wanted me now—out of his way. But without me around to stop Drake, I was afraid the murdering bastard might still get away. This I could not allow. Not again. Leaving in a hospital gown rankled, but any exit was acceptable at this point.

After carefully knotting the strings with which the gown was tied behind me, I poked my head out the door to check the hallway. It was abuzz with activity, but the sheriff's deputies were no longer in sight. I walked boldly along the corridor, down the stairs, and out the doors leading to ambulances. People come and go constantly to hospitals, so I didn't stand out quite so much at a glance. As I stole around the side of the building to the street, I spotted a silver security SUV vehicle parked near the hospital entrance, but there was nobody in it.

I encountered only a couple of passersby, and they seemed unfazed by my odd appearance. But that didn't mean that once out of sight, they weren't reporting me on their phones. Without my own phone or wallet, I couldn't call a cab or an Uber. I waited at a busy corner, hoping for one to appear. When one with a lit-up roof sign came along, I hailed him. The driver, a small individual with quill-like hair combed straight back from his forehead, seemed to take my appearance at face value and picked me up.

As I opened the back door, he asked over a clicking meter and radio static, "Just bust out?" His tone was belittling rather than witty. A prickly personality that matched his porcupine like appearance.

"Something like that," I said.

"Got any money?"

"You'll be paid," I said, with more confidence than I felt.

As I slid onto the back seat's worn fabric, I was assailed by the lingering odors of coffee, grease, and stale sweat. The dirty floor mats were littered with gum and takeout food wrappers.

Despite his doubtful expression in the smudged rearview mirror, the cabbie said, "Where to?"

"The Red Nebula Inn."

The springs in the seat squeaked loudly as we bounced over the bumpy road.

He stopped in front of the motel office, and I told him to wait while I went in to borrow the fare from Byron Hutchinson.

"Mr. Guthrie?" Byron said from behind the front desk when I came in. "What's happened to you? Have you been in an accident? Where are your clothes?"

"Where are yours?" I said, wondering why Byron was dressed like a little green man.

"You mean this?" he said, holding up his hands as if amazed I would need to ask. "I'm volunteering at the festival tonight. They always need help, especially at the end, when it's usually the busiest. But never mind me. What are *you* doing in that hospital gown?"

"It's a long story, Byron. But right now, I need your help."

"Of course. What can I do for you?"

"Uh, well, can you lend me some money to pay for my taxi?"

"No problem. I'll take care of it. I'll just charge the fare to your room."

"Perfect," I said, relieved. "Mrs. Tilford and I appreciate it. The cab driver is disagreeable, but he helped me out of a jam, so tip him generously."

"Got it."

"Thanks."

"Just part of the service," said the Vulcan eared one, as before.

While he went out to the cab, I dropped into a cushioned chair. My legs felt weighted with bags of buckshot. My lungs were as congested as Times Square on New Year's Eve. What a day. And it wasn't over.

"Okay, that's handled," Byron said, when he came back. "But tell me, why did you come here in a taxi? Where is your car?"

As I started to answer, Byron caught himself and said, "Sorry, that's none of my business."

"It's okay, I don't mind."

"In that case, please tell me more about this jam you were in. And how else I can help you?"

"Happy to tell you all about it. But first I have another big ask—bigger than paying my cab fare. Can I borrow that costume?"

Byron looked at me uncertainly. "Of course, I'd like to help, but I don't know if I can do that, Mr. Guthrie. They're sort of counting on me at the festival. I can't let them down, you know."

"You won't be. If you lend me the costume, I'll be happy to take your place wandering around the park and shaking hands and patting kids on the head. They'll never know the difference."

"But why would you want to do that? Don't you have other clothing you could wear?"

"It's a disguise."

"Oh, I see. Well, that's different. Why didn't you say so? I assume you'll need a room key? Let me get you one. I'll bring the costume right down to you."

Taking the key, I thanked him again and headed for room

seven. By this time, according to the bedside clock, it was after eight. Only an hour before Darlene Dooley's Big Moment. Spurred by the urgency, I stripped off the gown and showered away the smoke remnants. I was dressed in clean underwear, shorts, and a T-shirt when Byron knocked on the door carrying the costume. He had switched into cutoffs and a Red Nebula T-shirt. I put on the alien outfit, which fit fine. Asked if he could lend me a pair of shoes, Byron got some sneakers he said he thought would fit me, and they did.

"Now what's this all about?" he asked.

"If you'll give me a lift, I'll tell you all about it on the way to the festival."

"Sure. I'm going anyway."

"One last favor, Byron. Do you own a firearm?"

He gave me an incredulous look. "Of course, I do. What business owner doesn't?"

"Think you could let me borrow it?"

"What do you plan to do with it?"

"Catch some bad guys before they cause more harm."

"In that case, sure. I'll go get it." He returned with a 9mm semi-automatic he'd concealed under his T-shirt. "Will this do?"

The Glock 19 carried a standard fifteen-round magazine. Reliable and easy to use, it was probably the most popular handgun in America.

"Are you kidding? It's perfect. Have you ever fired it?"

"Only at the range," he said.

I was glad to see the nine was fully loaded. I sat down, removed the magazine, and quickly took it apart. Finding no problems with jams or failure to feed or difficulty operating the action, I put it all back together. Only a fool would bet his life on a weapon he hadn't checked out first. I stuck the Glock in my pocket under the costume.

"Is there going to be a shootout?" Byron asked.

"Not if I can help it, though I guess some might consider me an armed and dangerous alien."

"Don't say that," he said. "Around here, those are fighting words."

"Right. Don't worry, I'll take care of your gun."

"I never doubted it," Byron said.

To express my gratitude, I told him as much of the story as I dared while he drove us to Kelly Station Park in his ancient yellow VW bug.

"Will you ask the police for help?"

"No, I need to steer clear of them until this is over," I replied.

"Why?"

"I want a chance to take down this guy myself. I have to assume he'll be armed and dangerous as well. And he'll have no qualms about trying to kill me."

"Right there in front of the crowd and the cops?"

"At this point, I don't think he'd stop at anything. He's killed before and has nothing to lose by doing it again. But I have the element of surprise. He thinks I died in a fire he set today."

"Geez, Louise!" Byron exclaimed.

"And my own mother wouldn't recognize me in this getup."

I had green claws for hands and feet, a green cape, and bug-eyed green headgear. I worried that the headgear might interfere with my peripheral vision. Also, that the feet might trip me up. But I could shed that stuff as needed. I figured this costume would get me by the sheriff's deputies and fool Drake as well. It was lightweight, made of wick-away material. That helped, but the night air was so humid that my skin would soon have a sheen.

At 8:35, according to the dashboard clock, Byron pulled off the road and parked in a long line of vehicles a block from the festival grounds.

Twenty-five minutes to show time.

"Okay, Byron, I still need one more favor," I said.

"Ask it," he said.

"Will you lend me your wristwatch?"

He slipped it off. I slipped it on.

"From here on out, you are going to keep your distance from me, Byron, because doing otherwise would be dangerous and I don't want you getting hurt. Are we clear?"

"Aye aye, Captain," he said.

Katydids and crickets buzzed me as we got out of the Volkswagen. I swatted them away and stuck the Glock in my waistband and hustled along the pavement, trying to keep to the shadows. Up ahead, uniformed deputies were directing traffic and performing crowd control duties against a backdrop of flashing blue. Since I was in costume, nobody paid much attention to me as I entered the park near the designated flying saucer parking.

The smell of deep-fried cooking was pungent. I passed booths with tables full of merchandise, carnival rides, and refreshment stands. Children surrounded me to shake hands, pat their heads, and pose with them for photographs. It felt ridiculous at first. But I got used to it. Adults were standing around or sitting on lawn chairs and blankets. I was keeping an eye out for Darlene Dooley and John Drake. But when there was no sign of them, I began to wonder if Bonita had lied to me.

Recorded music blared through huge PA cabinets on the sound stage. To my surprise, as I walked by, I glimpsed a familiar face up there running the mixing board—none other than Weedy Fowler of the C-Note Saloon. I was still puzzling over that when I came to the staff dressing room tent, a place for performers to get undressed and shed layers of themselves as they got into character. Throwing back the flap, I went inside. I found the 20x30 space filled with clothing racks, folding chairs, bright lights, lots of mirrors, and a long counter space to spread out belongings. Since no costumes hung on the racks, I assumed the performers had already changed into their costumes, fixed their hair and makeup, and gone out to portray little green men.

I decided I might have a better chance of finding Darlene if I stayed here in one central location instead of roaming. But with time winding down, I kept checking Byron's watch. I told myself that, if necessary, I could catch up with Darlene after she introduced Bartholomew. But it became moot when she flounced up in a denim mini-skirt and a shimmering, low-cut sequined blouse.

"Hey, Darlene," I called, disguising my already muffled voice. I waved her over.

When she asked what was up, I said, "Let me show you," and opened the flap.

As she stepped unsuspectingly inside the tent, I grabbed her. Putting my forearm across her throat, I used my other hand to lock on my wrist for leverage.

The crowd flowed by, noticing nothing.

"We need to talk," I said.

She tried to lunge forward, bucking and writhing, but I tightened my grip.

"If you scream, the cops will come and arrest both of us. They will let me go, but not you. You'll be arrested for kidnapping and murder."

She coughed hard, continued to thrash about.

"John Drake will get away with all the money and you won't get to introduce Brother Bartholomew. Nod your head if you understand."

Darlene stopped struggling. I relaxed my grip enough for her to nod.

"Screaming is option number one. Option number two is you don't scream. We talk a few minutes. Then I let you go have your fifteen seconds of fame. Sound better?"

She nodded again. I let her go.

"You almost strangled me," she hissed, whirling around, rubbing her throat.

"Not even close," I said. "We need to talk."

"I don't know anything about any kidnapping or murder."

"Sure you do, Darlene. The cops have a witness and enough evidence to see you are convicted. I can't offer you a plea deal. But for you to have any hope of not spending the rest of your life behind bars, you need to come clean right now."

"What do you want?" she said.

"I want John Drake—Owen Pike to you, I guess. Help me nail him and I'll put in a good word for you. Tell me where Drake is."

"I don't know. He's here somewhere. But you can't take him."

"I can give it a goddamn good try." I glanced at Byron's wristwatch. It read 8:45. I pulled up two chairs, and we sat facing each other. "I assume you're intending to meet up and run off together with all my client's money, which means you probably brought it here with you. So, what's the plan?"

What she told me was so wild that at first, I couldn't believe it. Or that Drake went for it.

Darlene brushed that objection aside along with her hair, using the tips of her fingers.

"John didn't like it. I told him he didn't understand how much introducing Brother Bartholomew tonight meant to me. That I wouldn't miss it for the world. He said I must be nuts, that the park would be crawling with cops. Why complicate things further? I told him it was just show biz."

Before burning the van, Drake had pulled out the monolith and lights. After dark tonight, he was to reassemble the monolith in the same place as before. Nobody would see him in the woods. It was mainly just a matter of screwing the three sections together. Darlene had also enlisted Weedy Fowler, who, as I'd noticed, was running sound tonight, to take part in the scheme. During Bartholomew's remarks, she would phone Weedy to kill the guru's mic and instead play a recording of the famous music from the 2001 film. The music would cue Drake to light up the monolith using a wireless remote controller. The crowd would be so focused on the spectacle of the illuminated metal slab that Darlene and Drake would become invisible and slip away.

"And go where?" I asked. "Hollywood?"

"So, you've been talking to Bonita. She's your star witness."

"What if southern Cal got too hot for you?"

"You know, when I picked up that briefcase, I went home and dumped it over my head. The money waterfalled over me. I had to gather it up on my hands and knees before I could count it. We'll still have it when we slipped across the border where the long arm of the law couldn't follow."

"Darlene, has it ever occurred to you that Drake might just be using you the way he used Snuffy and Bonita?"

"God yes," she said, her eyes holding tight to mine. "But maybe I'm using him. Did you ever think of that?"

After going to so much trouble, I was confident she wouldn't run before introducing the cult leader, so I let her go. Looking for Drake, who was around here somewhere, I passed several booths offering information about local churches and organizations. Near the main Kelly Community Organization tent, I encountered Detective Sanchez, but managed to slip by without being noticed.

Leaving the midway rides and tented booths behind, I came to the flying saucer-shaped stone sundial, where a volunteer wearing a Kelly-Green T-shirt and hat was chatting with a woman who sported a tattooed upper arm showing a Martian with a spaceship flying overhead. I waved at them and continued toward the rear parking lot, where I'd be positioned between the stage and the woods. On the way, I skirted the huge flying saucer pavilion and came to an inflatable life-sized alien balloon—with Jessamine Barrett standing beside it.

When I halted in disbelief, she said, "Can I help you?"

"You sure can," I said. "Start by telling me what the hell you're doing here?"

She hadn't recognized me in my costume, but her eyes widened, and she smiled, knowing my voice.

"Tracking you down," she said. "When I found your hospital room empty, I knew this was where you'd come. You're still trying to catch Drake and Darlene, aren't you?"

She knew the answer. "Why won't you listen to me? This

place is too dangerous for you. I don't want to have to rescue you all over again."

"C'mon, Guthrie. We've been in on this together from the start. I couldn't let you do this on your own. How can I help?"

I took a deep breath and sighed. "All right, Jessamine. There is something you can do. See over there?" I pointed in the direction of the Community Organization tent I'd passed earlier. "Sanchez is there. Go tell him that they're both here at the festival. If he wants to catch them, he should let Darlene introduce Bartholomew and then follow her. She'll lead him right to Drake."

"How do you know this?" she asked.

Seeing the festival's organizer stepping up to the mic on stage, I said, "I persuaded Darlene to tell me a few minutes ago."

"How'd you manage that?" Jessamine asked.

The organizer was saying she hoped all the RV and overnight campers had been having fun.

"Never mind. Just get going. Darlene's coming up any minute."

Jessamine wanted to know more, but I walked away before she could question me further.

By this time, the parade participants had been thanked and the homemade costume contest winners announced. The crowd applauded when Darlene came up in her eye-popping outfit. Clinging to the microphone, she thanked them for the warm reception.

"Today, anyone who dares to believe in aliens risks becoming a laughingstock. Yet astronomers focus their powerful telescopes on the skies, searching for other worlds. With so many billions of stars in such a vast universe, how farfetched is it to think that another planet might exist which could support human life?"

This won her more applause.

After making a few more comments, she said, "For thousands of years, human civilization has been guided by prophets. But where did these ancients gain their understanding? What if wise aliens have visited earth to share their mind-blowing visions of the future? Some believe they have—and that they are still with us—like tonight's speaker, Brother Bartholomew of the Divine Tabernacle of Joy."

As Bartholomew joined her in the spotlight, Darlene bowed to him, pressing her hands together piously close to her chest, palms touching. The chubby hair stylist, who was wearing his yellow robe and gold slippers tonight, bowed back. First, to Darlene, and then to the audience.

"How can we find peace in a world filled with war?" Bartholomew asked after Darlene backpedaled, as if leaving a royal presence. The crowd parted before her like a red carpet had been rolled out.

I watched her as Bartholomew continued his remarks.

"How can we find love in a world plagued by hate? Find meaning in a world where there is none? Dear ones, listen, for I bring you the answer."

The audience seemed to hang on his every word.

"I met a man once on the road to Hopkinsville, who told me he had first traveled to earth millennia ago in a large space craft faster than light propulsion. I say a man because he looked like a man, talked like a man, acted like a man. But he was not a man. He was an alien."

The crowd gasped.

"The extraterrestrial said he had come in peace. I was in awe. I was joyful. We earthlings dream of aliens because we desire to be more important in this vast, forgetful cosmos. We want to be seen so we know we exist and have a unifying cosmic perspective. But then I was afraid. A visit from aliens who got here long before we were able to get there might indicate that they were so intelligent they considered us like Neanderthals."

The sound coming over the PA was crisp and clear, thanks to Weedy Fowler. No muddy notes or hints of distortion. Meanwhile, I moved toward Darlene as she closed in on the front parking lot.

"The alien seemed able to read my thoughts. He said we had nothing to fear from him or his kind, who came here long ago and have been among us ever since. He said an alien invasion would be a waste of their time. Eons ago, his race had learned how to avoid chaos and destruction. For millennia, they had been watching us from right here on earth. Their advanced technology could help us solve humanity's problems, he said. I asked if they would do this through advice and consent, or by forcible corrective action."

When Darlene stopped on the gravel by a silver Honda Accord, I was about twenty yards behind her. I did not want her getting into the car, but I assumed she'd wait for Drake. I ducked behind a car and took off my claws.

"The alien," Bartholomew said, "told me that a culturally and ethically advanced species like his would not seek to harm human civilization. But even if an ancient and advanced extraterrestrial civilization wished to help humanity, unintended consequences could occur. Humans could suffer from a loss of identity and confidence due to the aliens' technological and cultural prowess. Because of this, they might avoid all human contact so we could develop naturally at our own pace. This is known as the zoo hypothesis."

At the other end of the parking lot, a figure stepped in and out of the shadows, heading our way. I stayed out of sight.

"Unfortunately," Bartholomew continued, "the alien said he and his kind were not the only aliens—and that not all aliens have good intentions. Some may be plotting to take over the earth to deplete its resources like an invasive species of plant life that crowds out the native plants."

At this, the crowd groaned.

Even though I was expecting to see Drake, I was surprised when I saw it was him. Reaching under my costume, I brought out the Glock.

"Because of these aggressive aliens, mine said he'd decided

to change course and no longer avoid all human contact," Bartholomew said. "In the 2001 movie, the aliens used monoliths to help ape-men make a tremendous evolutionary leap forward by learning how to make and use tools. Fifty-two years later, in November 2020, a monolith very similar to the ones in the movie appeared in a remote Utah desert. Some believed this monolith was a gift from benevolent higher beings."

At Drake's approach, Darlene opened the Honda's trunk and lifted something out. It looked like Senator Barrett's briefcase, and I assumed it was still full of his money. I tightened my grip on the gun, knowing we were all within effective pistol range of each other. Drake halted while Darlene made a call on her cell.

"Soon after, another monolith surfaced on the far side of the world in Romania. And they kept coming, popping up all over the planet. More than a hundred monoliths. Various explanations were offered, but I say it was a sign—a sign that the Divine Joy was coming."

At that, Bartholomew's microphone went silent, replaced by an almost inaudible low-end humming that built slowly into a great bass rumble and then a stunning blast of trumpets— the opening fanfare of 2001. Simultaneously, Drake whipped out an electronic device and aimed it at the woods behind the park. Instantly, the clearing lit up, unveiling the monolith prop exactly where it had appeared two days ago.

Everything stopped. Then, heaving a massive sigh, the awestruck crowd began advancing as one toward the shining silver pillar. As they did, Darlene and Drake moved toward each other. It was time. I ripped off my alien headgear and, with a two-handed grip, aimed the Glock at them.

"Stop right there," I yelled, to make myself heard over the still playing softer parts of the music. "Hands up."

Darlene reached into her purse and pulled out a gun. Drake had one, too.

A second later, I heard the snapping twig sounds of multiple gunshots being fired. One slammed into my left shoulder, searing it with agony, and knocked me down. With the gunshots still ringing in my ears, I scrambled up to shoot back, but when I pulled the trigger, the borrowed gun jammed. I dropped behind an SUV. Tugging at the fabric of my costume, I found blood soaking through, but couldn't tell how badly I'd been hurt.

I peeked out again to see if they were coming to finish the job. By then, the panic-stricken crowd was stampeding away from the woods and scattering in all directions. Drake was running toward the woods with the briefcase clutched in his hand. And Darlene lay on her back in her cowboy boots. As she'd feared, Drake had double crossed her.

I stumbled toward her, gritting my teeth against the blinding shoulder pain, and kneeled at her side.

"Darlene," I said.

Her eyes were open. "It went well, didn't it?" she said, and died with a smile on her lips.

There was no time to think about this sad end to her sad life because Drake already had a good lead, and no reinforcements were in sight. With a sinking feeling that he was going to get away again, I picked up Darlene's .22 pistol and pursued him on shaky legs. A motorcycle was parked in the back lot. He jumped on it and kicked the starter again and again, but the engine wouldn't turn over.

A break at last.

Seeing me hobbling toward him, Drake took another shot but missed as I crouched behind a gray Chevy Eldorado. We exchanged gunfire until both of us were out of ammo. Then Drake bolted into the gnarled trees. Even though I doubted I'd ever catch up, I went after him. This was not Drake's planned escape route. That was clear. The land fell away sharply here, and when he reached the brink of a steep forty-foot drop, he stopped and spun around. He'd trapped himself.

There was no other way to go but through me, so he tried that.

I didn't see the knife he had in his right hand until I was

almost on top of him. He attacked, jabbing the six-inch blade at my throat. I made him miss, but he drove in again, slashing, pushing me backward. This time I saw it coming and, though he nicked me in the side through the costume, I countered by clubbing his wrist away with a hard swing of my right forearm. He dropped the knife, and we both dived for it, rolling over and over. When we came apart and jumped to our feet, we were only inches away from the ravine's edge and he had the knife. He smiled and waved it triumphantly, letting me know he wouldn't miss again. As I listened to the breath rushing in and out of my lungs, I knew I was in trouble. I had no choice. Drake was standing with his back to the drop-off. Before he could carry out his unspoken threat, I took a step forward and drop-kicked him in the stomach. It hoisted him over the edge, and he screamed as he fell.

Then there was nothing but the rustle of leaves.

My stomach churned with shock and nausea as I lurched over to where Drake had disappeared. He had plunged all the way to the bottom, slamming against boulders and brush before smashing headfirst into the rocky stream bed. His neck was bent at an odd angle that told me he wouldn't be getting up again. During the struggle, the briefcase fell, too, scattering bundles of bills all over. I slumped down on a smooth flat rock, breathing heavily, exhausted, wincing at the throbbing ache in my shoulder, and wiped at the blood on my little green man costume while I waited for Jessamine and Sanchez to arrive.

About the Author

Rick Neumayer's debut novel, *Journeyman*, was published in September 2020 by Fleur de Lis Press. *Hotwalker*, his first novel in the Jim Guthrie Mystery series, was published in 2021 by Literary Wanderlust. Rick has also published short fiction in many literary magazines, and three of his full-length Broadway-style musical collaborations have been produced. A career teacher, he has had a wide variety of experiences, including working as a newspaper reporter, book reviewer, literary magazine editor, and singer in rock bands. He is a Louisville native and resident with degrees from Spalding University (MFA), University of Louisville (MA), and Western Kentucky University (BA).

www.ingramcontent.com/pod-product-compliance
Lightning Source LLC
Chambersburg PA
CBHW061817190726
48289CB00007B/2228